MOONLIGHT MASSACRES

A NOVEL

MOONLIGHT MASSACRES

McKINLEY ZUMWALT

TCU
Press

FORT WORTH, TEXAS

TCU Box 298300
Fort Worth, Texas 76129
To order v: 1.800.826.8911

Design by Preston Thomas

We make war that we might live in peace.
ARISTOTLE

The earth also was corrupt before God, and the earth was filled with violence.
GENESIS 6:11

IN THE LATE 1870S, Texas governor Richard Coke tasked Leander H. McNelly with cleaning up the vast area south of the Nueces River, north of the Rio Grande, known as the Nueces Strip. To accomplish this enormous task, McNelly hired forty-one men and numerous spies who utilized three controversial tools—the Book of Knaves, *La ley de fuga*, and the Gospel of Jesus Christ.

CHAPTER

In the early dawn, surrounded by a thick brush forest of oak, mesquite, cactus, and cenizo, a lanky cowboy lay sleeping against a high cantle saddle, his face covered by a large black Stetson with a solid gold snake hatband. On the dark dirt next to him laid an empty tequila bottle.

High above the rocky creek, atop a twenty-foot live oak tree, a mockingbird sang a welcome to morning song. Without sitting up, the cowboy shoved back the hat, pulled one of his ivory-handled, silver-plated pistols and shot the mockingbird dead. In a flash of gray and white, the little bird tumbled through the limbs and landed on the leaf-covered ground at the base of the ancient tree. Although pleased with his amazing shot, the cowboy wasn't surprised by his skill. Hours of pulling the Colt single action Army had paid off, and he hit most everything he aimed at. He moved the hat back over his face in hopes of returning to sleep. His head throbbed from the tequila and the early morning sunlight seeping through the leaves.

1

Across from the ash-covered fire pit between them, his restless companion stirred the coals of last night's fire and threw on some dried mesquite sticks. In heavily accented English, the Spaniard commented, "They say it eese a sin to keel a mockingbird."

The cowboy mumbled, "That is the stupidest thing I've ever heard. Is it a sin to kill a cow, or a pig? It's only a sin to kill an innocent person."

As the sticks burst into flames, the beefy Spaniard said, "The mockingbird he does no one harm. He is innocent—eating only boogs, not destroying anything. So, you keel without reason. It eese a sin."

The cowboy sat up, glaring at his older companion. Awake, tired, and irritated, with no hope of going back to sleep, and after the night he had last night, it was just too danged early to start the day. Especially with a philosophical discussion. "I had a reason to kill, General—it was waking me up." He popped his pistol up and pointed it at the Spaniard. "Same as you!"

Like a snake striking, the Spaniard leaped across the fire, knocked off the Stetson, and grabbed the sleepy cowboy by his dark hair, pulling his head down into the dirt. A Bowie knife seemed to magically appear in the old man's hand, which he pressed firmly against the cowboy's throat. At the same time, the Spaniard knocked the pistol into the ashes near the growing fire and growled, "I may not be as fast at the draw as you are, *Señor,* but if you ever point *la pistola* at me again, you will find I am old, mean, and more deadly than you."

The cowboy knew it to be true. The old Spanish general was a ruthless son of a gun, a man without mercy. Money seemed to be his only motivation, and he let nothing stand in the way of his profits. The old man let go of the cowboy's hair. "We have tasks to complete. When finished, you may go your way, and I will go mine. But until done, you must act with some restraint."

The cowboy stood up, turned around, but didn't even bother taking a step before he began urinating into the brush. "Our partnership has been very profitable, General. I know what I am doing."

"Chu are a *serpiente de cascabel*—rattlesnake."

CHAPTER ONE

Buttoning his fly, the cowboy turned back and grabbed his hat from the dirt, then knocked it against his pants to clear the dust. "I like to think I'm a bird, not a reptile. We're birds of a feather—just not mockingbirds. We're probably more like eagles or vultures. To kill either one of us would not be a sin, for neither of us is innocent. And we sure do enjoy destroying things that stand in our way—if it profits us."

"Sometimes it is necessary to tear things down, in order to build them as you wish."

The cowboy retrieved his .45 by kicking it clear of the ashes. Then he picked up the tequila bottle, tossed it into the air, and shattered it with one sure shot. He was very superstitious, believing if he didn't fire his pistol once it left the holster, he would be the next one killed.

He knew what he wanted—to build the biggest ranch south of the Nueces River. Damn, he'd like to own the whole strip. And he aimed to get it, come hell or high water. He had never stopped to wonder what the general wanted. The fleeting thought entered his mind to try to find out. Then he quickly pushed that thought aside. Poking his nose where it didn't belong might get it cut off.

"Five families down, five more to go. *¿Bueno?*" The cowboy looked at his partner briefly. With the Spaniard's cold stare, he couldn't maintain the eye contact for long. Something about those dead black eyes seemed inhuman, unblinking, a bird of prey. The cowboy buckled on his fancy striped chaps before he hoisted his heavily tooled saddle and blanket. He shook the dead leaves off the blanket and threw it onto the back of his picketed gelding Yaller Lightin.

"*Bueno.* Then things shall be as I wish." The Spaniard spit as he slid his foot-long knife into the scabbard against his leg. He poured coffee into a tin cup, then doused the coals with the remainder before kicking the fire apart.

The cowboy wanted to whine about not getting a cup of coffee, but he wisely held his tongue. He'd chew some jerky and drink from his stale canteen. At the end of this week, they'd be in town and whisky and girls would command his attention, clearing the taste of the trail from his mouth.

The Spaniard bent over his massive gut as he lifted the left hind leg of his brown and white pinto stallion to clean the hoof. "The moon, she is full tonight, so we must work while we can see. But as soon as possible, we must find a farrier. My horse, he has knocked his shoe almost in half."

CHAPTER

JULY 24, 1877
ROSS RANCH
Six miles southwest of Frio City, Texas
○ *Full moon*

Bertha Mae Ross pulled a wrapper over her nightie, threw a flour sack packed with all her possessions out the window, and climbed across the sill into the bright light of the full moon. As her bare feet touched warm sand, her heart pounded with anticipation and excitement—tonight, her life would change. She grabbed the sack, and with her arms full, took off running to the outhouse, her moon-shadow racing before her.

She had to go out of the window. The door would have squeaked something terrible and she didn't want Mama to know she was running away in the wee hours before dawn with Harold Iversbach. Even though he was a Jew, Bertha wanted to marry him, and she knew with the deed done, Mama and Pa would come to love him as she did. Besides, she was much more suited to being a storekeeper's wife than a farmer's wife. Selling dry goods instead of pulling weeds would be a better life.

Of course, her folks would be disappointed with her decision not to tell them about getting married. She was their only daughter. But being fifteen, she was old enough to make up her own mind. Her daddy was a hard man, not inclined to having his decisions questioned, and there was no winning an argument with him, so it was better to avoid the argument all together. In time, Mama would smooth things over with Pa, and after the first grandchild came, he would claim the whole thing was his idea.

As Bertha Mae neared the outhouse, her daddy's javelina pig dog, Teeth, began to bark. Harold must have arrived early. She'd asked him to meet her on the back side of the farm, just so the dogs wouldn't set up a ruckus. She lifted her hand to her mouth to stifle her nervous giggle. Harold must be so anxious he couldn't wait and had walked all the way up to the house.

She stepped into the three-foot-square privy to change out of her nightie. She sure didn't want Harold to catch her indecent before the rabbi said the words that made it legal. The space was tight, but tall. She pulled her hope chest wedding dress out of the sack and hung it on the hook to the left of the door. As she lifted her arms to remove her nightie, a gunshot rang out.

Terror froze her to the spot. The Comanche moon lit up the sky, and she remembered just four months ago, a raiding party had come and taken twenty of her pa's best stock ponies and a dozen cows.

Peeking through the quarter-moon cutout in the door, she could see men in the yard. They were not Indians. Even with her limited sight lines, she could see two cowboys on foot and two mounted— one on a palomino horse with a white left hind foot, the other on a high-stepping paint horse. The small crescent hole in the door severely restricted her view, and she couldn't be certain of the number of men, but they raised a terrible to-do, shooting their pistols into the air, shouting and whistling loud calls.

Then her pa came onto the porch, wearing only his nightshirt and boots, hollering, "What's goin' on here?"

Bertha couldn't hear any reply. So she renewed her struggle with the voluminous clothes around her head as she tried to change into her dress. Were these men here just to hoorah the bride and groom? Had they found out about Harold's suit and intended him harm? Then she heard her mother scream, "Let him go."

A shot rang out. Then another. And another.

Bertha gasped when she looked back through the quarter-moon cutout. Her daddy laid half on and half off the porch. Her mama writhed as the short stocky man grabbed her around the waist and threw her against the wall.

Ma needed help. And what about her twelve-year-old twin brothers? Bertha struggled to disentangle herself in the tight space. She tugged at the door, but her sack of possessions blocked her way. Where were the boys? Were they still sleeping? Surely, they couldn't sleep through this cacophony.

The attackers sounded drunk—cursing loudly and laughing, shooting their pistols for no apparent reason. Bertha Mae, still snagged in the clothing, twisted to extricate herself from the flour sack on top of her feet and the nightie around her ankles. She hiked the nightie back onto her shoulders. As she reached to lift the latch on the outhouse, her mother screamed again. Bertha stretched up to look out in time to see her mother slump against the wall and slide down to the porch floor. By the light of the full moon, Bertha Mae saw a dark stain quickly spread on the front of her ma's nightclothes. Fright and shock immobilized the younger woman. Was her mother dead? Her daddy hadn't moved. Was he dead, too? Was this really happening?

With her eye riveted to the small hole in the plank door, Bertha Mae watched her world disintegrate. For the first time in her life, she was fixed with trepidation. Self-preservation demanded she remain where she was, quiet and still. What these men were after was not obvious to her, but they seemed bent on destruction.

"You shouldn't have killed the woman," the stocky cowboy shouted. "We could've had some fun."

Because of the bright lunar light, Bertha Mae could clearly see the faces of the men. One small man with a drooping black moustache dressed in loose white sack clothing wielded a knife that glinted in the moonlight. The short stocky ranchman set fire to the barn. Throughout the horrific spree, the high-stepping paint horse spun around near the water trough as its rider barked orders in Spanish. In the distance, riding a palomino horse, a fourth man with striped chaps rounded up cattle.

While the men ransacked the house, Bertha Mae stayed in the outhouse, silently weeping. Then, as quickly as they came, they were gone.

Before the dust in the yard settled, Bertha Mae sprinted from the privy to the house. Her pa's dog, Teeth, covered in blood and dirt at the bottom of the porch steps, twitched in a death throe, a perpetual snarl frozen on his muzzle. Her mama lay near the door, grossly eviscerated, mouth gaping, vacant eyes open. Bertha Mae lifted her fist to her mouth to stifle her moan. She had to get to the boys. Then her pa groaned.

He was gut shot, but alive. When Bertha hefted him back up on the porch, he screamed with her effort. She placed her hand over his bloody stomach to try and stem the bleeding.

"No use, girl. I'm done for."

She tried to stop her tears—to be brave like Papa would want, but he didn't seem able to focus on her. "Papa, what happened?"

"Don't know, Missy, but listen careful. I need you to take care of your ma and the boys."

Bertha couldn't bear to tell him that Ma lay dead five feet away.

"I will," she whispered.

"Git Uncle Von . . . "

Bertha knew the man he referred to was not really her kin, but the old Texas Ranger her father had known since the late '20s. The old bachelor Ranger had spent many a Christmas with them. She reckoned the man too old to go chasing criminals these days, but she wasn't gonna tell her pa that.

"I'll get him today."

Her pa coughed and bloody foam appeared at his mouth. "Sell the bull to Lambert and that'll keep y'all through the winter 'til the yearlings are big enough to yield a good profit."

"I will, Pa. Don't you worry about a thing."

"Don't let Francis Lambert cheat you . . . tell him his last offer plus twenty dollars'll do."

He coughed again and she saw a glaze cross his unfocused eyes. He wheezed, "Remind the boys what it means to be a Ross."

"Ever'day," she said.

As she struggled to lift his left leg onto the porch so she could make him more comfortable, she noticed the heels of his boots, well-worn on the outside edges, which had exaggerated the bow of his legs. He didn't seem to walk anywhere—he almost always sprinted, hurrying to close a gate or kill a snake. Although he carried a middle-age belly and thick neck, there was usually a gaunt, hard look to him that now disappeared into a ghostly pallor.

Then suddenly his eyes focused on her. "When you were born, Bertha Mae, I wanted a boy."

"I know," she whispered, remembering the times he had expressed his disappointment in her.

He patted her hand. "But that was before I knew how much joy and comfort a sweet girl can bring to her old pa."

Bertha Mae couldn't stop the tears then.

His voice had grown slow and scratchy with all the talk. "I thank God for ya, girl. You've been the best daughter a man could want. I love ya." She touched his face, and then she felt the fight go out of him. Her daddy was gone.

CHAPTER
THREE

○ *Waning Gibbous Moon*

I ride onto the Ross Ranch a day and a half after the slaughter. Because of my special skills at tracking, I've been sent by Captain Leander H. McNelly, at the request of old Ranger Von Richtenberg, to see if I can find any evidence that will lead to an arrest and conviction of the dastardly criminals who slayed four persons out of the family of five. The only problem here is that everyone in Frio County, and their dogs, have likely messed up any hope of finding a single usable track.

Unfortunately, this isn't the first time I've seen this happen, because Texans on the whole are generous folks who rally together when tragedy strikes—more focused on the living than the dead. What's done is done. No changing it now. So, they had all come to give comfort to the grieving daughter and in the process marred hopes of finding the clear trail of the renegades responsible for these crimes. Still, I plan to collect the information as best I can, noting it all in my little black book, to use if it ever comes to trial. I doubt it will get to court, but that's what is expected of a Ranger.

After more than twenty years carrying the badge, I'm getting too old to do this. Tired of chasing ne'r-do-wells. At forty years old, I want to ride nothing more than a rocking chair on my front porch. But crimes keep coming, and the cap'n keeps asking me to go. I know I will until the cap'n quits asking. But each morning after I shoot off the five rounds in my Colt, as I put in a fresh load, I realize I am slower and stiffer. Therefore, I need to be smarter and wiser.

So, before I enter the Ross Ranch compound, I hug the tree line and study the scene around the house. In my younger days, I'd have just waded in, but not now. No telling who's waiting in the shadows to call me out. I make a big target—not a wide one. I'm often called a bean pole, but being a head taller than most men makes me easy pickin's.

The morning heat is rising, causing me to constantly lift my hat to rub a dark blue bandana across my ever-widening forehead to dry the ever-present sweat of the July morning.

Under the shade of a large live oak near the edge of the yard, I dismount, loosen the surcingle and girth on my Texas/McClellan saddle, and ground tie my partner against crime, a big dun gelding I named Chief. Here he can crop the summer's fading grass. At least one of us will get breakfast.

When the animal twitches his smooth hide to flick a fly off his muscled shoulder, I give him a pat. Like many partners, we have a contentious relationship, mostly when the beast is tired and ready to rest, or whenever the weather turns cold. But I know I have no better ally in my fight against crime than the lineback dun. And I often regret the necessary ill treatment of the gelding when we are on the scout and a good bag of oats is impossible to come by, so I'm happy to let the horse graze whenever possible.

Glancing around the area to get the lay of the land, I walk over to the remains of the burned-out barn to the north of the house. There is nothing much left of the once well-built structure. A few pitchfork tines and a shovel blade without a handle, a charred metal pulley, and curled leather of burned tack peek from the smoldering debris. I kick at the large, blackened door hinge. The fire had burned fast but not hot enough to melt the metal. Smoke still rises from a hot spot in the corner and the smell is strong enough I lift my bandana to cover my nose and mouth.

The outhouse sits between the house and the barn.

These folks were obviously industrious and frugal. They had carved a good life out of brush and rock. In spite of the crime committed here, most everything remains neat and orderly. Solid corrals stand to the south and the north. Rock and concrete water troughs dot the area.

The house is deftly situated atop a rise where you could sit on the porch and look out over the sandy red fields and the green brush country. This was all a man could want at the end of a long day. But the one who built this would never sit here again.

The oldest part of the house is local sandstone carefully fit together in a crazy quilt pattern with only a few heavy-shuttered windows and several rifle slits. But the new pier and beam, board and batten addition includes that deep front porch with floor-to-ceiling double hung glass windows, guaranteeing to catch any lovely breeze that a summer night might bring.

I walk toward the house thinking of the four funerals happening in town right now. The bodies had been removed early yesterday and were being buried today, so the only soul on the place is an old Mexican woman on her knees, scrubbing blood off the porch's pine boards.

I hear the jingle of traces and spot Parrot's black-box vehicle coming up the road. Painted in white letters on the side of his tar paper house on wheels is the word "Photography." It doesn't surprise me to see the Ranger spy's wagon rambling up the lane.

When Parrot gets near enough, he hollers, "Good to see you, Preacher."

That nomenclature had been bestowed on me because Captain McNelly insists the Gospel of Jesus Christ be told to each criminal before they hang, and I am often the Ranger chosen to do the telling.

He'd say, "C. W., get over there and give 'em the good news of the love of God. Give 'em time to repent and choose between heaven and hell. Then carry out justice, swift and true."

Now, I'm not really comfortable with the label "Preacher" because I know I'm more sinner than saint. But if the cap'n can't do the preaching himself, the job frequently falls to me, and lately, the cap'n has been under the weather.

Parrot is a good ten years younger than me, but his balding head and whisker stubble, chewing tobacco often dribbling down his chin, belies the fact. Mr. Parrot is one of Captain McNelly's best-kept secrets. He travels around the country as bold as day, with his eyes and ears open. Things people would never share with a Ranger because it involves a relation, or longtime friend, tumble out around the spy. And when he cleans up, stands up straight, and wears a suit, you wouldn't recognize him as the same feller loitering near the stable or around the cracker barrel. Today he dressed up in trousers and a shirt with a string tie.

Parrot hops off the wagon. "Sounds like a bad one."

"Let's go see."

Our boots thump loudly as we walk up the double-wide wooden steps onto the porch to begin our inquiry in the house.

Serviceable pottery is stacked neatly in a homemade hutch. The town ladies probably had a hand in straightening things up. A hand-hewn table that could seat eight to ten people on benches dominates the room. No indoor plumbing, but a dry zinc sink rests under a window covered with blue gingham curtains. One door to the north leads to a bedroom. Two doors on the south lead to two small bedrooms. We glance in the first small bedroom and see falderal, ribbons and such, that obviously belong to a gal. When we go to the back bedroom, two small hand-built beds made from mesquite posts with ropes instead of slats sit along the walls.

"The boys were murdered here, in their sleep. One of them varmints musta snuck in with a knife before the shootin' started." The bloody sheets have been removed and the mattresses turned over, but when I upend the corn husk-filled ticking, it is obviously bloodstained.

The scene is horrific, and I feel anger rise in my throat over two young buttons who'd never grow into men. But the worst thing is, this is not the first time I've seen this.

"Just like before," Parrot confirms, "working with the full moon is like daylight. They can do any dastardly thing they please."

A similar crime had been committed in April, and another in June. Both crimes happened within fifty miles of here, during the full moon, when the light was so bright you could see exactly what you were doing and where you were going.

During the first crime, deep in brush country, thirty miles from the nearest human being, an old woman, Greta Müeller, and her two grown sons had their throats slit. But miraculously, right after it happened, they were discovered by a horse buyer who happened along and found them. If he hadn't come along, they would have rotted there a long while.

The second crime was perpetrated on a young newlywed couple, Antonio and Ramona Saldaña. Like the Ross Ranch massacre, Antonio had been gut shot and left for dead. The unspeakably brutalized young woman died when her throat was slit. The young groom stumbled and crawled to his brother's home over a mile away before he succumbed to his wounds.

If Parrot is right, a gang is committing robberies and murders every full moon. If that is true, then the Rangers have about thirty days to bring this gang to justice or risk another massacre.

I say, "Twenty-five days—it's likely to happen again at the next full moon."

"I'm ready for this lawlessness and killing to stop," Parrot pulls his handkerchief to rub a bead of sweat trickling down his neck. "If good men don't stand up for what's right . . . " his voice trails off as he states the obvious through clinched teeth. "I seen this stretch of Texas go to the devil quickly during this fool war. It's time to set it right again."

Evil always seems ready to overpower good. Standing in the gap between good and evil is not without cost. It cost me my youth and a chance at a family. It forces me into the company of men—some of them despicable. It compels me to live a solitary lonely life, but I soldier on with the ghosts of the innocent slain beside me.

As I step out of the house, I tamp down the fury boiling in my stomach.

Parrot says, "I could use a cup of strong coffee to clear the smell of death lingering in my nostrils."

I don't know if it's his suggestion or the anger I feel, but it sets my stomach to rumbling. I know I need to get on the scout. The trail will grow even colder if I stop for breakfast. It won't kill me to eat the cold biscuit in my war bag, but it didn't stop me from hankering for fresh bacon and eggs. "You're right, Mr. Parrot, civilization has to be more than just a collection of towns. It has to be law and order."

Trying to dispel the heat of the day, a twelve-foot-tall whirlwind of dust and sand cuts a serpentine track between the outhouse and the barn before it lifts back to the sky.

Parrot spits a brown stream of chewing tobacco onto the ground and nods toward the spinning column of debris. "Take more than a dust devil to draw off the evil that blew through here."

I dream about people being willing to "do unto others" in a just and right way. What kind of world would it be if more people would be willing to sacrifice their selfish desires for the good of the whole? But I know that is just wishful thinking . . . something my ma calls a heaven longing.

Parrot laments, "Texas has been ripped by violence for so long."

"Unfortunately, these killings have to be resolved with violence, because violent men beget violence. Ruthless men are willing to do anything to get what they want."

"Justice does beget peace."

I know I'm preaching to the choir. Parrot and I see eye-to-eye on justice. And the fellows that did this killing deserve to be dragged behind a team of horses for ten miles, then hanged at the end of a rope until their bones rot apart . . . dead as Hector.

When we walk around the outside of the house, I point out the girl's bare foot track under the window, but the track doesn't go far until it is obliterated by wagon and hoof tracks.

Parrot asks, "You believe what the girl said?"

"I don't think she was complicit, but we cain't count it out. She stands to be the sole heir of over a thousand acres."

Perhaps the outhouse will have evidence supporting, or disproving, the young girl's story. I step over to the small privy, open the door of the "fragrant" room that has a mail-order catalog hanging on a hook, a bucket of corncobs and a bucket of lime on the floor. I dip the tin cup into the lime bucket and sprinkle the fine white powder into the open hole before I step inside and shut the door.

"She said four attackers?"

"But there could have been five or six." I peek through the quarter moon. "She didn't have a very good view. If she was the perpetrator, she had to have help, because I don't think she could have killed them all and driven off the cattle, although she was having some problems with her folks because she admitted she was running away to get married. I think her only crime was being in the right place at the wrong time."

"Well, she's gittin' hitched this afternoon, after the funeral. I'm here to take the picture."

"She has nowhere else to go." I know my matter-of-fact manner might be shocking to some, but these circumstances didn't allow for a proper time of mourning, or courting. How could a fifteen-year-old gal take care of the farm and ranch alone? Marriages of convenience are the rule here, rather than the exception. Most people don't have the luxury of an "inconvenient" marriage of love. And marriages of convenience frequently lead to love.

"Hard way to start a marriage."

I traipse over near one of the stone water troughs. "She said one rider sat a high-stepping paint horse that spun around and around near the water tank."

I point to evidence of a horse that had stood in one spot pivoting on its hind legs. My heart leaps. "This might be just what I need. This horse has a defective rear shoe. See the distinctive slash near the toe?"

If I can find the rider of that horse, the girl might be able to identify him. If she can identify him, we have a good chance at conviction.

Criminals who get caught are often willing to point a finger at their compadres in hopes of a lighter sentence.

I reckon we've seen all there is to see here, so I whistle, and Chief raises his head, locates me, and begins to amble toward us.

"C. W., where ya headed next?" Parrot asks.

"Gonna follow the lead." I point out the distinctive shoe track. "Once I get past the hullabaloo in the yard, the trail of over a hundred cows and several dozen horses should be plain enough a child could follow it. I expect they're trailing south, toward the Mexican border."

"I'll take the weddin' picture, keep my ear to the ground, and when I'm done, I'll foller you."

"When the goin' gets rough, I'll leave you a path, every hundred yards or so. I'll use a yeller string tied high in the brush and a broken branch on the opposite side of the trail pointing in the direction I'm headed."

"Hey, what's going on here?" The voice rings out from the brush. "Who burned that barn?" A big chestnut Morgan horse gallops into the yard, its rider still shouting questions. "Where is Jacob Ross? What are y'all doing here? Who are you?"

In a puff of dust, the man dismounts as he fumbles with the catch on his pistol.

I raise my hands to show I mean no harm and say, "Slow down, feller, I'll expl—"

Before I can finish, he comes at me swinging, obviously having given up on getting the pistol out of the holster.

As his right arm windmills toward my head, I duck, and say, "Hold on here, Mister, who are you?"

I try to calm this event, but he doesn't seem prone to reason. I'm not in the habit of socking people without cause, so I shove him in the chest and at the same time with a sweep of my leg, drop him into the dirt.

Parrot stands there grinning at me. "A fistfight is a good way to get your blood pumping in the morning, isn't it, Ranger Wallace?"

The man on the ground bounds to his feet, fists held in a pugilistic stance. Like a raging bull, he circles me, and comes at me aiming for my gut, but again I dodge and he hits my pistol rig, causing the tie-down string to twist on my leg. It acts like a tourniquet, cutting off the blood to my leg. I grab my gunbelt to try to twist it back into place when the fellow comes at me the third time. I say, "You are assaulting a duly sworn officer of the State of Texas."

That stops him. He sputters, "Something's wrong here."

When Parrot speaks up and explains what has happened, the man bursts into tears. "Dead? All dead?"

"Who are you?" I ask.

"Francis Lambert, the neighbor to the east." I wonder if he could be a suspect. How could he not have heard?

"I've been in Corpus all week trying to buy a bull, since Ross wouldn't sell me his."

Parrot pipes up, "The bull is long gone, along with about a hundred cows."

Lambert wipes his dripping nose with his sleeve. "Poor Jacob, poor Marian, and them little boys."

After Parrot explains about the funerals and the wedding, Lambert dusts off his pants and says, "It's a shame about that bull. He was short-legged, but he carried a lot of weight. He'd add beef to those longhorns." He bites his lip and rubs his sleeve across his eyes. "They was good neighbors. I reckon I best be gettin' to town. That girl will be needin' my support. Sorry about the tussle. I figure neither of us are really much worse for wear. We'll call it a draw."

As he rides off, Parrot chuckles, "Draw my eye, you could have eaten him alive if you had to. I've seen ya do it with only one punch."

"It serves no purpose. And life's hard enough without the aches and pains of getting hit. Can you ask questions in town and find out who Lambert is and if he could be in on this Ross massacre?"

Parrot agrees with a snort. "I'd be surprised if he was."

My knees creak louder than new saddle leather when I mount. It'll be another hot day. I reseat my hat tightly onto my head. If I need to move out fast, I don't want to lose this hat. I've spent three years breaking it in and am quite fond of it. Of course, I could swallow my pride and loop a string around it like some of the other Rangers did, but I couldn't bring myself to do that—it'd be like grabbing the horn of a saddle, a tinhorn move.

I wave goodbye to Parrot, ease my calves into Chief, heading south at an easy trot. It's more than a hundred miles to Mexico, most of it through rough country with thorny bushes and low rocky sandstone hills. Up and down, round and round. These criminals have a good head start on me, but a lone rider can cover ground a lot faster than a herd of cattle. I reckon if the cattle are pressed, they might cover twenty or twenty-five miles a day. On days Chief and I push, we can cover forty. One time, the Company traveled a hundred miles in a very long, seemingly endless day. I hope never to do that again. But I know it will take a hustle if I am to overtake the herd before they cross into Mexico. Once they cross into Mexico, I'll be powerless. I know I cannot bring back the Ross girl's family, but maybe I can supply her a nice dowry by recovering her pa's stock.

About five miles from the Ross Ranch, near a water hole, I latch onto the tracks of a five-gaited horse with a deep dent in the toe of the hind shoe. The horse has a unique gait and the shoe has a unique mark. One I can easily track. I know I can pick that mark out from a large group of animals. I can place that track at the Ross Ranch. The girl said she could identify them. I hope that is true. It gives me hope that even if I can't recover the cattle, I can bring the murderers to swift and sure justice.

CHAPTER
FOUR

Parrot's picture-taking wagon served as his house and dark room. But wrapped in heavy black tar paper to keep the light out, it was hot as Hades in the summertime. The Jewish folks that requested these photographs were well-to-do. They had asked for three pictures instead of the normal single shot. As he prepared the plates for three tintypes, one for the groom's parents, one for the bride's family, and one for the new couple, he wondered if he should do three this time, in light of the bride's family's death. In the end, he realized the groom's family had paid for three photographs, and three photos they'd receive.

As he set up his camera in the meeting house that served as both schoolhouse and church, he surveyed the crowd and listened to their chatter. Most of it centered around the murders and the "poor" bride. If C. W. recovered the stock, Parrot figured she'd come out with quite an inheritance, all of her mother's possessions, and a nice little ranch. He wasn't sure "poor" was the best way to describe her.

He'd not seen hide nor hair of her since he arrived.

As the ladies laid out the wedding feast, a large fashionable-looking lady whispered to the women, "You reckon Jacob Ross was doin' somethin' crooked and got crosswise with his partners?"

Another lady scolded, "Annie Young, you don't go spreadin' rumors. You know Mexican raiders did this."

Old Mrs. Shriner piped up, "Least it weren't Co-manch."

Mrs. Young said, "It do put the fear a' God in ya, though."

They gossiped on, "I cain't believe this girl's gittin' married on the day they buried her family. This new generation ain't got no sense. She should be in mourning at least a year."

"Where's she gonna go, if she don't get married? Who wants a growed girl living under their roof with their husband? Not me! And you cain't expect her to live out there on that ranch all alone."

"She's just lucky the Jew wanted her. There cain't be no happiness comin' out of this."

"Hush, y'all!" Mrs. Shriner said, "You call yourselfs good Christian women. You'd best be praying for God's blessin' on that girl. She's got a turrible burden to live with, and she needs compassion, not judgement."

Then the rabbi called to the crowd. The crowd wore long and sorrowful faces—not what you'd want for a wedding, but it was what it was. The company measured at least fifty folks. Parrot wondered how many of those were true well-wishers and how many were just curious because of the ruthless slaughter of the Ross family and the promise of a free feast.

Parrot had never been to a Jewish wedding before. A little tent set up at the front of the room. The men sat on one side of the room, and the women sat on the other. The groom and his parents walked up the aisle together and took their places under the canopy. As Bertha Mae walked down the aisle alone, through the veil it was obvious tears dripped down her cheeks. Her young groom met her halfway and protectively held her arm. She gratefully accepted his assistance and weakly smiled at him. Parrot wished he could have made a photograph of her at that moment, but she was moving, and that sort of tintype just wouldn't make.

He did expose one photographic plate from the back of the room as the bride and groom stood under the little tent top. He hoped it would develop without too much blurring.

Most of the ceremony was in a foreign language. Parrot *habla*-ed German and Spanish pretty good, and it sure wasn't German or Spanish. The couple signed some papers, exchanged rings, then smashed a cup in a little sack with their feet. After that the bride and groom sat in chairs and were hoisted aloft onto the shoulders of young men. The newly married couple held a handkerchief stretched between them. Then a dozen or so Jewish men carried them around the room singing and dancing. It was a strange wedding indeed, but by the end of the chair ride, Parrot thought he heard the bride giggle and he could see her smiling shyly.

The ladies in the corner looked on the dancing disapprovingly, probably because many of them were Baptist and thought the bride should be in a more sober mood. In light of the murders and disapproving crowd, Parrot suspected the joy and hilarity of the celebration was truncated. One day, he hoped he could partake of another Jewish wedding under different circumstances, but Jews were few and far between in South Texas, although every Texas town of any size had a sole Jewish merchant, and like the Iversbachs, they often ran the most profitable businesses in town.

After the chair ride, Parrot requested the groom remain seated, and he positioned the bride slightly behind him for the official wedding photograph. He hoped it showed her lovely dress to its best advantage. The groom held his right hand up by his right shoulder and the bride clutched it with both her hands. The young merchant looked back and up at her. Like all brides and grooms, you could see the uncertainty of the future on their faces . . . fear, anticipation, excitement, and of course, the sadness and horror of the events of the last twenty-four hours. It was an unusual photo for Parrot, but memorable. Even though the bride had dark circles under her eyes and looked overwhelmingly sorrowful, she was also hauntingly beautiful.

As the wedding party retired to the tables piled with food, Parrot climbed into the back of the stifling hot picture wagon to process the photography plates. He splashed the tin sheets about in the chemical baths, counting the requisite minutes on the luminescent dial of his expensive pocket watch, all while working in total darkness. Finally, he emerged.

The photo under the canopy turned out well, with only a little blurring of a fidgety toddler standing on the left side. Overall, Parrot felt quite pleased with himself. When he first started taking pictures, he never experimented, remaining cautious because of the costs of the chemicals. Now, he'd really gotten the hang of it and was happy to take any pictures other than slain criminals in their coffins posed in a store front.

By the time he finished varnishing the photos, most folks had started home. The long distances and hungry animals to tend ensured most celebrations were short. He presented the photos to the bride and groom, wished them all the best, and started out after Ranger Wallace.

As he left the rough road and turned onto a nonexistent path into the brush, he fretted they would not be able to stop the next family from suffering like this young bride. Less than thirty days. They had a lot of ground to cover in less than thirty days.

CHAPTER
FIVE

Before dawn, the young widow Esther Stokes struggled out of a deep sleep. An odd dream about chickens and a coyote lingered on the edge of her memory. She couldn't quite remember it all, only the coyote's yellow eyes. But it left her feeling unsettled.

Instead of the usual rooster's crow, the dog barked. She thought *that's what woke me up.*

Immediately, her head cleared. Some varmint threatened her chickens. Panic surged through her. She grabbed the trusty old scattergun, then opened the plank door and slipped outside without stopping to pull on her boots or her wrapper. She couldn't afford to lose a single hen. Those birds were her only means of survival.

The night was pitch black. The moon hadn't risen yet, but familiar stars splattered across the Milky Way. A warm southern breeze swirled her nightgown around her knees as she crossed the yard.

With her free hand, she chased the fabric, finally taming it in her grasp, while gripping the heavy weapon tighter with the other. The smell of ripening peaches and turned earth wafted over her.

The dog stopped barking.

Esther halted.

What would stop that dog from barking? Had the coyote run away? Squinting into the distance, she could barely make out the silhouette of the single-story shed she called a barn. Even in the daylight her eyesight was poor, but at night it was much worse.

Quickly, she tiptoed down the worn dirt trail the dog had made between the house and the barn, hoping to avoid stepping on the tiny green stickerball grass burrs that would prick her feet and sting for days.

The dog ran up, tongue hanging out, his stump of a tail wagging his whole behind.

Scratching behind his ears, she whispered, "Worthless, what kind of watchdog are you lettin' some skunk kill my chickens?" Worthless wiggled faster in answer.

The barn had two sets of double doors—one set to the south facing the house, and the other to the north facing the hills. They stood open, except in winter. She saw a faint glow from a safety match barely illuminated through the north doors.

Before she could step in, she heard voices speaking in Spanish, almost too rapidly for her to translate. At least no critters were attacking the chickens. She sighed, grateful her only source of income was secure. Worthless was just alerting her to early morning visitors.

She wished she didn't have to offer the customary traveler's hospitality. But any civilized person venturing this far southwest into the land called the Nueces Strip was at least a half-day's walk from a hot meal and a drink of water. Leaning the scattergun against the barn, she smoothed her waist-length hair and twisted it into a knot. She wasn't dressed to receive callers, but it wouldn't be polite not to at least offer to bring out a cup of hot coffee.

Along with cigar smoke, the stranger's words drifted through the rough slats of the barn.

"The *caballero* has planned three more raids," a man's voice said in a thick Castilian accent, marking him a European.

Did she translate the phrase properly? The *th* lisp of his words sounded odd. Not like the Tex-Mex slang she was used to. What did he mean?

Hesitating, she debated whether she really had to interact with a strange man. It was a stupid custom for a woman alone, especially one wearing her night things. But what if she had been on the road all night? What if she hadn't eaten or had a drink in a day? Her late husband, Jobe, would want her to "do unto others." Guilt gnawed at her.

She opened her mouth to extend her hospitality when the voices broke into a heated argument.

"*Assesinato*," the Castilian insisted.

The phrase stuck in her brain. Was it idiomatic? What did it mean? *Assesinato*, assassination. Then suddenly she realized.

Bloody murder!

Horrified, she stifled a gasp.

A tenor voice said in Spanish, "I will not kill sleeping children again."

She pressed her fist against her mouth. The second voice belonged to *Tomás*, her hired man.

The stranger insisted, "You will do as your general commands."

"If I keep my promise, then the *jefe* must honor his promise to give me this land when the war is over."

"*El Rey* will determine that," the stranger added.

El Rey, the king? What king? Confusion washed over her. What were they talking about?

"Don't worry," the harsh voice continued, "the neighbors have helped you before, they will again. They will cut throats for anyone who will pay. You trust them, don't you?"

She heard Tomás spit before he said, "I trust no *gringo*."

"You killed that family, drove their stock across the river. You'll do it again. It's easy money. Kill, or be cut up yourself. It must happen for our plan to be completed."

Esther's heart pounded and her mind raced. *Who is this man and what family was he talking about?* What was this Spaniard's power over Tomás?

Normally she felt spurred on by things that set other women swooning. She couldn't, and wouldn't, abide such foolish behavior as fainting—it wasn't Christian and it wasn't practical to be afraid. And above all else, she was practical. She struggled to muster the courage to respond and act. But she didn't know what she could do.

Confusion riveted her to the spot. Something moved on the far side of the barn. The hair on the back of her neck prickled. Tears threatened to spill from her eyes. Her breathing became shallow and rapid. And she hated herself for it. She strained to hear what was happening on the other side of the barn. Her heart pounded and her breath sounded so loud she hoped the men couldn't hear it.

Easing behind the open barn door, she bit her lip to stop a cry as she stepped onto a patch of grass burrs. When she steadied herself to extract the barbed thorns from her foot, the barn door squeaked. It seemed a loud scream in her ears.

She stiffened. A horse snorted at the slight sound. In the distance, the dog, Worthless, barked again, but the stranger seemed intent on his own words and didn't notice. The wind gusted and the whole barn seemed to pop and sway.

"Early, at the next full of the moon, meet me at the *Cantina la Paloma*. I demand blood. This entire family must be destroyed, or *El Rey* cannot have the control he needs."

She was sick of the violence. Sick of the mayhem that gripped this country, claiming her husband and so many others. She longed for tranquility. Where was justice?

Hearing the squeak of saddle leather, Esther knew the Spaniard had mounted his horse.

The full of the moon. She had about twenty days to find help and save some family from bloody murder! And the killer was her hired man.

CHAPTER
SIX

JULY 28, 1877

Dimmit County, Texas

Tracking this herd is not difficult. The drovers make no effort to conceal their trail. The second day out, toward dark, when the shadows are long and the light dim, I try to move through the brush quietly, pausing every few minutes to listen. The last thing I need is blundering into these vicious fellers perpetrating such awful crimes. If they're smart, they'll backtrack, or set a sentry to be certain no one follows them. At times like this, although Chief does a great job of alerting me to the approach of anyone or thing, I think about having a human partner—someone to watch my back.

These criminals seem so bold and arrogant I would be surprised if they even bothered to set a sentry. Of course, they could be simply ignorant.

In this unpopulated land, the low rolling hills look green from a distance, but once you ride them, you see chalky gray dust covers every dry leaf. The hills are made up of fist-sized red rocks—some sandstone, some flint, and some iron, interspersed with spiny pear cactus. In brush country, the thick bushes, many barely taller than a mounted man's eye, restrict vision beyond six or eight feet. You can hear someone long before you can see them. The largest trunks of most of the bushes are no bigger around than a man's upper arm. And most of the brush, whether it is mesquite, catclaw, or cactus, grows thorns that grab, snag, and sting as you ride through them.

Zigzagging through the brush makes going tough. Although there are no roads, I occasionally cross a hog or deer trail that often leads to water. It's rough for Chief and me, and we become familiar with the slap of thorns as I try to ease the thickest brush out of our way, but I'm often forced to walk, leading Chief, to break the way. Thank goodness for a thick pair of chaps. I wonder how Parrot will ever get that wagon across here.

I can't keep my mind from dwelling on the senseless slaughter of an innocent family. These fellers could have stolen the cattle without killing the family, but they'd deliberately killed everyone. Why? That seems an important fact. Did they plan on squatting on the land? Did they hope by killing everyone that no one would claim the property? I can't help but wonder if the butchers are local. If they are local, wouldn't they have noticed that the daughter was missing? Wouldn't they have worried she could recognize them? Then I wonder if they would come back after the girl. Surely she would be safe in town. And she had changed her name. But you never can tell. I chew on it over and over.

I thought about the other people who had been murdered. During the first murder, the house had been pilfered and several hundred head of cattle taken. During the second, only a couple dozen cattle had been stolen. Nothing of real value in the house appeared to have been taken, just ransacked. Had stealing the cattle been the objective, or was murder the true intent of the criminal's drunken rampages?

I mull these ideas for miles until my mind clogs with them. My melancholy flees when the horse steps out of the thick brush onto a large patch of barren loam soil that someone has obviously cleared to plant. This brush country keeps secrets like a fog at sea. Even though few and far between, there are people out here cloaked by the green.

When I find the droppings of the herd, I set spurs into Chief and easily cross the open field. I ride fast and low in the saddle, because being out in the open makes me nervous. It wouldn't take much for someone concealed in the brush to get a bead on me, and with a squeeze of the trigger, I would never know what hit me. When the field ends, I need to fade back into the brush country.

CRACK. A shot whizzes past my ear before thudding into a mesquite branch just in front of me, cutting the branch in two and impeding my way.

"Hold it, mister," the utterance is young, just changing into a man's voice.

My heart pounds a wild tattoo as I raise my hands, glancing around, still unable to locate the shooter. Chief dances nervously.

"I'm a Texas Ranger, son."

"I'm not your son, or your boy, and you're trespassing."

Last thing I want is to get shot out here. My body would disappear and no one would know. It grieves me to think of my mama again waiting in agony for word about me. "I'm tracking a couple of murderers. Are you one of them?"

If he is, I don't expect a truthful answer, but my major concern is getting out of here alive.

On my right, a dark-skinned young man steps from some white brush holding an Enfield rifle that is a good ten years older than he is. The rifle is well maintained, and obviously accurate, but the kid makes no effort to reload, so I calm down.

"I am not a murderer, but yesterday some fellers drove Rockin' R cattle through my okra field, ruining my crop. When I'm hungry next winter, I'll be thinkin' of them with a curse on my lips. I hope you catch 'em."

"They did more than ruin a crop. They murdered four people in Frio County. Watch out for yourself. Don't take chances with 'em."

"I won't."

He points, "You'll pick up tracks over yonder."

"Thank ya kindly."

"Next time," he warns, "go 'round a plowed field. That one was just planted and you and your horse prob'ly ruined two dollars' worth of crops."

"Send a bill to the governor and say C. W. Wallace ruined your crop. I'll authorize it."

"Two dollars, cash money?"

"It'll be a draft on a bank, but any bank you present it to will give you cash."

The young man's grin is unstoppable. "Well, I'll be! That'd come in real handy come winter."

"Take that cash money and bargain for a repeating rifle. This is rough country and that Enfield won't keep you out of trouble."

I nod farewell and head toward where he pointed. I carefully travel around the field. As I ride away, I think of that young man. Negroes are as scarce around this part of Texas as Jews. He was around fourteen years old. For the next couple of years, he'll work from dawn to dark building his spread. He'll construct corrals, catch a few wild cows and maybe a mustang or two, raise a barn, and then a cabin. And that will be a lot of work, but in between, he'll have to fight anyone and any wild thing that tries to take it away from him. In a couple of years, if he is blessed or lucky, he might court a girl, in two after that, be a papa. By the time he's my age, he could be a grandpap with a growing legacy. I lament that happy fate bypassed me.

On the other side of the field, I note the tracks of the nicked shoe horse and another smaller hooved horse heading west, while the others continue south. Once again, I enter the cover of huisache, white-and-black brush, and scrub mesquite as I pick up the trail.

I decide to follow the herd for a half day, then if that doesn't pan out, I can come back and follow the horse with the nicked shoe. If I can recover the herd, that would be something. It wouldn't stop the grieving of the Ross girl but it could ease any financial burdens she might bear. If I can figure out who is driving the cattle—that would be better, but ever' day out, the odds of that happening become longer.

Two hours later, at the mostly rocky Nueces River, the herd disappears. They go into the river as a herd, but seem to come out one at a time, as if they'd just been turned loose. Maybe the thieves realize the law is behind them. I search up and down the bank and cannot find a good trail.

The cattle and those driving them are now deep in the Nueces Strip. And there probably isn't another lawman for a hundred miles in any direction.

By the time I turn back to where the horse with the nicked shoe and the other horse had separated from the herd, it's early afternoon. With the evidence of the horse wearing the nicked shoe here before me, the same shoe I had tracked from the Ross Ranch, I nurse hopes of bringing someone to justice. This nicked shoe offers pretty good evidence I can take to court. That horse had been present when cattle were rustled, and an innocent family murdered. And if the girl can identify the rider, although there would be no recompense without the recovery of the cattle, we can find some justice, even if it's small.

The sun hangs about an hour above the horizon when the two horses turn south again and cross deeper into the Strip, twenty miles north of where the herd crossed the water. I follow them.

The farther south I travel, the fewer folks live here. Any time I cross into the Strip, I cold camp, because the last thing I need is someone coming up on me. When it becomes too dark to track, I hole up under a hackberry tree and try to get some sleep. I long for a hot meal, a warm bed, and a soft woman. Three falling stars streak across the sky as a pack of coyotes sing to each other. Definitely tired of my own company, I could do with a little laughter and pleasant conversation. I've caught myself talking to the gelding more than I care to admit.

In Texas, the expansive property between the Nueces River and Rio Grande has long been disputed territory. An old treaty claims the land south of "the river" belongs to Mexico. Texas claims that "the river" refers to the Rio Grande. The Mexicans argue that "the river" is the Nueces. So the area is peopled by Mexicans and Texans, both thinking they are living in "their country," with each willing to fight to prove they are right.

The area is too large for the law to have much effect; smugglers, murderers, and cattle thieves have free rein to do as they please. The Civil War had opened a door to even more lawlessness. The State of Texas asked Leander McNelly to clean up the Strip. And Cap'n McNelly has fewer than fifty men to do the job. But we are a tough, determined lot who rarely travel as an army. We are usually sent one or two Rangers into the fray. With plenty to do, and only a few men to do it, the work is divided by territory. I usually ride the upper part of the Strip. There's good and bad in doing that—many people know I'm a Ranger, so there isn't much covert work I can do. That's why I need Parrot and a couple of other informants to keep me abreast of the happenings. They are my brush scouts.

Parrot often serves as a messenger/runner, carrying messages to and from the Company, bringing reinforcements when I need them. The only problem with the system is the time it takes for reinforcements to arrive. This is big country.

Fortunes can be made in the Strip, because the law is scarce and land plentiful. On this open range, wild cattle roam the land freely—in my younger days, some buddies and I followed the tradition of pulling unbranded calves from their mothers and slapping our brands on them—mavericks. When my mama found out, she took me to task.

"It's stealing," Ma said, so I quit the easy pickings. "A good Christian man wouldn't do it." At that time, I was anything but a good Christian man. Godless men are plentiful in the Strip. Unscrupulous people always look for an easy way to get rich quick without hard work.

It is those kinds of men who led me here time and time again.

But thank goodness, there are good people here too. People like that young man, working hard every day to make a better life for themselves and their families.

As I stretch out under the shadow of that old hackberry tree, glad to be out of the saddle, Chief plops down twenty feet from me and rolls on a patch of dirt to dust his sweaty back. In his prone position his eyes glaze over and softly close as he falls asleep until he gently stretches his head down and lies flat for a proper nap. He's tired too. I freeze as I hear a noise in the brush. Chief jumps up, snorting. I sit up, finger on the trigger of the Henry, heart racing. The last quarter moon rests high in the sky. I lie in the shadow so I don't think I'm exposed, but I can't see much of anything through the brush. Old habits die hard; every night I sleep with my hand on the cocked Henry, but I dream of the day when I won't have to. Chief snorts, then stomps a foot, but other than that, silence buzzes in my ears. Then I hear the deep scream of a wild cat.

Puma, cougar, mountain lion, panther, catamount—no matter what you call it, Chief and I don't want to tangle with it. I slap my hand against my leg and push air through my lips hoping with my hiss, the cat will scat. Better a cat than a felon.

This rugged country poses many dangers. But thank goodness the good Lord has given the majority of the wild creatures the good sense to run away from danger. Of course, cornering most any animal will bring a different ending to the story. Whether skunk, bobcat, or even deer. I've seen a cornered deer gore and paw a man to death before any of us could pull the creature off him. In my life's work, I have had to corner the most dangerous of all critters, man, who becomes unbelievably vicious when trapped by his own machinations.

As I lay back down to rest, my mind boils with thoughts about the horse with the nicked shoe and a young girl trapped in a privy while she watched her family slaughtered. I knew it would take a miracle to find enough evidence to get a conviction in court, but catching the evildoers is just the first step toward ensuring no other young girl goes through what Bertha Mae Ross endured. With overwhelming evidence, agreed upon by two or more witnesses or a confession, the captain taught us how to dispense swift justice to one and all at the end of a rope. But my preference is a jury trial. Bringing criminals before their fellow citizens encourages everyone to obey the law.

It's a fine line between justice and vengeance. I question my motives every time I'm placed in the situation of meting out justice. I like to think I'm doing it for the victims, but it's probably closer to the truth that I'm doing it for Texas. More and more godly folks are moving here, and I hope to make this a safe place to raise a family. For industrious folks, this is a wonderful place to become prosperous.

But as long as good people have to worry about whether they are going to get shot in the back, this will be an uncivilized country.

Before the sun rises, I saddle and head south. I know I'm getting close to Mexico. Sometime tomorrow my trail will end in the Rio Grande. If I don't find them this morning, I probably never will.

CHAPTER
SEVEN

In the half light of dawn, while my horse crops breakfast, I sit on my haunches under a scrub mesquite bush studying the little homestead in the valley below me. Glad to be out of the saddle for a while, I hope the six days on this lead will pay out today. The horse with the nicked shoe had come this way, and the rider of that horse was involved in robbery and murder. I hope he is down in that little unpainted house right now.

Brush country sets my nerves jingling. I'd cut Indian sign early this morning. Most likely Kickapoo. They were headed east. High in a tree, I'd left a message for Parrot to head to Uvalde, the nearest sizeable town, and send a Ranger to investigate the Kickapoo. The Kickapoo are generally peaceful, but their concept of ownership is different from ours, and things tended to turn up missing when they are around. They believe if you're not using it right now, they have the right to use it until you need it again, or they're through with it.

Although the murdering Comanche raids are fewer and fewer, they still cause concern. The last Indian raid in Frio County occurred just this past spring.

As I squat under the mesquite tree, I reach over with my gloved hand and pull green barbed prickly pear cactus thorns out of the gelding's foreleg. Left too long, they can fester, and the last thing I need in this country is a lame horse. Chief snorts his protest.

The verdant rolling land looks like a sea split by a sandy brown path—a single path. No wagon or buggy passes this way often enough to make ruts. Through-travelers cutting across the open range are probably rare because it is easy to get lost out here in the brush. The trail coming from Moses Hindes's place dead-ends at this tiny cabin. And although I feel pretty familiar with this part of the country, I hadn't known this little homestead was here.

The sun had not yet risen over the hills, but gray dim light of dawn brightens every minute. I'm grateful for the rise in the land that lets me see over the tops of the brush and down into the valley. In the dim light before dawn, I continue to study the small house and barn for movement. Nothing below stirs. Only thing saving this little homestead from more trouble is the distance off any road or trail—and they didn't own anything anyone would want.

As a Special Force Texas Ranger, I've been some sorry places and done some unsavory things, and I've learned to live by a few maxims— watch the weather, eat when you can, and sleep when possible. A ten-minute nap can mean the difference between life and death. Sleep sharpens your reflexes, clarifies your decisions, and helps keep your temperament in check. That's what I'd learned from my captain, and that's how all the Special Force Rangers live. Branded "little McNelly's," in part slander against the captain's diminutive size, but mostly as a lament over the effectiveness that a single Ranger like me poses—a force of one. We strike fear into many a criminal's heart because of the book we carry. That book, as incomplete as it is, carries the names of known lawbreakers who are wanted by the State of Texas.

Until the sun peeks over the horizon, enabling me to see any danger plain and clear, I plan to sit here and nap. I relax with my rifle across my lap, trusting Chief to alert me to any peril. I shut my eyes for a few minutes.

Then I awake with a start, immediately alert, heart pounding, and up on one knee scanning 360 degrees. A dream about my deceased brother Jesse flickers through my mind. I can almost hear his laughter and see his unruly towheaded curls and the gap between his front teeth, but I can't quite make him out as clearly as I want to. The trouble between me and Jesse seems another life ago. I tend to dream about Jesse when something important is about to happen in my life, like the time I was almost kilt by a black widow spider bite in Nueces County.

Chief twists his head to try and nuzzle under the saddle for the bag of oats. I swan that horse tells time better than I can. Every day a half hour after the sun hits the horizon, I try to feed him four double handfuls of oats, and he recognizes that time to the minute. I'm getting short on oats and today he's only gonna get three handfuls. I put the oats in my hat and hold them out for him to munch. I doze again as he grinds away until the eastern breeze picks up and a dog in the valley catches my scent and begins to bark, bringing me alert.

And a rooster crows.

Shadows still linger over the valley and I spot a match flare in the east window of the rundown house. But as the glow fills the small window, nothing moves outside, not even shadows. I listen for children, but only stillness hangs in the air. I can't help but wonder what I will find when I ride down into the clearing.

The daylight grows stronger, and I can see the green hills have been baked to a dusty gray-green under the midsummer sun. The steady southeast wind covered the leaves with caliche dust. In a month or so, if no rain comes to nourish them, an unnatural "fall" will come and the leaves will begin to drop.

I study one of the poorest places I'd ever seen. Indians live better. The yard is cleaned—no grass or manure, mostly hard-packed dirt. The windmill, made of an old wagon axle, is missing a blade and can only turn when the wind blows from due south. The tiny clapboard house and the barn that is not much more than a shed are sorely in need of paint. And the barn roof needs patching. To the north there is a five- or six-acre garden struggling in the droughty weather to grow. Pitiful.

Nearby sits a large fenced chicken coop with about a hundred hens, but the corral is empty—no cow, no sheep, no goats, no swine, no horses. In most of brush country, the soil isn't good enough to have a profitable farm. Game is plentiful; goats thrive on the brush; but only a small number of cattle thrive on the sparse grass.

This shiftless man doesn't take very good care of his place, I thought. He probably takes to the bottle too much. Many do. But someone scraped out the barest of living on this poor, rock-strewn plot of land. This is what I'd expect from someone up to no good. After all, the tracks had led me here. I wonder if I'd find the nicked shoe horse stabled in the little barn. It certainly is not turned out in the corral.

I pull my Colt and check the load, although I know the weapon is fine. Just force of habit, as the familiar apprehension I always feel entering a new area washes over me. I prefer the Henry, although I find the pistol an effective weapon for slamming against a mis-deed-doer's head.

In a place like this, there are an awful lot of areas for someone to lay ambush for me, and in the Strip many people don't welcome strangers. Especially when that stranger is a Ranger. No one wants you buttin' into their business, and they are willing to keep you out by force. Being tired and hungry often leads to mistakes, and I am both tired and hungry. I can't afford mistakes. It only takes one to end a feller's life.

With a deep breath that I hope isn't my last, I tighten the saddle girth, then mount Chief. Easing the reins, we head down the hill.

The dog sets up a ruckus. An Anglo woman comes onto the porch. She wraps her arm around the rough cedar porch post as if holding on for dear life, and stands watching me. She is not armed.

It is a Texas custom to offer travelers a drink of water or a cup of coffee. Travelers are so few and far between most decent folks rel-ish the company, but her apprehension is visible. Then she seems to plaster her face with an unnatural smile.

A ranch hand stumbles into the yard from the barn carrying his straw sombrero under his arm and rubbing the sleep out of his eyes. He, too, is not armed. Like many Mexicans, he sports a heavy black moustache, flour-sack pants, and huarache sandals, triggering my memory about the knife-wielder of the Ross Ranch massacre. Supposedly one of the criminals had worn flour sack pants and had a big moustache.

I hear him utter, *"Buenos Dias, Señora."*

The woman's gaze never wanders from me.

"Rider," she points.

"Sí."

The smell of ripening peaches drifts over me as I trot my big dun gelding past five scraggly trees that might be called an orchard. A black-and-white bobtailed collie near the house porch continues to bark.

When I take a hard look at the woman, I realize she is trembling, and she clings to the rough cedar porch post in an effort to still her shakes.

"Quiet, Worthless," she commands.

Before the dust settles, I swing off the horse in a practiced movement that allows me to continue clutching my rifle loosely in my left hand. If need be, I can squat and fire. Chief will block anyone shooting at me from the right, and with my back to the horse, I can blast toward anything in front of me. I lost a good horse that way one time, but she saved my life.

I quickly sweep my eyes across the area. Nothing moves but the woman. I try to study the surroundings without appearing to do so. Is she a decoy to draw my attention away from villainy? Nothing seems to move.

"Howdy, ma'am. " I clear my throat in hopes of stopping my voice from being so scratchy.

The words garble in my mouth. I don't know if it's because she is such a handsome woman, or because I've spoken less than six dozen words in the last week, and most all of those to Chief. I self-consciously run my thumb down my handlebar moustache. It's so untrimmed it covers half my mouth. I struggle with words.

"Mighty pleasurable summer mornin' we're a-having."

"Yes, sir," she smiles with relief, perhaps because I speak English. Not many in this area do. When I look at her, she blushes like a schoolgirl. Her honey-brown braided hair wraps around her head like a crown. Her complexion is a healthy brown from hours in the sun. She's about thirty and lovely—not delicate or pretty, but sturdy, like a good wife should be.

"I'm Esther Stokes. Can I offer you a cup of coffee and a bite of breakfast?"

So, I landed at the Widow Stokes place. I'm a lot farther south than I intended. I've heard about the widow from the Hindes family, but I pictured her as an old decrepit woman.

I slap my hat against my dusty chaps, glancing down at my filthy boots. I've been living in these clothes for more than a week without so much as washing my face. I figure I'm a sight and certainly not clean company for a lady, but how can I resist?

"I reckon that's the best offer I've had in a month, ma'am."

"I don't have much," she confesses, "just eggs and tortillas."

"Eggs sounds mighty fine. I hadn't et one in a fortnight."

Like a proper guest, I reach into my saddlebags and extract a paper-wrapped pound of smoked bacon—obeying the unwritten Texas code all civilized folks follow that declares one always gives more than they take.

"If you'll let me contribute, the outfit I work for supplies us with a good slab a' meat, but eggs is hard to carry on an ole' wind-suckin', gant-up, moon-eyed, pelter like Chief here." I pat the horse on his thickly muscled neck.

The ranch hand tries to take the horse, but I shake my head no. The well-trained animal remains motionless, reins dragging in the dirt, ground-tied.

As I extend the slab of meat toward the woman, our hands touch, and the strange contact feels as if I've hit the funny bone in my elbow.

I hadn't touched another human in so long. With a thank you, she takes the meat from my hand.

The Mexican man disappears around the side of the house, and that makes me anxious until I hear the squeaking handle of a water pump being pulled up and shoved down.

I prevaricate, "Ma'am, I was bound for the old Spanish road, but I wandered off the trail in the moonlight. I've been ridin' most the night. Would ya mind if I stuck my horse in your pen to let him roll a bit?"

She simply nods and goes into the house. I hear her mutter, "Now, what could make a man ride all night when decent folks should be in bed?"

As I walk Chief to the corrals, I hear her call, "You didn't tell me your name." But I ignore her and keep walking, worried she might recognize me as a Ranger and clam up. I hope to get a little information out of her before she decides to keep any information to herself. In a bit, I hear the ring of the cast iron skillet as it slides onto the stove top.

Pulling the saddle off, I throw it over the corral rail. When I turn, I notice the woman glancing out the window at me. I move slowly, surreptitiously studying the ground looking for tracks, until I become aware of her growing curiosity. So I step to the pump, take off my gunbelt, keeping the butt of the handgun within reach, and place it carefully next to my Henry rifle. Then I pull my shirt off over the top of my head, so fast she doesn't have time to look away. I knew any refined woman would be embarrassed to watch. She glances away but I wonder if she noticed the myriad of white scars lining my upper arms and chest. It bothers me to think she might have seen them. I begin to wash.

When I finish, I don my only clean shirt and yearn for a mirror so I could trim my scraggly mutton chops and thick moustache—I'm getting tired of chewing hair.

She hollers out the door, "How do you want your eggs?"

"All stirred up is fine," I call back.

Looking for tracks, I quickly slip to the southwest corner of the barn. In the dust, plain as day, is the fresh print of the nicked shoe, again and again. So, the horse from the Ross Ranch massacre has been here. And stayed quite a while. Standing in one place for at least a half-hour. Come and gone. As the imminent threat of ambush diminishes, relief washes over me. The tracks hadn't come near the house. But they definitely stopped here at the barn. Perhaps the rider palavered with the Mexican.

Maybe the woman orchestrates the whole malicious crew. It wouldn't be the first time I'd found a woman acting as the brain of weak men.

Something is going on here. I don't know what, but I know I need to try to find out. This nicked-shoe horse is definitely the one I've been tracking.

Wearing my gunbelt slung over my shoulder like a bandito, I duck my head and step onto the shack's narrow porch. I stomp my boots on the uneven boards to announce my coming.

The aroma of frying bacon fills the air. I try to appear relaxed as I entered the woman's tiny domain, but the minuscule one-room house feels like a trap. I'm a big man, more accustomed to sky than roof. As I survey the cabin, poised to go for the Colt, I realize there isn't anywhere to hide, not even a closet, just a couple of pegs on the wall. I relax and place my hat and the rifle on the wedding-ring quilt that covers her bed.

Surprisingly, the room feels homey and comforting. She hums a tune I recognize as a hymn as she cracks at least two dozen eggs into the bowl. The table is set with flowered Dresden china. Apparently, she hasn't always lived in poverty.

"Smells like heaven will," I say.

With her back to me as she cooks, she laughs, a deep throaty sound. When she turns, her brown eyes lock with mine. "I like to think heaven'll smell like flowers and babies."

"Prob'bly will to women, but to men, it'll smell like leather and horses and bacon."

My inclination is to come right out and question her, the way I would with a suspect. Flash my peso badge, demand answers. But I'm under orders to keep tight-lipped, so I have to be careful how I go about this, although question after question keeps popping into my mind. Why did the nicked shoed horse stop here? What is the rider's name? Where was he going? What is your relationship? How do you make a living?

She nods toward a cane-bottomed chair, but I move past her and sit in an old ladderback facing the door.

In the tightness of the space my body brushed hers, and for a second her pleasant scent seems to overpower the strong smell of the bacon. I shake my head to rid my nostrils of the unnerving sensation.

Before I sit down I hang my gunbelt over the back of the chair, pistol butt where I can easily grab it. An opened, half-packed carpet-bag is shoved partway under the head of the bed. She is obviously planning a trip.

Where is she going, and who is she going with? How is she traveling? I've seen no horse. Is the man with the nicked-shoe horse hiding in the barn or coming back for her? I want to ask, but know asking will be poking my nose where it doesn't belong . . . and poking your nose in other people's business is dangerous. I need to tread carefully now, and maybe I can get the information out of her.

To my surprise, the hired man comes in and sits down at the table. It is unusual for Anglos and Mexicans in these parts to eat together, even more unusual for employers to eat with hired hands. She is an interesting character. What would cause a single white woman to invite her hired hand inside her home? Perhaps they are partners, not boss and servant.

Noting my reaction, she says, "I know it's not customary, but it's a tradition my late husband, the Reverend Jobe Stokes, started, and I didn't see any reason to stop when he died. Feeding Tomás outside would only mean more work for me."

"Mister . . . ah," she pauses for me to supply my name, but I don't, so she says, "This is Tomás."

"Howdy," I nod my head toward the thin middle-aged man who glares at me.

It's not honest for a man not to introduce himself, I think. But I'm under orders not to tell anyone my name. She dishes the eggs and bacon onto the plates and then pours the coffee.

She asks, "Would you say grace?" Then she bows her head and waits.

The request didn't surprise me. Decent folks say grace. I just hadn't been around decent people in a while. Taking an opportunity to organize my thoughts, I clear my throat. "Almighty Father, giver of all good gifts, thank you for providin' all we need. Bless the hands that prepared this food. Keep us all safe. Amen."

For a few moments, only the scrape of utensils on china breaks the silence that hangs between us as we eat. The crisp hot meat and moist scrambled eggs taste like home.

I'm itching to tell the widow my name, but Western etiquette demands she not ask me again, if I didn't offer. *She probably thinks I'm up to no good.*

I pause between bites, searching for something to say. My thoughts are never far from Bertha Mae Ross, stuck in an outhouse while her family is killed, and I think about Miz Stokes's privy. "Clever work on your latrine." It just burst out of my mouth as if I had no will of my own.

Embarrassed, she ducks her head. I feel myself turning a deep shade of red after realizing my blunder. A feller should never talk about the unmentionable, especially over food, with a lady. I clench my teeth, wishing I could take back my thoughtless, impolite words. I have been too long gone from civilized people.

She dabs her lips with her napkin before speaking, "The late Reverend Stokes was an inventive man. He built the building with a hinged roof and door, so in the summer and fall we throw back the roof and prop open the door using a cloth drape for modesty. In the winter, or when it rains, we close it all up."

"The open roof sure is smart—" for a moment I think about mentioning the smell, but I recover by saying, "makes it much cooler and keeps the yeller jacket wasps from nestin'."

"Yes," she agrees, "Except under the seat rim—I have to remove one or two nests every summer."

My eyes must have been wide as saucers, because she glanced at my face and burst out laughing. I chuckle too, relieved that the conversation is concluded. I reach for my coffee and say, "I'm on the scout for a photographer feller named Parrot."

I see goose flesh rise on her arms. She suddenly looks nervous. Suspicious. I can't tell if she is suspicious of me because she just keeps glancing at the hired man. Cautiously she says, "That's an unusual name. Is he an Anglo?"

I, too, watch for Tomás's reaction. But the hired man doesn't even look at us. Perhaps he doesn't speak much English.

"Yes, ma'am," I continue. He has a big, tall wagon with his name painted on the side and he's always taking pictures of thangs. He's sorta hard to miss."

In fluent sounding Spanish, I suppose she asks Tomás if he had seen a photographer or his wagon. I sure aspire to speak and understand Spanish, but I never seemed to grab more than the basics—howdy, numbers, and such.

Tomás shakes his head no, but the murderous glance he gives his mistress when she turns away unnerves me.

"We haven't seen him." She bites her lower lip. It seems as if she wants to say something more, but she closes her mouth and looks down at her plate. I wonder what she isn't saying.

CHAPTER
EIGHT

CANTINA LA PALOMA
Piedras Negras, Mexico

The man was strong as a bull, mean as a toothache, and plain unhappy. He was drunk enough to pretend this woman was young and pretty and wanted him. He didn't really want her, but the one he did want acted so high and mighty, so far above him he couldn't touch her. He planned to stick it to this little substitute until she screamed. He would imagine she was the one he desired.

He put his two dollars on the bar, thinking about pretty, straight teeth instead of rotten ones, and pale white skin with the tendency to freckle instead of dark brown skin. Grabbing this woman by her black hair, he pulled her upright and dragged her toward the dark corner reserved for such deeds.

"Ouch, that hurts, *señor*. *Alto*. Stop pulling my hair. A girl wants words sweet and a pretense of love. Romance."

He yanked her hair harder. He would show her hurt. Her words made him want to cut her. Cut her deep. He found cutting exciting.

He jerked her hair until her head slammed against the wall, causing the windows to rattle, making her to stumble and fall to her knees. Then he dragged her the rest of the way kicking and howling like a dog.

He wanted to be feared and remembered. Respected. But she was well beyond tipsy, on her way to smashed, and he doubted if she would remember him. He told himself he didn't care if she remembered him tomorrow, but he did. He wanted the whole damned world to remember him. When he had more money and land, people would know and remember him. They would respect him.

Perhaps it would be even better if she didn't remember him. The anonymity gave him freedom. He pulled his blade and slashed down her aging cheek, leaving a three-inch tear. She would carry the memory of him forever on her face. He would show her what hurt meant.

Her hand flew to her cheek as she screamed in pain. When the man behind the bar started toward them, a silver peso tossed in his direction stopped him. Yes, money solved everything.

As the man unbuckled his gunbelt and his pants belt and let them drop to the floor, he was already thinking about the next full moon when he and his *compañeros* would go raiding. Every raid was different. He liked that kind of excitement. Now that would be real fun, and a great leap toward his goal of getting rich and powerful. When he was rich no one would say no to him. No one would tell him what to do.

He pinned the woman to the wall with his left hand by holding her voluminous black hair. Her cheek continued to bleed. She whimpered, screamed, occasionally spewed strings of Spanish as he pulled open the buttons on his pants. He let them fall to the floor near his feet, not caring that his buttocks were exposed to the whole room.

The door sprang open and light shattered the darkness. Framed in the doorway was the unmistakable silhouette of the Spanish general—pistols on his hips, bullwhip in hand, shoulder-wide sombrero. It took the Spaniard only a moment to assess the situation, and the whip lashed out across the room, landing on bare buttocks.

"Let her go, you fool. If you're going to go whoring, do it elsewhere other than our meeting place. Pull up your pants, *el puerco*. We have work to do."

CHAPTER
NINE

After breakfast, I thank the widow, saddle up, and ride southwest. Before I get out of the homestead's sight, I pause on the top of a hill long enough to watch the widow walk out of her home and begin a brisk stride toward the Hindeses' place, her shoes, tied together, hanging around her neck, the obviously loaded carpetbag clutched in her left hand.

What would make a woman with no horse set out to walk six miles barefoot carrying a heavy bag? I wonder. *What would make a woman live way out here alone?* My mind leaps and bounds across the morning's events like a newly penned mustang. I can't help but wonder about her. I spy on her long enough to be certain she's heading to the Hindeses.

Then I turn to the task at hand—tracking the man on the horse with the nicked shoe. If I don't catch up with the fugitive, I plan to come back and confront the widow about her surreptitious behavior.

Unconsciously, I track signs of rabbit, beetle, quail, deer droppings, and javelina ruts. I can hear the voice of my adopted father in my head. He taught me years ago to watch the ground.

"Learn to watch. Beware, many things can be hostile—Indians, Mexicans, whites, scorpions, black bears, rattlers, and spiders—but treacherous men are the most dangerous." I can almost hear his voice. Like mileposts in the dust, I mark the trails of passing creatures . . . cat track, skunk path, armadillo hole, coyote dung, hog rub. This time of day, the deer huddle in the shade, chewing their cud; the hogs dig into mud if they can find it, and the armadillos curl into a ball instead of blindly digging for grubs.

About a hundred yards from the house, I pick up the suspect horse's trail. The distance between hoofprints indicate a slow gallop. Three or four miles later, the chalky ground turns hard as rock and tracking becomes more difficult. It isn't rain that mars the trail because it doesn't rain here often, and when it does, it is often a "gully warsher" of at least an inch of hard-blowing rain, but it hasn't rained in a long while. Within a six-foot radius, there should have been prints in the fine dust or a nick on the caliche. I dismount to study where the next print should have landed, about a twelve-foot radius. It is as if the horse has taken wings and flown. I move forward—twenty, then thirty feet, looking for a scuff in the ground, a broken blade or twig. But there is nothing. It seems my pursuit of the dastardly buzzards who'd murdered four people in cold blood ends here. I am probably three miles or less from the Mexican border. In all likelihood, they've taken refuge across the Rio Grande beyond the reach of Ranger law.

My maternal uncle loved to tell tales about the Coahuiltecan Indians who occupied this land a hundred years before the foot of any white man touched it. They were so primitive they didn't hunt or farm. They existed on bugs and snakes, mesquite beans, and cactus. He'd say, "South Texas is the closest place to hell you can get on earth," (and here, my mother would tap him on the shoulder and give him her "watch your language" look) "fitten' only for thieves and smugglers." It is true. Anyone who chooses to live on this poor land has his hands full trying to survive.

I retrace my path back into the woman's yard. Before I enter the yard, I unbuckle a spur from my boot and drop it into my saddlebag. I plan to use the pretext of the lost spur as an excuse to look around.

She lives in an excellent spot to be a conduit for supplies to smugglers. Her corrals are large enough to hold a herd of stolen cattle, although they show no sign that they have. But I've known more than one innocent-looking woman to be a snake.

Just as I predicted, when the dog begins to bark, the Mexican shows up to find out what's happening. He looks as if he'd been sleeping—in the daylight, before noon, at the time he should be working the hardest. But the cat's away, so the mouse is playing. At the sight of me, he nervously steps out of the shadows of the barn.

"No *estamos aqui*, Señor." The slight man gestures with his hands pointing down the trail toward the Hindeses. "Señora *para alla*." He furtively shifts his gaze back and forth.

Although I parley Apache pretty good, I don't get along with Spanish. Making the words flow is impossible. The whole language seems upside down to me. And my lack of understanding has often proved a detriment to me. My ma speaks like a native.

"The Señora is gone?" I ask.

"Gone." Tomás confirms.

In the hope of finding out what she is up to, I intend to thoroughly search the house. Now I just need this feller to go back to his own business. Through sign language, I indicate to Tomás that I've lost the spur, then I hand him a bottle of medicinal tequila I always carry in my saddlebags. The *hombre* calms down as he gratefully takes the bottle and disappears back into the barn.

Pulling open the door to the little cabin, I realize again how little she owns. There is no lock on the door, although it can be barred from the inside. The only things of value are the mirror, the iron bedstead, the cook stove, and some old books. The floors are clean. The bed is neatly made. The carpetbag is gone. A high-collared wedding dress hangs on a peg in the corner, but it is the only clothing I see.

I knew her to be a generous woman. I had read suspicion in her eyes, but she had invited me in and fed me without expecting anything in return. She let me mind my own business without probing. She was a good egg cook. She was probably a good woman—I just needed to confirm that for sure.

In an apple crate nailed to the wall near the head of the bed stand a dozen books. I pull down the heavy family Bible and thumb through it. It is well worn. I've known more than one person who hid their loot between the pages of the Good Book. But all I find are a few pressed flowers and some obviously well-read beloved passages. The other books include a volume of poems, a complete Shakespeare, *The Rise, Progress, and Prospects of Texas* by William Kennedy, *Swiss Family Robinson, Pilgrim's Progress, The Count of Monte Cristo*, and a few theology books. It is quite a library for a poor Texan. I thumb through each one, and in the poems, I find three love letters from Jobe. I quickly scan through them, but there are only words of love and mentions of ongoing Christian work.

I open the flour bin, find it almost empty, and incapable of concealing a weapon or money. Nothing in the sugar bin, less than a handful of coffee beans, and about five pounds of pinto beans. I sift through the dried beans and find nothing. Jars of canned vegetables—okra, corn, potatoes, squash, green beans, and black-eyed peas—line a shelf that hangs a foot down from the ceiling. There is no meat, smoked or canned. It doesn't look as if her supplies will take her far after her garden peaks. Perhaps she's gone to resupply.

A shotgun lies under the bed, a half-empty jar of shot next to it. The gun is clean and loaded. The corn shuck mattress ticking is fresh, as are the linens. I check the floorboards and under the table and chairs. Nothing is loose. No evidence she is involved in anything nefarious.

I guess there is nothing left to do here. I'm out of leads and out of options. Once again, the criminals triumphed. I reckon I'd head to the Hindeses' place to see what she is doing. If I could just pick up one more lead. If not, my investigation is ended.

The bright sunshine causes me to squint and pull my hat lower over my eyes. The hired hand is nowhere to be seen when I swing onto Chief and head to the Hindeses, not taking the trail, but keeping in the brush.

As I top a ridge, the July sun sits a quarter-way up from the horizon, causing the distant land to shimmer with illusionary water holes.

But even though it is only late morning, before I go a half mile, moisture dots my upper lip and back. It is probably eighty degrees and will soon climb to about a hundred. The ground will be burning by midafternoon.

It doesn't take me long to catch up with the woman on foot, even though I keep off the beaten track, which means meandering around in the brush. My biggest concern is that she will hear me crashing through the bushes, or Chief's hooves striking on the rocks.

Topping another rise, I spot the widow in the valley sitting on a fallen tree log in the shade to catch her breath. I almost miss her. I dismount and watch through the scraggly branches of white brush. Pulling a glass Mason jar out of her bag, she takes a drink of water. The exercise of walking fast made her "glow." Tendrils of brown hair slip from under her bonnet. She looks around, perhaps sensing she is being watched. I pull back a bit.

After repacking the Mason jar, she stands up, brushes off the back of her skirt, and lifts the valise to the top of her head before she starts walking again.

Thirty minutes later, she tops the little grade she's been climbing for the last fifteen minutes and pauses again to catch her breath. In the valley below, about three-quarters of a mile away, I can see the salt cedar trees surrounding the Moses Hindes's place. The Nueces River runs clear and green to the north of the cattle pens.

Albert Hindes's homestead sits across the Nueces River—on the north, Texas side. I can see the obscure images of two animals and two of his children playing in the yard. But it is to Albert's late father, Moses's place, in the disputed territory south of the river that the woman heads.

Five red-and-white hounds send up the alarm when they see her. Their clear mournful bays resound across the distance. I'm grateful for the distraction they cause, because anyone around will be less likely to notice me, if their attention is focused on her.

The Hindeses' house, built before Texas won independence from Mexico, is constructed in the old style of two separate log buildings tied together under a single roof, with an open space between the buildings called the dogtrot. A plain, simple woman, Inez Hindes steps from under the dogtrot, waves her apron, and "woo-hoos" when she sees the younger woman approaching down the trail.

The wash on the line flaps in the breeze and the windmill turns with a gentle squeak. Chickens scatter in the yard as the hounds follow the widow woman to the house. The dogs, cats, goats, pigs, and chickens in the yard are uncountable—more than you can shake a counting stick at.

I'd stopped by here yesterday and asked Miz Hindes about Parrot, and she said she hadn't seen a stranger here since the first of the year.

Inez Hindes's youngest children, eight-year-old Mariah Jane and six-year-old Billy, come running toward Esther Stokes. I hear their high little voices ring through the brush.

"Where ya goin' Miz Stokes?" Mariah Jane inquires as she takes the carpetbag out of the older woman's hand, and with a great effort begins to carry the heavy gear toward the house. The widow smiles sweetly at the little girl and reclaims the bag. Relief washes over the little girl's countenance.

"Ya takin' a trip?" Billy asks. He carries a fishing pole almost everywhere he goes, and it's in his hand now.

"Can we go with ya? We promise not to whine."

The children keep up continuous questions until they reach the house, so Esther didn't say a word. Mariah Jane's dress is clean, but two sizes too small. Two dark braids hang almost to her knees. Billy, on the other hand, is a mess. Dried mud covers many of the freckles on his hands, feet, and cheeks. His overalls, two sizes too big, are rolled up into deep cuffs with threadbare knees, and the torn back pocket is a flap that hangs by a thread. His front pockets bulge with a million hidden treasures. I reckon the boy's been awake and running full speed for hours before the sun rose. One day he'll make a good Ranger.

"You're off mighty early, Miz Stokes," their mother says.

Inez Hindes, although only fifty-five years old, has been married forty years. She loves to boast about her twelve living children, thirty-three grandchildren, and two great-grandchildren.

I ground-tie my horse, then sneak behind the outhouse.

I feel like a criminal myself, always sneaking around. When this batch of trouble ends, I am going to go home and quit Rangering. I'm tired of consorting with criminals. Tired of always watching my back and suspecting ever person I meet is up to no good, I want to consort with the honest and good folks in this world, like Inez Hindes.

Shooing a dog with her apron, Inez gives the children a look that tells them they best go play.

"Come in for some coffee and tell me what brings you so far from home."

I can't help but admire and respect the homely, honest woman who always wears her hair pulled back into a tight bun on the nape of her neck, making her look stern. Although she looks stern, there is a kindness and humor about her eyes. She reminds me so much of my own ma, it makes me homesick. Miz Hindes has always welcomed me to her clean-scrubbed hand-hewn table, in spite of my squabble with her son, Albert. I love hearing her tell the stories of early Texas—including the one where her mama gut-shot a Comanche coming in the door with no good intent, and living though the Runaway Scrape.

I hear Inez ask, "Did you have a visitor today?"

Esther hesitates. I watch as she nervously shifts her bag from one hand to the other before setting it down at the door.

Inez continues, "Cornelius Wallace stopped by late last evenin' askin' about a picture-makin' man."

"Tall feller, blonde moustaches, big dun horse?"

"That's him." Inez confirms.

"I fed him breakfast, but he didn't tell me his name."

"He always was a strange one."

Uncomfortable with her comment, it is my turn to duck my head and shift my weight.

"You know him, Miz Hindes?"

As the women enter the house, their voices garble. I move from behind the outhouse to crouch in the shaded south corner of the dogtrot. Then I could hear them plainly again. A hound comes over and nuzzles my leg. I scratch behind his ears, then shoo him on with my hand.

"Everybody knows his family. His uncle's that famous Texas Ranger, Bigfoot Wallace."

"I've heard tales about him."

"I knew Nels's ma when we lived over to Atascosa County, before they moved up the country and we came to Zavala County—before he had trouble over that girl. The boys always call him C. W., but his mama calls him Nels. For a couple of years, Nels an' Albert seemed great friends. Then somethin' went 'skewed. For years I hadn't seen hide nor hair of him 'til last evening. I always figured he got sidewise to the law. He said he didn't have time to jaw—had to hunt up that tintype man. Promised to come back one of these days and catch me up on all the news."

Esther says, "I don't really have much time for visiting either. I'm needin' to borrow your rig to go to Austin."

No lone woman would travel a hundred and eighty miles for nothing. She is definitely up to something.

"Oh?" Like a good Texan, Inez would never ask anyone's business, but I know she is as curious as I am as to why a trip to Austin is necessary. *She'll get it out of the woman one way or another.*

"I'm hoping to find a buyer for my place there. I've given up on the folks in San Antone, so I've written the banks in Galveston and Fort Worth, too."

I wonder if that is the truth, or a cover-up lie. Could she be going to meet someone?

"I wisht one of us had the cash to he'p you out." I hear Inez clattering around, and my mouth begins to water when I smell her strong coffee and a plate of freshly baked kolaches. Her version of the Czech pastry is famous countywide. No one ever leaves her table without a sample of the yeasty, sweet old-world delicacy.

"You know," Inez continues, "I've said it before, and I'll prob'ly say it again, but Albert needs a wife and you need a family."

Esther laughs. Whenever I see Miz Hindes she wants to matchmake for me, too.

"I keep telling God that, but he hasn't seemed to listen to me."

"Oh, he's listened," Inez says. "He just ain't ready yet. I know

Albert ain't no preacher man like Jobe, but he'd take care of you. He's doing right smart for hisself these days. He even got a new bull."

I can't stop from wondering what my old "friend" is up to. Albert could never hold on to a nickel. He'd been one of my maverick friends, but I'm not sure he ever stopped branding calves that weren't his.

"Mamma!" Mariah Jane hollers. "Billy's riding the goat."

I scramble from behind the house when I hear the chair scrape against the wooden floor as Inez stands up, grumbling about the young'uns, and rushes outside to take care of the problem. Then I hear her heavy footsteps as she comes back into the single room that serves as kitchen, living room, and guest bedroom.

"I wisht we still had Jobe to ride the circuit." Inez laments. "He made those Bible stories jump-up and live for Allie Mae and Isabel, but the little ones don't remember him a-tall."

"The new parson is a bit dry," Esther agrees.

"But he's willing to risk his life on this circuit. The superintendent is callin' it the blood circuit. . . . The Book tells us we might have to lose our lives for the Gospel, but I don't reckon many take it as literally as Jobe did."

I step back when the pack of hounds enter the dogtrot. The same one immediately comes my direction, wagging his behind, wanting me to scratch right above his tail. When the children step up onto the dogtrot too, I take another step backward into the shadows. I hear them ask. "Mamma, can we go with Miz Stokes to Austin? We ain't never been to Austin."

"You ain't been invited," Inez scolds.

"I could be your chap'rone," Mariah Jane offers as she shyly runs her hand along one of the oak logs.

"And I could be your guard." Billy pretends to draw six-guns.

The noisy confusion and my increasing distance muffles any response until they all step out of the dogtrot into the animal-filled yard.

"Would you consider takin' 'em over to my sister's at Castroville? She'd be happy to have 'em, and I'll send Albert up after 'em in a couple a' days."

"I'd love to have the company, if you could spare them. They'll help the miles zing by."

"If you want to put up with 'em, they're yours."

"That'll be fine."

"Give me a second to put up some food for 'em and get their clothes ready."

With a whoop like wild Indians, the two children run out of the house, down to the barn, passing within feet of me, but never noticing. I take advantage of the situation by slipping back into the brush. In only a few minutes, they return leading a little black horse hitched to an old black two-wheeled buggy.

For me, it's easy to face down a criminal. Yes, my heart pumps wildly, and I may sweat rivers, but no criminal scares me like a child. Their innocence amazes me. And I worry that I'm going to be the one to corrupt them and end their enthusiasm for life. Perhaps it's because I didn't have a carefree childhood and I can't remember being innocent. My own childhood was strange and extreme. Perhaps I find it splendid that, in spite of the violence in this part of the world, children seem to quickly move past any trouble and continue to live life with a gusto and joy I envy.

"Wash your face and hands," Inez admonishes. "Billy, go put on clean clothes. And Mariah Jane, don't fergit Dolly—put enough oats into a tow sack for ten days."

I hear the children furiously working the pump handle up and down, probably splashing water everywhere. Then I see Mariah Jane run to the barn, only to emerge moments later struggling to carry the burlap bag full of oats which she drops, then half drags, half carries to the vehicle. Mrs. Stokes helps her lift it onto the back of the two-person rig. The children climb into the open-topped buggy, folding their hands in their laps like little angels as they eagerly wait to start.

I bet that "angel" business won't last long.

"Mamma?" Albert Hindes calls from near the barn. "I cut a new door hinge from that beef I slaughtered."

I hunker down on my haunches when I see him through the fronds of the brush.

He stops short when he sees Esther, but the look crossing his face isn't surprise. I slip over into the shadows to give myself a darker silhouette. All I need now is a visit with my old pal. The last time I'd seen Albert, only the law had stopped us from turning deadly.

"Howdy, Esther."

I crawl back farther into the brush. The last thing I want is to be discovered. I reckon I'd learned all I was going to learn here. Another failure. McNelly would be disappointed. My attention swerves back to the group in the yard when I hear Inez scolding Albert like she did when we were youths.

"Albert! You shouldn't be so familiar with Miz Stokes. I don't think she invited you to call her by her Christian name."

"Sorry, Miz Stokes." He doesn't sound sorry to me, only insolent.

The children giggle.

"Yer learnin' 'em bad habits," Inez mutters. "Yer 'sposed to be an example."

I peer around the corner to see Albert set his tools down and walk to the buggy.

"Where ya headed, Miz Stokes?"

"Austin," the children chorus together.

"That's a long way to go alone."

"She's not going alone," Billy says. "We're goin' with her as far as Castroville."

Albert looks up at Esther. "You're in for big trouble takin' them two bobcats with you."

Esther pats Mariah Jane's leg. "It'll be a better trip with them than without them."

"What's goin' on in Austin, Miz Stokes?" Albert tries to sound nonchalant, but his voice comes out oddly possessive. It makes me want to slug him again. I suppose everything about him makes me want to take a poke at him.

"She's hopin' someone'll buy her place," Mariah Jane says, the know-it-all creeping into her voice.

"We'd better get on the road," Esther lifts the edge of her dress as she prepares to step up into the buggy.

I watch as Albert lays his hand on her arm, delaying her. "Why don't you wait 'til tomorrow, and I'll go with you? Without these two brats, Ma can watch mine."

Esther freezes, a look of horror obvious in her eyes, even from this distance.

"I'd go today," he says, "but I killed a deer this morning and I've got to finish dressin' it."

Bad time to kill a deer, I can't help myself from thinking, *he's libel to get worms.*

"I'm afraid my friends will be expecting me," Esther stammers. "If I'm a day late, they'll be worried sick."

"You've corresponded?" He leans in, inches from her face.

She nods hesitantly. It is obvious she is lying.

"Visitors been totin' yer letters instead of me?"

She nods again. "We'd best be on our way, or they'll be fretting."

"When'll you be back?" Albert asks sharply, his thick lips curled as he tries to be friendly.

"Oh, Albert," Inez cuts in, "she'll be back when she gits back. We ain't needin' that buggy. Quit bein' a mother hen. You can go git Mariah Jane and Billy in a couple a' days. I'm not worryin' about 'em, why should you be?" Inez enters the house and comes out carrying a shotgun and a bag of shot, which she puts in the floorboard behind their feet. She kisses each child and presses something into their hands.

Albert lays his hand on the horse's rump, "Y'all be careful."

Inez mutters. "For petey-sake, Albert, she's a grown woman. She's gone further from home than you'll ever go." Inez bends to pull weeds from a bedraggled bed of corn flowers and bachelor buttons near the door. "Do your courtin' when she gits back—if some city feller hasn't snatched her up while you are markin' time."

Mariah Jane begins chanting, "Albert and Miz Stokes sittin' in a tree k-i-s-s-i-n-g," she spells.

Billy joins in, "First comes love, then comes marriage, then comes Albert with a baby carriage."

Giggles draw my attention to three of Albert's children hiding behind the live oak tree in the front yard. From their position, they have a clear view of me. Their grubby faces wear shy smiles.

Albert pulls hard on Mariah Jane's pigtail. She cries out.

"See what you got to put up with all the way to Castroville?" He turns toward his own children, "You idiots git home."

"And we better get on the road," Esther pulls the horse's head around to the north.

"We'll be back when we git back," Billy cries. "Maybe you little kids can go next time."

"You bring 'em a candy," Inez calls. "Don't forgit it—and don't you eat it!" she warns.

"You mind," Albert cautions.

As I scramble for my horse, I hear Inez scold, "They usually do, Albert. They aren't like you."

CHAPTER
TEN

At my wit's end, I decide to go back to San Antonio and see if any of the other Rangers have ideas on how to stop these villains.

Something isn't adding up. Nicked shoe horse goes to the Stokes's farm. The widow packs up, hikes six miles, borrows a horse and buggy, and leaves the country. It stands to reason that she is too scared to stay, or carrying a message to someone. As the only lead I have, I am very interested in where she is going and who she'll talk to next. But I'm also aware that the clock rapidly ticks toward the possibility of another slaughter. I need to do everything in my power to stop the malefactors from raiding another ranch.

Esther Stokes doesn't seem like a common lady lawbreaker. Most women who drift across the law's thin line do so out of necessity. She certainly isn't living high on the hog, and she seems too smart to be some man's tool. But the horse with the nicked shoe did come to her place.

My thoughts rarely drift from the senseless slaughter of a good family and the sorrow of a young bride, an old woman and her two grown sons with their throats slit, and a dying rancher crawling over a mile to his brother's house while grieving his dead wife. May. June. And now, July. If the pattern holds, the clock ticks toward another tragedy. But there is no way to know when or where the dastardly murderers will strike. I hope as word spreads among other ranchers, they'll set guards, especially during the full moon.

"Stop, Miz Stokes. Stop!" I hear Billy scream in horror.

Although I am almost a quarter of a mile behind them, I hear the cry. I touch spurs to the gelding and the animal leaps up the hill. I see Esther jerk Dolly's reins. The mare's mouth flies open in pain as the chain cuts into her jaw, skewing the buggy to the left.

I don't see any immediate danger, so I spin Chief around and go back below the rim of the hill where I dismount, wait, and watch. There seems to be no reason for Billy's scream. From the top of the hill, I can make out the distant blur of the church spire at Castroville.

"What is the matter, Billy?" the widow demands.

"The point of the Lone Star is headed down, and the field of red is flying over the white. Somethin's wrong. That's a distress signal."

I creep under a scrub oak and wait. With all their attention directed forward, I lie on my belly, lifting my head over the ridge trying to see what Billy sees, praying that they'll not look backward. A sharp rock digs into my hip, so to ease the pain I inch forward. It will also help me hear better.

"What nonsense are you talkin'?" Mariah Jane demands.

"The flag—look at the flag. It's signalin' somethin' wrong."

Nothing stirs in the town except the red, white, and blue flag that shifts and dances in the southern breeze.

"Sure 'nough somethin's wrong," Mariah Jane confirms.

"We'll never know what, until we go down," Esther jiggles Dolly's reins.

Before the rig moves ten feet, an old man on a gray donkey starts up the hill to greet them. He stops at a distance and raises his hand as he calls to them.

"Howdy, folks. I seen ya hesitate, so I reckon you got our signal— we didn't mean to scare nobody—but just wanted to let ya know we got the worst outbreak a' measles I ever did see. Folks that done had 'em already are gettin' 'em again! I figger it's some foreign kind."

Esther calls back. "I have the Hindes children and I'm supposed to leave them with Helen Reese."

"Don't you go a-stopping in Castroville, Missy," he warns. "We've had lots a' folks die, and Helen Reese don't need no more kids to worry about. Her man's got more spots than anybody in town."

"Oh, my goodness!" Esther responds, "Would you tell her we were by and I'll be taking the children with me to Austin?"

The children yell, "Wahoo!"

"Shore, I'll be tickled pink to tell 'em. I was the first to get them pesky little dots and the first to get well. The Reeses will be plum sorry to have missed y'all."

The old man lifts his hand over his head in a farewell salute as he trots his donkey back toward town.

When Esther pulls Dolly's head around, I can see the frustration on her face.

"What we gonna do, Miz Esther?"

Then she smiles, and the sun literally comes out from behind a cloud and shines on the buggy and its occupants. It casts a golden glow about them that makes them look saintly with the quaint old Alsatian town in the background. If I could paint a picture, it would look like this.

"We're going to go callin'. You'll have to be on your best behavior, and maybe we'll be invited to supper and to spend the night on a soft goose-down bed."

I trail the little company about six miles to a big hacienda surrounded by a shoulder-high rough rock wall that has cactus growing on the top. Arched over the entrance to the compound, a stone structure is embedded with white round river rock that spells out Montemayor.

I recognize the name because Alberto (Bebo) Montemayor is a prominent rancher and politician. I've heard talk of him running for governor.

As Mrs. Stokes drives the buggy under the arch, big dogs begin to bark. I ride along the wall, but cactus prevents me from seeing much. A queenly older woman comes out the massive dark mahogany door and embraces the widow, kissing her on both cheeks.

I hear Esther say, "*Buenos dias*, Yolanda," and they begin to blather in Spanish.

Three children come out of the door and in seconds, I glimpse Mariah Jane running and laughing after them. The women sit on a bench in the shade fanning themselves with Spanish lace fans, chattering away in Spanish and English so fast I can't comprehend a word.

I reckon the widow and children are set for the night, so I head east, figuring to stop at the Menger Hotel for food, a bath, and a long sleep. Tomorrow, if I can, I'll talk to any Rangers that are in town and catch up on the news. I should be able to pick up the widow's trail again somewhere between Schertz and New Braunfels.

ELEVEN

T he sheriff of San Antonio stood six feet one inch tall, and was 250 pounds of muscle and toughness. Sometimes he thought he'd been selected like the Old Testament King Saul simply because of his size. That size was a blessing as he knocked sense into some of these folks. But most likely he was elected because he spoke German, Danish, Dutch, Spanish, and English. The rigors of the job had turned his hair white even though he was only thirty-five years old. Thank goodness San Antonio was no open cow town like the old days. Most of the townspeople nowadays were decent folks.

The city was growing so fast, it was hard to keep up with new faces—almost nine thousand residents now. The once-sleepy little mission town was a mecca for people wanting to capitalize on Texas. There were now more hotels, bars, businesses, and churches than you could count. German speakers were being replaced by English and Spanish speakers.

Three of his deputies were white boys, two were Spanish, and one was colored. The colored deputy dealt mostly with the army post. Those military types were particular about how justice was administered to their boys.

The front door of the jail opened and the colored deputy, Charlie Goodman, marched in a prisoner at gunpoint. Draped over Charlie's shoulder was the cowboy's heavily tooled gunbelt with distinctive twin ivory-handled, silver-plated pistols.

"Don't you lay your black hand on me again, boy, or I'll kill you."

The sheriff stood up, dwarfing the lean cowboy. "What's going on here?"

Charlie spoke up. "This civilian fleeced some of the post boys in a poker game. I had to cold-cock him to disarm him." Charlie lay the pistols and a tortoise shell-handled switch-blade knife on the sheriff's desk.

"Thanks, Charlie, I'll take over from here."

Charlie left the room and the cowboy turned to the sheriff, "That nig . . ."

"Watch what you say, sir. That man is a duly appointed sheriff's deputy of Bexar County."

"He ain't got no right . . . "

"In Bexar County, he has the authority of the law to shoot you and no one would ask a single question. I think that means he's due your respect. Now have a seat and tell me your side of the story."

The cowboy sat and the sheriff stood over him in a domineering fashion.

"There's nothin' to tell—" a stern look from the sheriff made the cowboy go on. "I was playing poker and these soldier boys started screaming I was cheating 'em."

"Was you?"

The cowboy looked down at his Royal Bengal tiger-skin chaps, then he looked up at the sheriff with a sheepish smile, "Not exactly. One feller had an easy tell—pulling his ear. The other boy got a frown line between his eyes if he had a bad hand and laugh lines around his eyes if it was good. Now, would you call that cheating?"

"You're King Fisher, aren't you," said the sheriff, motioning toward the striped chaps.

"Yes, sir." Fisher smiled at the sheriff's preoccupation with the tiger skin. "These cost me three months' wages." It was just the effect he intended and usually got. "I procured the hide from a big cat what was stolen from a circus traveling through the country. The Bengal had escaped from the thieving scallywags. They were inattentive, though, and the tiger took them for lunch. I took the tiger. The circus owner required cash from me for my troubles. So, of course, I had to require something of the tiger."

"I cain't decide if you're a bounder, or on the level," the sheriff replied, "but you seem to have a knack of being in the wrong place at the right time. I'm gonna release you. But you get in one more squabble in San Antone and you'll be behind bars. You hear me?"

The cowboy straightened the flashy golden silk kerchief tied around his neck as he stood with an easy grin. "Yes, sir. You're saying do my mischief out of Bexar County."

The cowboy reached for his gunbelt, but the sheriff laid his paw on top of it. "I'll just keep these until you're ready to leave town. I hear you're quite the hand with them."

The cowboy gave him an "aw shucks" look, then said, "I work hard at it. I shoot a minimum of forty rounds a day."

"What do you shoot at?"

The cowboy shrugged self-consciously, "Tin cans, tequila bottles, mockingbirds . . . "

CHAPTER
TWELVE

The cacophony of the city excites Chief. The animal's nervousness telegraphs up the reins to me, forcing me to concentrate on controlling the powerful, shying creature. The horse, head collected, prances across the cobblestones as if on parade.

San Antonio, founded by Spaniards, has existed since the 1700s. Old adobe buildings are dwarfed next to the modern three- and four-story limestone buildings. New wooden structures spring up willy-nilly, causing me to wonder if the spaces in between are alleys or streets. Alleys are problematic. There's no better place to stage an ambush.

The thing I hate about criminals is they seem to run in packs. Just when you think you can handle one, another comes out of nowhere to shoot you in the back. I don't consider myself a *pistolero*. I'm much more accurate with the Henry. Being a big man, six-two in my stocking feet, makes me a big target. It seems to me many of the people who come after me are little men—literally. When I pull my pistol, they seem to shrink. Shooting from the hip I have a fraction of a second to aim at my target, squeeze the trigger, then move, hoping my opponent hasn't been able to sight me in faster. I've lain awake many a night calculating how to move. If I extend my right arm and step back with my left foot, moving me out of the line of fire, I hope to create a slimmer target. If the shooter is right-handed, they tend to skew to the right when hit, so after firing, I usually step back again and to my right. If they're lefties, as many noted gunmen are, I have to do a different dance. No pistol is accurate beyond a dozen feet. But people often get fatally shot by accident when bullets start flying. And by accident, or on purpose, you're just as dead.

Being in the city always makes me review these things. I've earned a few enemies over the years, and for some reason, probably because the city means less work, criminals tend to congregate here. Over the years, I've decided most criminals are lazy and impatient. I always take those two qualities into account when dealing with lawbreakers.

This city is known locally as "San tone ya" or "San An tone." San Antonio is a busy place. I haven't seen more than two dozen people in the last month, so the city is a wonder to me. Some streets are paved with bricks. Most are winding cattle trails that head to the railhead and stockyards downtown. Wagons, burros, trains, children, dogs, and people exist in the swirling dust.

As I stop in at the Bexar County sheriff's office to report my presence in town, the front door opens, and a cowboy with a big black Stetson and fancy striped chaps steps out the door. He grins and laughs, nodding toward me before walking down the street. He whistles a dance hall tune and does a little sashay step in his shiny patent leather boots.

When I enter the sheriff's office, I notice a fancy ivory pistol apparatus on the desk. The big man picks them up, empties out the bullets, and puts them into a drawer.

"I'm C. W. Wallace, a McNelly Special Force Ranger."

The sheriff extends a hand that is the size of a cast iron skillet. I shake it, noting the calluses. This is a working man.

"I just wanted to let you know I'm here for the night and to inquire about any other Rangers in town."

"I know of no other." He twists the key in desk drawer lock, then removes it and deposits it in his pants pocket.

"I'm headed to the Menger for the first bath and shave I've had in over a week."

He laughs. "Sounds like you have an agenda after having been on a hard scout."

"I do. I intend to sleep in a real bed in the buff and have all my clothes washed and pressed overnight while I get the first solid sleep I've had in a month."

"That sounds like a good luxury. Besides sleep, what brings you to town?"

"I'm trying to unravel the Ross Ranch massacre."

He purses his lips in disgust. "I heard about that. A true tragedy. I wish you all the best, and I appreciate your efforts."

As I head to the Menger Hotel, I start out tipping my hat to every woman, but soon it becomes too constant a task, so I just nod when I can. Every race, nationality, and creed is represented here—freed slaves, German immigrants, Mexican peons—each person hoping for a better life. Along with the jingle of wagon traces, voices of children, the slamming of doors, and stomping of boots, phrases of different languages tickle my ears that are not used to such noise. I hate the city. There seems to be danger for me everywhere and no way to ascertain where the threat is coming from until it's upon you.

I can't help from imagining bushwhackers behind every window. Many people don't like Rangers. Those people came to Texas to have the freedom to do as they pleased, even if their pleasure means harm to someone else. Rangers try to make sure everyone has an equal shot at freedom and prosperity.

From my childhood, Texas Rangers have rescued me from life-and-death situations more often than I like to admit. I'll always be beholden to them.

From downtown San Antonio, trails to other Texas cities lead out like spokes on a wagon wheel, trails created over the years by myriads of cattle. Early tomorrow, I will head out on the northeast trail to the state capital, Austin. But until then, I intend to crawl in between clean sheets at the Menger Hotel.

The Menger is an oasis of civilization down on old Alamo Plaza. It has a big mahogany bar, high ceilings which help the rooms stay cool, and the best food, so it attracts anyone with coins from carpetbaggers to European royalty.

A sign on the door into the hotel asks people to remove their spurs, so I sit in a ladderback rocking chair on the porch to unbuckle mine. My ma has the same rule at her house. Spurs sure can tear up a wooden floor. As I lean over, a pair of tall patent-leather boots with fancy spurs shaped like a gal's legs step onto the veranda. I look up once again to see the man wearing tiger-skin chaps who had been coming out of the sheriff's office. Without removing his spurs or glancing in my direction, the man shoves into the door and walks into the hotel.

Now I recognize him by reputation. King Fisher. A known *pistolero*. His name is not in the book, but it probably should be. A brawler and show-off by reputation, he lives in the Strip—Uvalde County—but his reach is long, and he likes to party at the bar here.

I am surprised to note he is not wearing his infamous ivory-handled pistols, and then I realize Fisher's pistol rig was the one the sheriff had slipped into his drawer as I entered the office.

When I step across the hotel's lobby to register, I see Fisher leaning against the door to the bar. He boldly watches my ever' move, and I'd be worried about turning my back to him if he'd been wearing his guns, because I've heard he shoots equally as well with either hand.

After I finish signing the book, he calls across the room, "Are you a Ranger?"

I ignore him and ask the clerk, "Could room service bring me a bath and a shave, clean my clothes, and fix me a big plate of greens, potatoes, beets, beans, and cornbread?"

"You want meat with that, sir?"

"No beef, pork, or venison. I been eating enough of that."

"Very good, sir."

Before I can head to my room, the pistolero grabs my arm. "Have a drink in the bar with me. You must be thirsty."

McNelly does not allow cursing, liquor, or cards in camp, and he discourages them when we are on the job. But I can see this fellow has a bee in his bonnet, and I reckon I'd better swat it, or I'll never be allowed to move on.

"I'll join you," I say. "What can I do for you?"

He summons the bartender, "I'd like beer, and whatever this feller wants."

I'm a teetotaler, usually. I ask the bartender, "You have milk?"

He responds that he does, and I ask for a big glass of it.

"With the cream, or without?"

"Definitely with." I turn to Fisher and ask again. "What can I do for you, sir?"

"I want to know if my name's in the book."

"The Lamb's Book of Life?" His brow furrows. Now I know good and well what book he means, but I'm not going to let him know that. It is widely known in South Texas that Leander McNelly issues each Ranger in his Special Force a book with the names and descriptions of all known wanted men. It's also known as the Book of Knaves, the Crime book, or the Bible II. On an everyday basis, I don't worry too much about the book, but each night after supper, I pull it out and read a few pages, hoping to fix the details in my mind. On a daily basis, I don't come into contact with enough people to worry about it much. The book has become legendary, causing many a man with a guilty conscious to confess because he thought his name was in the book, even though it wasn't. Lawbreakers always want to know whose name is in the book so they can warn anyone they know who is wanted. The book is a warrant for the arrest or execution of known murderers and criminals. After years of foiled legal proceedings and countless assassinations of witnesses, jurors, lawmen, and judges, the book makes it legal for me to put to death anyone whose name is in the book based on *La ley de fuga*, the concept that those known criminals are fleeing from law. Although controversial, the book is the governor's last desperate effort to bring law to Texas.

Fisher's eyes narrow, "You know the book I mean . . . McNelly's book. Let me see it."

We are not in the habit of showing people the book, and I certainly would not hand it to a stranger. I down the milk. It is wonderful. I stick out my hand, and he grabs mine in an ill-conceived power struggle, trying to crunch my bones together. As he squeezes hard, I squeeze harder, not letting go.

"I sure do thank you, Mister. That milk is just what I needed. That and a good night's sleep." As I crunch his hand, I give him my best steel-eyed glare. "I hope tonight's party will be quiet. I aim to have a good night's sleep. I'm not in the mood for any midnight serenades or shenanigans."

When I finally let go, Fisher moves his hand toward a pistol that isn't there, then in vain wipes his hand on his chaps.

Suddenly Bertha Mae Ross's description of someone in striped chaps pops into my mind. As I cross the lobby, I turn back and look at the man at the bar. From a distance, those chaps do look like stripes. I wonder what else might make chaps look striped. I decide to cogitate that more fully later, when I'm not so tired. I turn and go up to my room.

The night passes quietly, and by dawn I am clean, rested, and ready to hit the trail. The Menger's service is truly "Strict High Middlin," which is as good as it gets. My clean starched shirt feels good against my freshly shaved neck. My trousers are brushed clean and my boots are shiny as a soldier's on parade.

I do not regret leaving San Antonio behind. Town makes my ears hurt. I prefer the coo of mourning doves, the cry of killdeers, or the varied songs of mockingbirds to the racket of the streets.

After a good morning's ride, I top a hill overlooking the Comal River. I sit easy in the saddle, allowing the big dun horse to pull a mouth of grass from under an ash tree. The animal's coat, curried clean last night, now glistens with sweat that runs in rivulets in the hot morning sun.

As I figured, there on the road below me is Esther Stokes's buggy, making haste toward Austin. She is clearly on a mission and hell-bent to see it through. One minute she travels like she's on a picnic, the next she pushes that little mare to the limit. In San 'Tonya, I'd inquired about the Montemayor family and about Mrs. Jobe Stokes. It seems the Montemayors are a well-to-do family that became Methodist. Esther Stokes is just a young poverty-stricken widow. But, according to Inez Hindes, she hadn't left her place in two years. Now all the sudden she appears to be on some sort of quest. It didn't make much sense, yet.

Something is up, I just don't know what. But I aim to find out, and I reckon direct contact is the best way to do that.

CHAPTER
THIRTEEN

I lift Chief's head and lean forward slightly in the saddle. Using a running walk, the big gelding begins to pace, closing the gap between him and the buggy.

Billy's head nods up and down as he dozes. The late afternoon sun forms a golden halo around the boy's head. I chuckle to myself; that boy is nothing like an angel.

On the other side of the buggy, Mariah Jane trails a long thin branch behind the left wheel of the buggy and softly whistles some nameless tune.

When Billy stirs, Mariah Jane leans over Esther and pokes him.

"Some guard you are."

Billy stretches and yawns. "Whaddaya mean?"

"An Injun's been trailing us a quarter mile." Their high voices carry clearly down the road.

Billy twists around to study the trail behind them.

Esther scolds, "You mustn't tease like that, Mariah Jane. Didn't you ever hear the story of the boy who cried wolf?"

"No joshin', Miz Stokes! Some feller's a' coming on a big horse."

CHAPTER THIRTEEN

Esther swings her arm onto the back of the buggy seat, twisting around and squinting into the sun.

"You see him, Billy?" she struggles but fails to keep the fear out of her voice.

"Yes, ma'am, he's a' comin' at a nice shuffle, but it ain't no Injun. It's Chief."

"You mean an Indian?"

"No, Uncle See Dubya's Chief. No Injun pony paces like Chief. He's like ridin' the rockin' chair on Uncle Albert's front porch. He's one of Cap'n King's Quarter-thoroughbreds."

"Maybe he'll tell us a Bigfoot story," Billy stands up and turns backward.

Mariah Jane follows suit and stands precariously on the seat, flapping her arms up and down as she screams, "Uncle C. W.! Uncle C. W.!"

It quickly became obvious to me that this interview is likely to be directed by children, who many thought should be seen and not heard, but these two had not been raised that way. They are lively as flames—dancing and moving constantly. I just don't want them to get burned if the widow is up to something nefarious.

CHAPTER
FOURTEEN

"How are you, Uncle C. W.?" Mariah Jane asks.

"Where ya headed?" Billy chimes in.

I can't help but chuckle as I direct the big dun horse alongside of the buggy. I doff my hat at them, feigning innocence. "Evenin', Miz Stokes. Are y'all off to some place in particular, or just gaddin' about?"

"Miz Stokes is taking us to Austin."

"We ain't never been to Austin before."

"Yeah, she's tryin' to sell her place, 'cause she don't wanna marry Uncle Albert and give it to him."

Esther tucks her chin with an unmistakable look of disapproval on her face.

I smile at her over the tops of the children's heads. Although her bonnet is skewed, she sure looks pretty with tendrils of her hair coming loose from its crown and framing her face. The shotgun lies inaccessible on the floorboard under her carpetbag. What kind of femme fatale is she? It would take her at least a half a minute to pull, cock, and aim that old weapon.

"Looks like you got your hands full."

Anger replaces the disapproval in her eyes. With sarcasm she says, "You seem familiar to me, sir. Reminds me of a scruffy trail hand who came by my place two days ago. He wouldn't give me his name—carried bacon, but no razor."

Mariah Jane interrupts, "This here is C. W. Wallace. He's our uncle."

Billy chimes in, "Not our blood uncle, but our close family friend kinda uncle."

I'm not proud of the fact I'm always sneaking around. But it is a necessary aspect of doing my job safely and well. To stop sneaking around becomes another tally on the reasons why I'm ready to quit Rangering. Her shaming me did not sit well with me.

"Are you goin' to Austin, too, Uncle C. W.?"

"Yep."

"I'm tired of this buggy. Can I ride up there on Chief with you?"

Esther warns, "Children, let Mr. Wallace alone!" Her anger and suspicion toward me quite apparent.

The children sit contritely for a half second, then Billy turns to Mrs. Stokes.

"Could Uncle C. W. tell us a story? He's a right fine weaver a' tales."

"I know he is." She glares at me. "Whoppers seem to surround him."

"We're bored. A story sure would help the time gallop by."

She reluctantly says, "I'm sure Mr. Wallace has more important business, and will want to ride on."

"Pleeeease," the children whine, "stay with us."

I smooth my mustache and say, "Since we're headed to the same place, we might as well travel together, and since we're travelin' together, we might as well jaw."

"Do wax eloquent," she snipes.

The children settle back against the buggy seat, their legs dangling several inches off the wooden flooring. They fold their hands into their laps as if on the settee in their parlor. It is obviously the first time in days they sit still.

"Tell us about how you traded for Chief."

"Na," Billy argues, "that's a girl story. Tell us about bein' in the army or fightin' Injuns."

I wink at Billy, "Those stories might be a bit rough for the fair ladies with whom we travel."

With a sigh, Billy nods his acceptance with great regret. I'm never sure how to handle the little humans. I try to imagine them as adults. That helps a little.

"But perhaps I can tone it down a bit."

Billy nods eagerly.

"I was born the same year Texas was born, 1836. My pap was off'ta war and ne're once saw my countenance, for he was defendin' that Thermopylae of America—the Alamo, from a demon of a man, San'tanna. And you both know the fate of those brave Texians."

Billy looks at his big sister. "I don't git it."

"His pa died at the Alamo."

I take the interruption in stride, but I can't stop my smile. I try to blend my words with the clippity-clop of the horse's hooves, hoping to lull the "wiggly worms" into a stupor. Although I haven't often dealt with children, I have a passel of nieces and nephews that I rarely see. Even a new great-nephew. Texas is exploding with children. I think I could learn to cotton to kids, if I ever had a chance.

I start my tale again, "In '45, when I was just about your age, Mariah Jane, I hap'ly changed my nationality from Texian to American."

"We joined the Union, didn't we?" Mariah Jane's earnest gaze fixes on my face.

"That's right. But Adam's curse caused the wind a' war to blow too oft across this thorny land and when I was twenty-seven, the Stars and Stripes ripped in two and the blood of many fine lineages poured onto the mountains and plains in that most wretched of wars between the North and the South."

"Did you fight in the War of Secession, Uncle C. W.?" Billy asks.

"I served out west all durin' the war, Billy, but ne'er saw a Yankee. Ever' day we fought Plains Indians, keeping folks like yer ma safe."

"Tell us about one of your battles."

Every time I've been around this boy, he asks about fighting. It wouldn't surprise me to find him in the Rangers in a half-dozen years.

"We cut acrost the trail of a dozen Kickapoo, but two branched off in the direction of Frio City," I gesture with my hand. "Now the Kickapoo have long lived on the Rio Grande River, and gen'rally aren't hostile, but there have been exceptions. Like many native people, their concept of ownership is different from ours. They believe if you're not usin' it right now, then they have the right to do so. We call that stealing. But with so many men away at the war, our job was to protect Frio County folks and thangs, so we headed out after them Poos to see what mischief they were up to."

Dolly's walk slows, so Esther taps the mare with the buggy whip. The widow doesn't make eye contact with me, and I wonder what she is thinking.

"The lieutenant ignored them ten Indians that started toward Mexico, and we headed after the two that set out north. Flankers were sent out so we wouldn't miss the trail, in case the southbound Indians doubled back to attack us from the rear. And it wasn't but about as long as it takes a dog to scratch his . . . ear, when we heard guns a-blastin'."

The children inch toward the edge of the seat.

"We tore out toward the ruckus and found it comin' from a rust-red sandstone gully, what folks now call Brand Rock. It's a water hole on the old Spanish Trail used by many a drover. You can still see some of the brands they carved in the bluff when they camped there.

"Our flanker, Henry Locke, dismounted up on the east side of the hollow, shootin' down on ten Kickapoo. We fired down the gully. As long as Locke held his position, we put them warring devils in crossfire. When an Indian would rise from behind the brush to shoot, the boys in front could see him plain."

Here, hoping to create some suspense, I take off my hat and wipe my forehead with my handkerchief. Then donning the droop-brimmed hat again, I tip it back with my forearm, until it touches the back of my neck. This way I can study the Stokes woman better, without seeming to. She appears to ignore my story, and that makes me want her attention all the more.

"Lieutenant took a ball in the shoulder. The shot came from right close to me, whizzing past my head. So I figured to use Indian tactics and jump across the arroyo to draw fire. Then I reckoned Locke could get a clear shot."

Using his thumb and forefinger, Billy motions with his hand as if he is shooting.

"I leap, but the rocks slip out from under me. I thrust out my hand to break my fall, and my gun goes skitterin' into the draw. So, there I was unarmed, on the ground, out in the open. Bullets flying all around me." I take a long dramatic pause.

"What happened, Uncle C. W.?"

"One of them red fellers rushed over and lifted his firearm point blank into my chest." I pretend to hold a rifle and pull the imaginary trigger. "He squeezed the trigger and 'click,'" I snap both eye lids shut and hold them shut, "he kilt me dead."

"Ha," the lady laughs in spite of herself.

I let out my breath slowly and pop open my eyes, causing Mariah Jane to jump. "The weapon misfired. I can account for the miracle a' my escape only by believin' it an act of Providence."

I look up to the heavens and take off my hat, placing it over my heart. The children look up, too. Widow Stokes stares straight between the mare's ears. Maybe she is planning her next caper . . . or taking a nap with her eyes open.

I study the high white mare's tail clouds that wisp across the blue sky. At last I meet both children's gazes and continue, "The rest of my company was so entranced by my perdicament, that none fired nary a shot. What had been a deafenin' roar of gunfire only a moment before, was now dead silence. I could hear the slight breeze blowing through the mesquite trees. Then, suddenly, a sound that freezes an Indian's heart as fast as a gringo's split the air."

"What sound, Uncle C. W.?" Billy demands in rapt attention.

"The whirring of the vilest critter on earth, a diamondback rattlesnake. I looked down to see we had routed a creature three inches in diameter and six feet long. That there snake bared his fangs at us and darted out his tongue. My red-skinned opponent and me stood froze, neither of us wantin' to make a move that might end in death.

"Our companions dared not shoot, on the chance of missin' the snake and hittin' us with a bullet ricochet off the hard red rocks. Although the hot rocks were cuttin' my back and the cold barrel of a rifle rested against my ribs, I didn't so much as blink an eye.

"That Indian standing o'er me stood still as a cigar store statue. Thank goodness that day was hot and the rocks blisterin', 'cause a snake with a belly full of jackrabbit only wants a cool place to catch a nap.

"What happened, Uncle C. W.? What happened?" Billy demands.

"After what seemed a millennium, that ole' snake turned tail and slithered off. Slidin' right next to me and 'tween that feller's legs. Relief washed over me and switched on my giggle-box. I started laughin'."

I laugh with a joyous hearty sound that echoes between the trees and down the lane, "and much to my *surprise*, that wild man lifted his gun into the air and started smilin' too. Soon laughter slipped from under bush and rock, as the other men, Rangers and Indians, joined us.

"Hoots and hollers followed. It was a fine brew-ha-ha. Then, the leader of that Kickapoo party brought their ponies and they mounted and rode south. To the best of my recollection, that tribe never raided Frio County again. And 'tis the only time I ever heard tell of God using a snake to save a roughneck's hide."

"How fortuitous your misadventure didn't end in violence," Esther said earnestly. I wonder if her sharp edge is easing.

"It is indeed," I reply.

"I wisht I could see an Injun," Billy sighs.

"Was that the same year the Comanche brave came sneakin' in the door at our place?" Mariah Jane asks.

"I reckon it was about that time, and speaking a' time, soon ole Sol will bid us adieu. Seein' as how I been in the saddle ten straight days, all I want is a couple of hours to embrace the sweet charms of Morpheus."

"What's that mean?" Billy whispers to Mariah Jane.

Mariah Jane in her best big sister voice says, "It's a poetical way of sayin' he's tired and sleepy."

"Oh," the little boy bows to his elder, and clearly more knowledgeable, sister.

"Were you plannin' to stay the night with friends, or would you allow me to set up camp near you, Miz Stokes?"

By the set of her mouth, I can see my suggestion is not well received.

"Pleeease," the children plead.

I point to an oak mott. "That looks like a fine campsite. We can kick up some dried leaves to make soft beds and the trees'll help cut the dew."

Gently pulling on the left rein, Esther directs Dolly to step off the road.

"Uncle C. W., can I sleep next to you?" Billy asks.

I study the widow before responding, "If it's all right with Miz Stokes."

She smiles at Billy and nods.

I direct, "You young'uns gather some dry wood, while I take care a' the animals. Then you can roll out our beds on the upwind side of the fire."

The children hop to their tasks as Esther brings out the provisions for supper.

"You liked eggs so much the other day, I reckon you won't mind having them again, Mr. Wallace."

"If it's made by your hand, Miz Stokes, I'll like it fine."

As before, after receiving my plate, I bow my head and pray out loud.

After she says, "Amen," she adds, "I traded eggs for fresh rye bread from the German bakers in New Braunfels."

"It's tasty," Mariah Jane begrudgingly admits. "I didn't think I'd like that seed."

I eat second helpings, and so does Billy. I help the widow wipe the plates with sand, then declare, "I'm plumb tuckered out."

It is not quite dark, but the light has turned golden.

I watch the widow as she gathers the food into a tablecloth and ties it up into the tree to keep out the skunks and ants. It is obvious the days without much sleep have left her pretty frazzled. The children are still bouncing up and down, playing chase between the trees.

I know if I can keep them still for ten minutes, they'll fall asleep. I carry two books in my saddlebags, McNelly's criminal tally and a well-worn Bible. I call the children over as I draw out the Bible. The children settle back, resting on the ground on either side of me. I randomly open the Good Book and it falls onto the story about Jesus and the little lost lamb. "We're just like that lamb," I say. "Jesus watches over us. And we're not tall enough to see everything he sees, so we have to trust him to care for us."

When I finish, the light has dimmed to where I can't read anymore. Mariah Jane and Billy are sound asleep. I pick up Mariah Jane and carry her to the pallet near Esther.

"Goodnight, ma'am." Out of habit, I lift my hand to my head to tip the hat that isn't there, then lamely finish the gesture by running my fingers through my thinning hair. I turn and retreat to my own bedroll.

As I carefully lay out my carbine and pistol within easy reach, I become aware of the lady watching me. I find nothing nefarious about her. Would a criminal be so kind to children? In my experience, criminals are only concerned about themselves.

I lay in the dark and listen to the sounds of the night. I can hear her breathing. She fell asleep the minute her head hit the ground. I wonder what it would take to remove those worry lines between her eyes. I reckon she is carrying an awfully big burden trying to provide for herself out in that godless Strip.

But something else is driving her. I don't know what, and I don't know how to ask her. Her big brown eyes are always wary, scared, like an animal caught in a snare. I know one wrong move and she'd shy off, and I'd never catch her.

If she is caught up in something criminal, I might be able to get her out of it.

Almost twenty years ago I'd given up chasing skirts for chasing Indians and bandits. Even my mother has given up asking, "Do you have a special girl, Nels?"

I don't know what it is about this woman that attracts me—it certainly isn't her fancy clothes, since she has none. And, it isn't her gay laughter. Since she didn't have that either.

I stare at the waxing moon creeping over the horizon. It is like a ticking clock. Were criminals plotting their next raid at the full moon? What reason could they have for slaughtering a whole family? I find no answers. The horse with the nicked shoe had stopped at the Stokes place and spent some time. Why? What did the widow know?

Then my mind drifts to the nagging thought that I need to slow down and settle down. The constant saddle time is starting to bother my left knee and hip. A fact that I'd admitted to no one. Even more threatening to me are the thickening knuckles on my right hand. My pistol pulling is not at a staying-alive speed.

What I need is a nice little woman and a couple of happy kids to remind me there is good in the world. A man is known by the company he keeps, and my problem is I am wearing thin on myself. There are good people in the world, and I need to spend time with those folks. It's hard on a feller always trying to watch his own back, suspecting everyone is out to get you.

Suddenly my perspective on Mrs. Stokes is different. Maybe I just feel sorry for her living in that shack way out in the middle of nowhere. Maybe I just think we might be in the same boat. Alone. I need to settle down—have some children. I am getting too old for this running around the country. She needs someone to love and cherish her. Someone to make her smile.

She stirs in her sleep.

She had obviously made the most of her little patch of ground. She has an economy of movement that I appreciate. She didn't sashay, flit, or dither about. She moved efficiently from task to task with focus. And she was handsome. I wouldn't call her pretty, nor beautiful, but she seemed to be pleasant. On the other hand, maybe she is just a good liar. I laughed at myself as I thought, *I sound like I'm weighing the merits of a horse before buying it.*

Billy rolls over against me and moans.

But it is true, children are life. They bring purpose. I reckon I am Rangering to make Texas a safe place for women and children. Although I've neglected to get a wife and babies for myself.

She looks to be about thirty, a little long in the tooth for babies. So am I. I don't know if marriage and family are in my future, but for the first time in a long time, I let myself think about it and the type of woman I'd like to take home to Mama.

CHAPTER
FIFTEEN

The golden shafts of dawn seep through the live oak trees, casting long shadows. I saddle and hitch the horses as quietly as possible while Esther and the children sleep. I put bacon in the pan, and in a bit, it sizzles, lifting the smell into the air. When the light breeze moves the aroma to her, she sits up and runs her fingers across her crown braid, pushing the wild hairs and loose pins back into place.

She looks more rested.

Rousting the children, I begin packing their blankets as I announce, "Hurry, we have all the honey we can say grace over."

The children head to the brush to do their business. When they return, I hand each child a thick slice of flame-toasted bread wrapped around a slice of bacon. After saying a quick grace, I pour thick brown honey over each piece.

"Eat up, chillun'," I holler, hoping to budge Mrs. Stokes from the brush. "We best commence the scout. We're burnin' the day."

"Can we ride Chief, Uncle C. W.?" Billy asks.

"Please," Mariah Jane adds with her mouth full.

CHAPTER FIFTEEN

I pick the little girl up and place her into the buggy. Esther, on the opposite side of the buggy, hoists her skirt and puts her foot on the metal step. Although I hustled to assist her into the buggy, she beats me to it. I hand her a bacon-filled biscuit.

"Chief's the colt of a wild Apache pony and a prize-winning England horse. So he's fresh in the mornin'. Maybe after an hour or so, the spunk'll be outta' him and you can ride him." I swing up onto the spirited horse.

We ride in silence for a mile, enjoying the morning, the children still half asleep.

Dolly eagerly pulls against the traces and the buggy lurches forward over the rocky ground.

"Look up yonder, Uncle C. W." Mariah Jane points north.

The sun flashes on one of the silver *conchos* that decorates the oncoming rider's saddle. My heart begins to pound in my chest as I recognized that saddle and remembered my orders concerning it. Quietly, deadly, I say, "I see 'em, girl, and I smell blood."

I draw my rifle out of the scabbard and dismount simultaneously. "Miz Stokes, best get them children and hug the ground. We got trouble brewin'."

I see my tone has frightened her, and she doesn't protest my order.

I grab Dolly's bridle and pull her into the ditch next to the road. I have to get the children out of harm's way because I suspect this will not go down easy. The buggy dips precariously as Esther jumps down. Grabbing the children, she draws them to the side of the road and onto the ground into the bar ditch.

The horse and rider grow larger as a man gallops easily toward us.

Swiftly as a snake strikes, I lift the carbine, raise it to my shoulder, and fire. The blast explodes into the air. A second later, the man falls out of the saddle.

With the gun's report echoing in our ears, Esther screams. The smells and sounds of violence tear the air. Gunpowder and blood. Then Esther rises up and runs past me toward the man I'd shot.

CHAPTER
SIXTEEN

Esther's screams rend the silence. She lifts her skirt, sprinting down the wagon-track road toward the figure sprawled
in the dirt.

I bound after her, unsure whether he is dead or alive. I grab her
arm, turning her around, away from the downed fellow. I wrap my
arms around her, locking her arms to her sides, as I try to explain.

"Let me go!" she demands, tears streaming down her cheeks. "Let
me go!" She twists vigorously in my arms.

"Miz Stokes," I say quietly like I would to a frightened animal.
"Miz Stokes, calm down."

But she continues to scream. "Murderer!" Stomping on my boot
and kicking my shin, she twists out of my grasp. She stumbles toward
the fallen man writhing on the ground. I know the nature of the man
in the dirt and know she stumbles toward unknown danger.

"That man is riding a stolen saddle." I call. "He's probably armed
to the teeth and deadly as a rattler."

The children behind her wail loudly, hysterically, and although I
repeatedly order her to stop, I am uncertain if she hears me.

The downed man crawls toward the walnut-handled pistol that fell out of his holster.

"Stop!" she cries.

But his outstretched hand moves closer to the pistol lying in the dirt.

"*Alto, por favor!*" she screams.

His fingers wrap around the pistol's grip and shakily, he raises the barrel toward her.

I have no choice. I lift the Henry to my shoulder, pull the trigger, and feel the kick. In front of her, the man on the ground jerks, then drops back into the dirt. Smoke curls from my rifle's barrel, obscuring my view.

As Esther Stokes kneels beside the dying man, the rapidly growing red circle on the man's right shoulder is mirrored by a smaller circle on his left breast. A strange pallor lights his tanned skin.

With trembling hands, she rips the hem of her petticoat. She plops into the dirt and lifts the man's head into her lap, tearing open his shirt and jamming her petticoat into the largest bloody hole. As I reach her side, I see the life go out of the man's eyes.

Like the flash of a mirror, a light reflects on her face and causes her to pause. I glance over to see the man's black mare grazing by the side of the road. The saddle's dozens of beaten silver discs, made of coins the Mexican's call *conchos*, flash in the early morning sunlight. I would recognize that saddle anywhere. About a dozen of the fancy Dick Heye saddles had been stolen months ago. It is in the Book of Knaves to shoot on sight anyone riding that saddle.

The children come up and stand expectantly in front of Esther.

"It's no use, Miz Stokes, he's dead." Mariah Jane puts her hand on Esther's shoulder.

"Yes," she screams, "and that man killed him! Get away—get away from us!"

I reach down to help her up, but she slaps my hand away.

Esther commands, "Get in the buggy, children."

Wide-eyed, Mariah Jane leads Billy away.

Again, I offer my hand to her, "Let me explain. *La ley de fuga...*"

"You owe me nothing. But you owe this man and his family an explanation." She can't seem to control the volume of her voice. Everything comes out as a scream. "When I see the governor, he'll hear about this, and you can give your explanations to a jury!"

She eases the dead man's head to the ground, stands, fighting my hand on her elbow. She turns, lifting her skirts, and runs to the buggy. The children huddle together in the seat whimpering. As Esther snaps the whip over Dolly's rump, the startled mare springs into a trot as if she can't get away from the scene fast enough.

Passing the point where the man lies in the middle of the road, Esther refuses to look at me as I kneel beside the crumpled body.

I search the man's pockets. There are papers, some in Spanish, others in English, a purse with silver *pesos* and double eagles, a monogramed handkerchief, and an onyx-handled switchblade knife about five inches long. I put the knife in my pants pocket, wrap the *pesos* in the kerchief, and shoved them into my shirt pocket along with the papers.

I look up to see Esther and the children staring over the back of the receding buggy at me. Regret washes over me when I see the sorrow, hurt, fear, and pain reflected on their faces. Could I have handled this another way? I don't regret shooting this no-good murderous thief. But I do regret shooting him in front of those little children and the woman.

Taking someone's life is never an easy thing. Even if the person committed a heinous crime, while they are alive, they have a chance to repent and change—set their lives on a new path. Once they're dead, they don't have that chance. The act of killing any living creature plagues my soul. It brings to my mind all the lives I've taken. And there have been too many. Not just this thief, but all the lives over all the years. They fixate in my mind. I can't quit dwelling on them; over and over the scenes play in my thoughts, keeping me awake, tormenting me in my solitary hours, living in my dreams. The only thing that gives me peace is dropping the burden at Jesus's feet in prayer. And that is easier to say than to do. Standing in the gap between lawbreakers and lawful folks often costs my peace. But if I didn't stand up against lawlessness, who would?

Against my better nature, I leave the body where it fell, because of the directives in the Book.

I gather the reins of the felon's saddled black mare, mount Chief, and put the spurs into him, tugging the little mare onward. I hug the brush until I pass the buggy. One thing I know, I need to beat that woman to Austin.

Thirty minutes later, as I top the hill on the south side of the Colorado River, I can see the large white flat top of the capitol in the valley. *Thank goodness, we'd been closer to town than I thought.* I slow to a trot as I cross the bridge. Obviously not happy with the hollow sounds of the hooves on the wooden bridge, the little black mare tugs wildly against the bridle, jerking my arm back. I pull her nose up to my knee, which didn't make Chief happy.

Oh, the capital city—it's noisy, and smelly, and in addition to pompous politicians and snobby know-it-alls, it is full of sinful distractions—ladies of the night, liquor, and showboats who see a man with a pistol as a challenge. It seems everyone wants to make a name for themselves at the expense of others. People with any sense live in the country.

As soon as I cross the river, danger seems to lurk behind the reflection of every window and in every alley. All cities are the same. A glass breaks down an alley and my hand reflexively springs to my pistol. I am always on edge here and know I will find no relief until I put the city behind me. As I drag the little mare, I know a compadre of the dead man might recognize her and demand accountability from me. I pray there will be no more confrontations today.

Once I cross onto the capital grounds, I think about the report I need to make. I don't use my tongue often enough to tell the story smoothly without rehearsing it. I tie the horses to the hitching post, remove the Dick Heye saddle, throwing it over my shoulder before I climb the steps to the governor's office.

A formidable bespeckled man sits behind an imposing cherrywood desk. "May I help you, sir?"

The man raises his eyebrows in an expectant manner, as if he is waiting for more information, but I don't intend to give him any more, so I simply state, "I need to see Leander McNelly and Governor Coke."

I stand the saddle on the floor with a thump, horn down to protect the fenders. It is a handsome saddle, and heavy.

The secretary motions toward a chair, "The governor's appointment calendar is filled all day. Let me tell him you're here and I'll send a runner for Captain McNelly."

"I'll find the cap'n myself. Tell the gov'ner we'll be in shortly."

I walk down the stairs and down the hall and knock on the door.

"Come in," the scratchy voice calls. I was not sure he would be here. The captain is not in good health and is spending more and more time at his farm. Relief washes over me at the sound of his voice, no matter how weak. I know one day I'll knock on this door, and there'll be no answer.

When I greet the diminutive captain with a hearty handshake, I note that McNelly looks pale and frail, although his neatly trimmed dark beard covers most of his face. He looks years older than his thirty-three years. We talk as we walk up the stairs and down the hall to the governor's office. He's panting as we enter the reception area. The captain confided, "I'm on my way to San Antonio. From there I'm heading to Oak Island. I'm glad you caught me. Have you made progress on the full moon murders?"

I shake my head. "I may have just blown the only lead I had, but I recovered one of the Dick Heye saddles."

I can tell Cap'n is pleased with the recovered saddle, but a coughing seizure prohibits him from answering.

"His name may have been George Haines." I hand over the things I'd pulled off the man's body. McNelly gives them a quick glance. He dumps the kerchief onto the desk, then picks through it. He puts all the silver pesos into his shirt pocket.

"I'll have them cut." He means he will take them to the jewelers and have the jeweler cut the five-pointed star into them. Those coins are often taken by civilian spies to another Ranger to prove that the bearer has come with a legitimate message. These silver tokens are proving to be a handy tool in McNelly's fight against criminals. They've become a type of badge.

When the inner door of the governor's office opens, Esther Stokes is telling her story, the blood still on her dress. But with her bonnet in place, her view is blocked and she seems unaware we are in the room.

"That morning, my dog barked before dawn, when I went out to investigate, I overheard a man behind my barn with a thick Castilian Spanish accent plotting with my hired man to murder one of my neighbors by cutting their throats when the moon turns full. They said a king and a general were involved."

"A king and a general?" The governor's eyebrows pucker.

When McNelly turns to me, I can only shrug. I haven't heard this story before, and I don't know what she is talking about. I had only known something about her was off, and now it seemed to be this secret.

She continues, "Those criminals plan to meet at the *Cantina la Paloma* at the full moon."

"Lee," the governor says. She turns around with a startled expression on her face.

"Mrs. Stokes, this is Leander McNelly, captain of the Special Force Texas Rangers and one of his corporals. Lee, this is the Widow Esther Stokes from Maverick County."

The captain responds, "Pleased to meet you, ma'am. Thank you for bringing forth this information."

The governor adds, "These outlaws have to be stopped here and now. We can't have noble ladies worrying about having their throats cut."

McNelly thoughtfully rubs his chin. "I have spies in that area, but they've had trouble coming up with anything concrete. This information about the Cantina La Paloma may be our first break. I'm hoping to know more in a short while. My man here didn't have time to completely brief me."

"There's more," Esther insists as she nervously fingers the tie on her bonnet. She points at me. "That man is a cold-blooded murderer."

CHAPTER
SEVENTEEN

Esther springs out of her chair, "That's him! He's the murderer."

I stand near the door with my hat in hand, embarrassed. I sputter, "I had orders to empty that saddle on sight, Miz Stokes. Cap'n said no palaverin' with the rider. I also had orders to leave the man where I dropped him, no burying, just bring in the saddle. I tried to explain, Miz Stokes, but you wouldn't let me."

I look to the captain for help. Mrs. Stokes looks to the governor, but no help is forthcoming for either of us.

"I tried to wing him, for the children, I tried . . . "

Leander McNelly interrupts, "Mrs. Stokes, let me introduce you to Corporal Cornelius Wallace of the Texas Rangers. The man Corporal Wallace killed this morning was a proven criminal, like all those charged in the Book." He thumps the thick book that rests on the Governor's desk. "He was riding a stolen Dick Heye saddle—on a stolen horse."

"We weren't close enough to see who was in that saddle!" Esther protests.

CHAPTER SEVENTEEN

The captain quietly says, "Those saddles are heavily studded with silver set in a pattern you can tell a half-mile away. Those saddles were stolen near Corpus Christi, and no others have been sold or made. Corporal Wallace did exactly as ordered. And it's going to take such swift and forceful action if we're to stop this bloodletting in Texas."

The governor says, "You must send Corporal Wallace to follow this Paloma lead, Leander."

I know I have fallen out of Mrs. Stokes's favor. It will be very uncomfortable to be near her again, so I backpedal. "I'd go, Cap'n, but I don't savvy Mexican too good, and I'm not real certain of the geography."

"But you know Parrot and our other connections," the captain insists. "Besides, I don't have anyone else. Mrs. Stokes, what you don't know is three Texas families have been murdered in their beds at the full moon. C. W. had been following their killer's trail when he was near your place."

I know there is a lot of bad blood between us. She hasn't yet forgiven me for concealing my identity from her. Now she probably figured out I was following her, and then to top it all off, I'd shot a man in cold blood.

McNelly turns to her. "Mrs. Stokes, you obviously speak Spanish, would you consider acting as Corporal Wallace's guide and interpreter? I'll pay you standard Ranger wages, forty dollars a month, and all the grub you can eat."

Esther's mouth flies open. She looks from Captain McNelly to Governor Coke, then back to McNelly. They are obviously waiting for her answer. She hesitates for quite a while.

"Forty dollars?"

From the way she's been living, I know this is a fortune to her.

McNelly says, "Employment for one month or until your mission is terminated."

"I . . . I don't, don't know what help I could be," she finally stammers.

"Go to the cantina, identify the man who spoke of the killings, translate what he says, and assist the Ranger any way he deems necessary."

"I don't have a horse."

Captain McNelly speaks up. "I'll provide a mount. You can take that black mare you picked up today."

I try to put on my poker face so they can't see the apprehension in my eyes. Can she forgive me enough to trust me? Could I keep her safe? "I think we need to explain the risks involved in dealing with these people."

"I wouldn't suggest taking on a lady spy with anyone else, Preacher," McNelly wears a grim expression and his hand firmly rests on my shoulder. "But the danger is imminent, and you must take immediate action. The moon will be full soon, and the opportunity will have passed. Report downstairs and draw your pay. And, take good care of Mrs. Stokes. Do your best to keep her out of harm's way."

"Yes, Sir," I intone soberly as I wonder what I am getting myself into.

McNelly digs into his vest pocket and hands the lady a silver peso with the star cut into it.

"If you get into trouble, send this coin to any Ranger, and we'll try to come assist you."

She takes the coin and examines it.

"The Lone Star," the governor says, before extending his hand toward her, "Thank you for bringing in this information, little lady. I know it was at great personal sacrifice, but you may have found the key that will open the door to end the lawlessness that has terrorized South Texas for the past ten years. Texas appreciates your service."

McNelly turns to me, "Be sure and draw a month's pay for Mrs. Stokes before you leave town."

I nod.

"And Preacher," McNelly continues ominously. "Even though you're in the presence of a lady, never hesitate to administer extreme unction to those who can't be handled in a more genteel manner, and don't hesitate to send for help if you need it."

I smile shyly, "One riot, one Ranger, Captain, and you're sending two." When I nod toward Esther, the men laugh.

Extreme unction—the last rites, a death knell.

CHAPTER
EIGHTEEN

I worry how to make amends to this lady and those little children. I wonder how I can work in close proximity to such a gentle woman. I'm a man well acquainted with violence; it seems to follow me wherever I go. Although I no longer suspect her of wrongdoing, I now fret she could come to harm. She makes me more nervous than ever. Would she be able to forgive me and get on with the business at hand?

I lightly hold her elbow as we walk down the capitol steps. Conflicting emotions race through me.

"We have a hard, and probably impossible, job before us," I confess. "I'll do everything in my power to protect you."

"We're dealing with unscrupulous desperadoes, Mr. Wallace. I'll do the job to the best of my ability. But do not think I'm a helpless damsel in distress."

The children chase each other on the lawn. When they see us they run to the steps.

"Can we go in the tallest building now?"

"Where do all these people live? Where are their farms?"

"I'm hungry."

"I need to go to Ole Egypt, and I ain't seen a single one around here. Don't they have 'em here? Where do they do the necessary?"

I hold my hand up to halt their barrage of questions. It surprises me that they obviously aren't concerned with explanations of the morning's events. It saddens me that they are so familiar with violence that they had not been traumatized by it. I'll make it right with them if I can. I know Inez would take me to the woodshed for harming her children. They couldn't unsee what they had witnessed.

I can tell Mrs. Stokes is wondering how she should act toward me. I know I am everything she disdains—brutal, cruel, and violent. Her heart, like mine, is probably broken with the fact that the children are so used to violence that the morning's events didn't seem to impact them.

"Miz Stokes probably has some errands to run. What if you two wild Injuns come with me?"

The children, jumping around like popping corn in a hot pan, appear to have no problem accepting my presence with her.

I say, "Tell me where you're staying, Miz Stokes, and what time I should drop the children."

She points to the steeple of the Methodist-Episcopal Church and explains that they will stay in the parsonage next door. With a nod of my hat, a child hanging on each hand, we begin walking toward the tallest building on the street.

I glance over my shoulder to see Miz Stokes headed toward the business district. I determine to clear my mind of all silly notions about her and focus on the governor's mission. I am not the sort of man she needed to be associated with anyhow. How foolish I'd been to daydream of courting her. She deserves someone much better than a man of blood like me.

We enter the cool building and begin the trudge up the worn marble steps. My boots echo in the stairwell, to the delight of the children whose voices rise in volume with each step. I wonder if the children are going to make me climb all four floors. I'm grateful when they paused next to the third-floor window to look out onto Congress Avenue.

CHAPTER EIGHTEEN

Mariah Jane points, "There's Miz Stokes window shopping in front of that store. She looks so little."

"What's a Baum's Department Store?"

As I explain, we watched Esther. She seems to catch sight of her own reflection. She tucks some stray locks back into the bonnet before smoothing her hand down her skirt and continuing to walk south. She had put an apron over her bloodstained dress.

The enthusiastic children head to the fourth floor, their joyous voices bouncing off the marble walls. An older gent with a disagreeable expression on his countenance sticks his head out of one of the doors and motions with his finger to his lips for them to quiet down. They continue climbing slightly quieter than before, but our footsteps still echo off the polished floors.

At the fourth-floor window Mariah Jane says, "There's Miz Stokes going into the bank across the street."

Billy adds, "She's pretty smart. That's a good place to find a buyer for her farm."

And I think, a good place to cash that money order from the state. But because of the violence and the drought, the real estate market in the Strip isn't good, and forty dollars wouldn't last her through the winter. I wonder how she'll make it.

NINETEEN

As I relax in the Methodist Church parsonage parlor, I wish I could take my boots off and get really comfortable. The children run on the lawn out back, noisily playing with a litter of pups, and the old pastor leaves me be for a much-needed break. I flip through the pages of the month-old *Brenham Weekly Banner*. The old newspaper is new to me, but barely intriguing enough to keep my mind off the woman.

I know the minute Esther mounts the porch steps. Mrs. Hilda Matthews rushes toward the porch and pushes open the screen door, smothering the younger woman in a warm embrace. I watch them. They seem totally unaware that I can see and hear everything they are saying out on the porch. The whole experience seems unreal to me.

The short, buxom woman leads Mrs. Stokes through the double doors into the finely appointed entry, and they disappear up the oak stairs. Their voices drift down.

The older woman continues, "Oh, my dear child, we are so pleased to see you and your little family! The children are examining our new puppies with James and your Mr. Wallace."

I look out the window and see the portly pastor chasing after the children and dogs as if he is twelve years old. I hope he doesn't have a conniption.

Mrs. Matthews's voice filters down the stairs. "I know you'll want a bath, but I'm afraid you'll have to hurry. Dinner is in forty minutes. I built a fire in your room so you could dry your hair." I can't hear Esther's comment, but I do hear the elderly woman say, "I'm so delighted to see you in the company of Mr. Wallace. You need a man to take care of you."

Suddenly Esther's voice rings clear as she sputters, "I'm not really in the company of Mr. Wallace. I'm working for him."

Hilda chuckles. "You've had enough time alone. Jobe wouldn't want you to spend the rest of your life mourning for him. He'd tell you to go on with your life."

Blood rushes to my face as I hear her gentle voice intone, "Even after all his colorful escapades, that man has the best of reputations in political and religious arenas. He's a Baptist, you know. I've invited him to stay for dinner. James has wanted to get to know him better for ages—but he's always gadding about, hither and yon, for Leander."

At that, I decide I've overheard enough, so I fold the paper and head for the back porch, but not before I hear Esther respond, "I met Captain McNelly this afternoon. He seems in ill health."

I can't hear a response because I'm slipping outside, but once I'm under the open window I hear her say, "I'm going to slip downstairs and see to dinner, but you don't worry about a thing. James and I will take care of the children."

I detect a note of sadness in the older woman's voice as she says, "It will almost be like having grandchildren for the day. You know we lost both of our boys in the War Between the States."

Outside, Mariah Jane and Billy continue to chase six roly-poly puppies through the shaded yard under beautiful pecan trees. Panting, James Matthews drops into one of the ladderback chairs on the back porch, and I join him.

"Mr. Wallace, tell me, how is Mrs. Stokes really making out?"

I debate what I should tell the kindly older gentleman. I try to measure how much the pastor really wanted to hear. I don't like meddling in other folks' business, but the pastor seemed to really want to know.

"She has a good-size garden," I say cautiously.

James nods, chewing on a toothpick he's pulled from his shirt pocket. "She was always industrious. I wonder how she's making out financially."

I squirm. Would she really want me telling her business? Something in the kindly old man's eye made me say, "She has no livestock—just a hundred or so hens."

James laughs. "Leave it to a Methodist to have a chicken for Sunday dinner."

"But that's about all she has," I blurt out. I couldn't stop myself. "I'd say she lives in constant danger in the most treacherous part of Texas, and her next meal is always in question."

James thumps his chair down on the wooden porch and turns to face me.

I continue quietly, "When I searched her place, her larder was near empty. She has no clothes except those in her valise. She has no horse. Her hired man's not worth shootin', and I reckon he's a threat to her." I feel my ire growing. "I know Jesus would be ashamed at the way we're taking care of that widow woman."

Tears spring into James's eyes. "She's not the only widow woman we're neglecting. The Methodist Church is failing in our duty towards widows and orphans."

"Yes, sir," I say. "I reckon you are—I reckon we all are."

Hilda calls, "Dinner's about ready. Come wash your hands."

The fireflies light the lawn as the guests enter the house, the spring on the screen door screeching before the door pops shut behind them. I note Mrs. Stokes's new sky-blue dress as she walks down the stairs toward us. It is nothing fancy—no lace, gussets, or frills, but very serviceable, modest.

As the pastor leads us into the parlor, the children's laughter rings throughout the house. For the first time, I see a genuine smile on Mrs.

Stokes's face. James comes forward and wraps her in his embrace. Her eyes glitter with tears. The tender moment even silences the children.

When the preacher drops his embrace, Esther steps back to survey the room, and because she did, I did too. A maroon velvet camelback sofa sits in the cove under the bay window, and voile curtains drape the windows that look out on the fading dappled light of the pecan tree-shaded wonderland of a yard. A tri-cornered what-not shelf with porcelain figurines stands in one corner, and a graceful bronze gaslight is mounted on the opposite wall. Not used to such gentility, the whole scene seems strange to me.

Esther whispers to Mariah Jane, "Reverend Jobe and I were married in this room."

James says, "It's so good to see you, dear Esther. Since annual conference, I've been meaning to write you a letter, but time gallops past me every day."

"Thank you for thinking of me, Brother James."

He says regretfully, "At annual conference, I brought up the widow's pension again, and I pray something will be done about it before next conference. It is immoral for us to leave the widows without provision—especially when Jesus specifically told us to look out for widows and orphans."

She purses her lips tightly together. I know she can't go another year without some funds. Even with the forty dollars in her pocket, her prospects are bleak.

"The children and Mr. Wallace tell me you're still trying to sell your place."

She nods.

"We'll get to praying for you, and I know God will do something special for you."

From the dining room, Hilda sticks her head through the doorway. "Soup's on."

Mariah Jane grabs Esther's hand and leads her toward the elegant room. Mariah Jane whispers, "She let me help set the table. Have you ever seen such beautiful thangs in all your life, Miz Stokes?"

The crystal and silver glisten and sparkle in the candlelight. A bowl of pink summer roses sits in the center of the ivory damask tablecloth. With her eyes twinkling, Esther squeezes the little girl's hand in agreement.

Much to my relief, Hilda sits me next to Mrs. Stokes. At least I don't have to have her across from me, scrutinizing my manners all through the meal. But as the food is passed, my hand keeps contacting hers. Each time, involuntarily, I make eye contact with her, which causes her to turn away to speak to Hilda. This situation is all so confusing to me.

Although I feel like the proverbial bull in the china shop, I resolve to relax and savor the fine company in the beautiful setting. The contrast between this civilization and my daily life is amazing. I turn over the silver butter knife that gleams in my hand. It is hard to imagine that people actually live like this all the time. Relaxed, pleasant, restful meals, never glancing over their shoulder, no trail grit in their teeth, no stringy jerky or mealy bread.

The children are bathed and dressed in their best, which means Billy has on patched pants, but they are clean. Their faces animate with joy at all the attention they receive from the adults. Hilda and James obviously delight in the company of the children.

I have never spent much time around high-class women. I know there are certain things I'm not supposed to do, and certain things I'm supposed to do, but I'm not sure what those things are. My boyhood was unusual, to say the least, and then both my father and my adopted father died before they'd been able to teach me these things.

Billy and Mariah Jane relate the exciting events of their day in town. I note the omission of the slaying of the outlaw this morning. Perhaps they had already forgotten the incident, or maybe, sadly, they understood too well the explanation that the horseman was a thief, and therefore deserved the sentence he received.

Children and women are such odd creatures, I think. And as I watch Esther lift her white linen napkin to her full lips, I feel a sudden unexpected desire to kiss her. That desire unnerves me. I'm not sure what I should do. I wondered if this is falling in love or if it is just pure-dee lust. Either way, I need to wrestle my wayward thoughts to the ground.

I know I have to talk to her about today's events. I'm just unsure what I need to say. I'd been thinking about it all day, and I'm still not sure. The shooting in front of the children weighs heavily on my conscience.

I must have her help until this escapade ends, and I realize my growing affection toward her could bring disaster. I also realize unrequited love is not a good thing. The last time I'd fallen in love with a girl who didn't return my affections it had almost been my undoing.

Hilda's mashed potatoes melt in my mouth, as do the freshly cut pencil-sized sprigs of asparagus. Relishing every mouthful, it is as if I hadn't eaten in years. I can't remember the last time I'd eaten asparagus. Perhaps the taste of the food is especially good because it wasn't made over a campfire, or eaten alone.

Everyone laughs but me. I try to enter into the festivities by concentrating on Billy's contorting expressions. Suddenly the boy's eyes grow wide. He clamps his hand across his mouth and sinks down in his chair.

Hilda asks, "What's wrong, Billy?"

"I forgot, my ma said chil'run should be seen and not heard, especially at the dinner table."

Everyone laughs again.

Hilda reassures him, "She's probably talking about children who don't have anything important to say."

"Oh," he sighs with relief and sits up ramrod straight.

Then James bids me to tell another "exciting" adventure, and I search my memory for one fit for women and children.

"We have a brush scout in our company who is Jewish. He wears this little hat all the time, even when he sleeps. He comes from somewhere over in Europe and he speaks seven or eight languages, but English isn't one of them."

They all laugh.

"How does he talk to ya?" Billy asks.

"We got a feller who knows Greek and Hebrew, and they yammer on. But he's learnin' English fast as can be, although he gits stuff mixed up. He once asked Captain McNelly if he wanted the 'empty horses' instead of asking about the remuda."

"*Remuda* is a Spanish word for a herd of ridable horses," Mariah Jane says with authority, to no one in particular.

"That feller, whose name is Sy, is pickin' up Spanish pretty quick, and he already parleys Comanch better than me."

James sighs, "I wish I could speak all those languages—then I could take the Gospel to the ends of the earth. Sometimes I seem to have trouble getting my point across in English. There's a little fellow about your age, Billy, who pretends to sleep all during my sermons. He yawns and snorts if I go on too long. He's a better timekeeper than my watch. And sometimes I wonder if he's understood a word I've said."

Hilda rises and goes to the kitchen bringing back a plate of molasses cookies. As she passes the plate, Billy squirms with anticipation.

Our hostess askes Billy, "What do you think of Austin?"

With his mouth full of cookie, Billy says, "The night's too bright here. I cain't tell what season it is. Them pole lanterns make Austin weird. Ever' night looks like a full moon, 'cept you cain't see no stars."

The mention of the moon brought my mind back to the reality of our mission.

James reaches for another cookie. "It is brighter in town than in the country."

After dinner, we retire to the parlor. James produces a guitar which he thrusts into my hands, saying, "Play that piece Mama and I heard you play last summer at Ranger Miller's funeral."

That was a long time ago, and my fingers hadn't plucked strings in weeks. I twist the tuning pegs back and forth, plunking a mournful wail, then I say, "Let's start with something fun," and I began playing a rousing chorus of "Oh, Susanna." They all sing along. Hilda singing the soprano, Esther taking the alto line, James adding the tenor, and me on bass. Billy sang something. I wasn't sure it was a tune.

Next, I play, "Crown Him with Many Crowns," and several other hymns. The children fall asleep during the second chorus of "Sweet Hour of Prayer."

Hilda says, "We make a good quartet. You should stay over Sunday and we'll sing it for the church."

I look at Esther, then back to Hilda, "Wish we could, ma'am, but duty calls."

Duty. The word didn't promise pleasant things. I knew we'd have to do our duty regardless of what it cost us. It is what Rangers are trained to do. I am not sure Mrs. Stokes is prepared for what might come.

James says, "Let's close the day with prayer."

But as I bow my head, discordant emotions rage through me. It is wonderful to be quiet and comfortable around civilized people—not worrying whether someone is aiming a weapon at your heart. Tired of always living wary, being alone, and afraid, I again resolve if I live through this, I will quit Rangering.

CHAPTER
TWENTY

rom the other side of the screened door, I watch as Mrs. Stokes sits on the front porch swing and stares out at the flash of fireflies. The chains of the swing squeak gently. The summer evening has wrapped a warm darkness around the city like a shawl. Lantern lights on poles sparkle down the city streets like fallen stars awaiting a reluctant moon to rise. Gray clouds labor in the night sky, unable to birth the new moon. Its absence portends the threat of murder.

From inside comes the companionable murmur of conversation as Hilda and James wash up the dishes. They insisted on doing it alone. The cicada and chirping crickets almost muffle the distant night sounds of downtown Austin. The porch beams softly groan as the swing moves slowly back and forth.

I look up the hill to see a half dozen two- and three-story houses with lights shimmering through their leaded glass windows. They look so beautiful they make my chest ache, longing for things that will never be. She deserves to live in a house like these and serve as a gracious hostess for grand parties and ladies' aid societies.

But it seems her destiny lies elsewhere—on a patch of ground in Southwest Texas.

The horrible words she had spoken in the governor's office dance in the breeze and whisper in my mind. "*Asesino, sanguinario.* Bloody murder!" Awful words.

As I watch her through the screen, I wonder if the hired man has run off with the Spaniard to commit murder and mayhem. More importantly, I question whether one woman and one Ranger can stop them.

So as not to startle her, I slowly screech open the screen door, then allow it to bang shut. The footfall of my boots thunder across the wooden porch. Hat in hand, I approach her nervously. I know her feelings toward me are mixed, so I figure I am the last person in the world she wants to sit with on the porch.

As if our relationship isn't strained enough, Hilda spent half the evening matchmaking the two of us. What Hilda didn't understand is just how short my life is likely to be. I am not a good husband prospect. I engage in work that puts me into jeopardy every day. The last thing the widow needs is another dead husband.

I'm not the type of man a decent woman should fall in love with, but poor Hilda doesn't know that as she drops hints like "he's never been married." Of course there are reasons I've never married. And those reasons are not going away.

But now, the unpleasant task of trying to set things right with the widow lies before me, and I'm not one to let unpleasant tasks go undone. Best get them over with.

"Mind if I join you, Miz Stokes? I need to talk at ya a spell."

I know she doesn't want to talk to me because her life goes topsy-turvy when I'm around, but what could she do? It would be rude to send me away when she has to work with me for a month, to earn that forty dollars.

I place my hat on the painted porch floor and sit in a big rocking chair. Instead of leaning back, I lean forward, putting my elbows on my knees and resting my chin in my hand, thinking of exactly what to say. After sitting quietly for a minute or so, she begins to squirm. When I finally speak, she jumps, my voice startling her.

"I'd like to apologize for gettin' off on the wrong foot with you." I pause, wishing she would say something. But what could she say? That things are fine when they aren't?

"The first time I met you, I wanted to tell you my name so bad I almost busted, but I had orders not to go spreadin' around who I was." I take a breath. "It's a sorry lot for a man to have to hide who he is, but sometimes you have to do things you don't like in order to catch criminals."

She responds curtly, "I now understand your breech of social etiquette, Mr. Wallace, and you are forgiven."

"There's more. I was trailin' you." I sit up. "I tracked that Spaniard to your barn, so I figured you were cohorts. After the Spaniard swam the river, I went back to yer place and went through yer thangs."

She gasps in indignation. "You searched my belongings as if I were a common criminal? You had no right to . . . "

I calmly say, "I know I had no moral right, but this little badge gives me a legal right." I pull the Mexican Peso out of the breast pocket of my shirt, fingering the parts of the silver that have been cut away to form the lone star. "I did not know if you were a criminal yerself." The carbonite street light glints off the metal as I turn it in my hand. "For all I knew, you were headed off somewhere to ambush the Rangers."

She glares at me through the darkness.

"Then," I continue, "I reckon I need ya to forgive me for shooting that no-good horse thief today. He was one of God's creatures, even if he was a slippery rattlesnake. I didn't like those orders, but orders are like God's laws, for my own good . . . so it won't help to question 'em too much. I just got to do what I'm supposed to do."

The look on her face said she wasn't convinced.

"Cap'n showed us we could shoot a man in the leg, disarm 'em, and preach the Word to 'em before they die, but that no-good scoundrel, he just kept comin'."

Esther shudders.

"I know I'm a rude, crude man without much education." I know she will work for me because she desperately needs the money, and she wants to prevent a crime from happening, but I also know she doesn't like or respect me.

"You don't have to like me, but you've got to trust me. Without trust, both of us will be in trouble before we know it. We've got a tough job ahead of us."

Then I reach out and touch her knee because I really want her to hear me. She jerks as if a branding iron seared her. Her gaze rivets to my face, so I shift my eyes to stare blankly into the distance.

"I'm hopin' you'll forgive me for puttin' you and them little chil'run in the sight of it all. That is my biggest crime. You'll prob'ly never forget that vision until the day you die.

"I had a long talk about it with the young 'uns, and I'll tell Miz Hindes about it when we git 'em home, but I'm powerful sorry you had to see it. And I need ya to forgive me," I pause as my voice breaks, "and I need you to understand." I can't stop my voice from dropping to a low growl, "I hate killin'."

It always tears me up inside. Makes me wonder if I could have done something differently.

I catch myself nervously twisting my moustache. I pick up my hat, stand up, and walk to the edge of the porch. I lean against the milled post and stare into the darkness.

"Takin' another person's life, whether they're guilty or not, is a turr'ble burden. That feller cain't forgive me. It's too late for him, but it ain't for you. Will ya forgive me for all the wrongs I done ya, Miz Stokes?" When I turn back to look at her, I can't stop wringing my hat in my hands.

"Yes," she says uncertainly, "I forgive you, Mr. Wallace. Tomorrow we'll start out fresh."

Then I say softly, "I'm much obliged to you, ma'am," before I turn and walk down the tree-lined street.

CHAPTER
TWENTY-ONE

AUGUST 9, 1877
● *New Moon*

L eaving Austin, I feel unexplainably cheerful. Even Miz
Stokes seems happy. Perhaps all is forgiven, or perhaps
she smiles because of the new gold-rimmed glasses sitting
across her nose. Whatever causes her to smile, I am grateful.

The sky is blue. The day is new. And all feels right with the world.
The threat of war in the Strip seems far, far away. The looming doom
to an unsuspecting family seems distant and foreign. How can anyone be cruel and barbarous when the world looks so beautiful?

I point to the stolen black mare tied behind the buggy.

"See that brand, that animal belongs to the Gill family. When
we're finished with it, it will be properly purchased for your use by
the State of Texas or returned to the Gills at the end of your month
of service."

"What happened to the fancy saddle?" I know she means the saddle with the shiny silver conchos.

"The Dick Heye saddle will be returned to its rightful owner. The saddle on her back came from a barter with the livery man."

"Bartered what, Mr. Wallace?"

"In my travels, I collect weeds that I barter to local doctors who crush them to make medicines. Old Dr. Winters doesn't ride anymore—jest uses his buggy, so he was happy to be rid of the saddle. I bought a new surcingle in case that old girth decides to break."

"You must let me pay you for it," she insists.

"When we're done," *If we make it through*, I think. "I'll take it with me. Yer jest borrowin' it for a time."

"I don't want . . . "

I pull Chief back behind the left side of the buggy. Done with the conversation, I can see she is like a dog with a bone, she will never let it be done until she feels honor has been achieved. In my book, honor is accomplished.

Although each click of the horses' hooves becomes a marker moving us farther away from civilization, I feel fateful destiny—a finality—moving toward the end of this sortie that began under a full moon a hundred and eighty miles away.

As the miles and the morning click away, the children chat gleefully about trivial things—butterflies, birds, flowers—but now their heads nod in a mid-afternoon *siesta*.

"Be nice to be able to drop off with a clean conscience like that, wouldn't it?" I say quietly. I can't see Mrs. Stokes's face, just the bonnet. Sitting in the buggy with the children puts her about a foot below me.

She turns toward me and nods.

"In a minute," she whispers, "they'll be up, bouncing around, wondering how much farther. Billy's very homesick, whether he'll admit it or not."

"Miz Stokes, I don't reckon it would be wise to tell everyone who I am and what I'm doin'. I don't like deceiving folks, but if the choice is getting shot in the back or lettin' folks believe something that's not exactly true, I'll take the latter."

"So, what do you propose we tell people?" she asks.

"I'm studying on that," I say, "and I'm frettin' a bit about how to keep you out of harm's way once we git to where we're going. I need you to do exactly as I say, without stopping to argue with me."

"Don't worry about me." I see her feathers ruffling, but she says, "I'll follow orders. During the shooting incident I did what I thought best, but I didn't have all the facts. This time I'll understand."

I hope she can use her head instead of her heart.

"Tell me about the Texas Rangers," she says. "I've heard of them, both good things and bad."

I push my hat back and scratch a mosquito bite on my forehead.

"Somehow," I say, "Texas got a reputation as a haven for criminals." My horse shies at the sight of an armadillo digging under a tree. "Since the war, criminals, ne'er do wells, and plain lost souls have flooded into Texas. Those who come here don't realize how vast the state is, yet most ever' man knows his neighbor—strangers are spotted in a second."

Esther whispers, "Wicked strangers who appear before dawn, plotting murder."

"Yankee malefactors who come here are stunned to find it's forty days of hard ridin' from the east border to the west, and its more than likely your horse'll die if you ride that hard."

She appears distracted, "Families also recognize that this is a bountiful land of plenty where a little hard work goes a long way. But criminals seem to want to take what others work for."

I look into her eyes and ask, "Have you ever been from one end to the other?"

"No," she breaks contact with my gaze. "I have been to Galveston, on my honeymoon."

"Then I reckon you know Texas goes from sea level to tall mountains. We got oceans, forest and desert, sand, clay, loam and rocks. My ranch is mostly rocks."

"You're so much of a rolling stone…"

I finish the sentence for her, "You're surprised to learn I have a ranch. Southern Kendall County, four thousand sixty acres."

She ducks her head with embarrassment.

I continue, "That varied Texas terrain means we got fishermen, farmers, ranchers, loggers, storekeepers, teachers, and preachers. There's folk here of ever' race, color, and creed...Cath'lics, Jews, Africans, Chinamen, black, yellow, brown, red, and white folks—most of 'em good law-abiding citizens just wantin' to be left alone and happy. They speak ever' kind of language you can imagine. But men are like dogs—some are domesticated and protective, others are like wolves, wild and runnin' in packs."

Instinctively, I knew she was wondering which category I fell into.

"Texas is a hard place—exacting an unfair tax in the terms of drought, late frost in spring, floods, tornadoes and hurricanes, spiders, lice, ticks, scorpions, tarantulas, mosquitoes, and a dozen other pestilences. But the folks that stay in Texas are a hardy stubborn lot with a streak of goodness a mile deep."

She nods, acknowledging the truth of this statement. "What does this have to do with Rangers?"

"So back in the twenties, before law or a police force existed, when things got tough, men like my pa formed the Rangers to protect what was theirs. In the early days, those folks pursued mostly Comanche raiders and renegade Meskin bandits. They hunted down outlaws and stamped out revolutionaries. But these days we fight white folks too—people lookin' to get rich off other men's work.

"They take other men's cattle and drive 'em across the river, murder and defile women and children. They figure it's legal if they can git away with it."

"Someone got away with Jobe's murder."

I don't know what to say to that. I wait a minute to see if she will say more, but she doesn't, so I clear my throat and continue as if she had not spoken. "The Rangers have been an on-and-off organization. We've banded and disbanded a half-dozen times. Some folks like our methods, others don't. Mostly, Rangers are good folks. One or two Rangers I've known had to hunt down kinfolk. But they did it, because it was the right thang to do. Honor, justice, and duty are important to us."

I lift the silver peso from my pocket and twirl it between my fingers. "I carry this coin so that the five-pointed star reminds me of honor, justice, duty, truth, and mercy."

I slip the coin back into my pocket.

"Justice and mercy seem to be opposites," she says.

"But it's the same coin," I add. She didn't say anything more, so I move my hand back to the saddle cantle and twist around to look at her better. She stares ahead, and I realize she is thinking about what I've said. I turn forward in the saddle and unconsciously finger the leather string that locks my revolver into the holster. I can't help but check and recheck it—it has grown into a habit over the years.

She whispers, "It seems as if there are too few Rangers to do any good."

"We do the best we can, ma'am. Now I'm not tryin' to say the Rangers is perfect. We've made our share of mistakes—hung an innocent man, burned a bar that criminals frequented, and it spread to the school or church. But we work hard to be sure such errors are rare. Most of us don't want the job, but someone's got to do it. We bridge the gap between good and evil, and it's a fine line to walk. We don't apply a law of revenge—only self-defense."

She looks up at me with skepticism. I know only time will tell her the truth.

"And, when we can, Leander McNelly wants us to show mercy. We're not a reg'ler army. We don't wear a uniform, but we're well mounted, and doubly well armed. There's no enlistment terms. When we're ready to quit, we jest march in and turn in our papers. A Ranger makes forty dollars a month, a soldier makes thirteen."

"The pay is good."

"Cattle raisers often kick in a reward when we recover their herds."

"That's kind and generous."

"It's good business. In a sense, all Rangers are generals—when a man is detailed to do a job, he don't need another feller telling him what to do. Each Ranger is a little standin' army within hisself. In the army, soldiers and officers have no social intercourse, but we Rangers have no such rules. So, if I want to talk to cap'n, I jest speak right up. Ranger policy is to readily discharge any man who wants out, because an unsatisfied Ranger is not efficient. I've been Rangering twenty-six years—since I was fifteen. I spent the war with Company D."

"But why do you do it, Mr. Wallace?" she searches my face for an answer.

"Because of men like the cap'n," I quickly reply, as various emotions rage in my heart. Then I pause so long trying to get my emotions under control she probably thinks I'm not going to say any more, but eventually I do, although we've gone almost a quarter of a mile before I can wrap my mind around the right words.

"The men in our Special Force are tough as boot leather. We ride like Meskins, trail like Injuns, shoot like Tennesseans, and fight like the devil. We'll make a meal off nothin' but dried mesquite beans. But for the most part, we're good-humored with a pleasant manner. Honorable men. Good men."

I stammer again as I stare toward the horizon; then taking a deep breath, I continue, "The cap'n seldom praises a man, but when he does, it means something. He requires you keep pace—live up to code. But he's fair, and honest, and noble. He dispenses justice or mercy with a manly decisiveness. I've learned how to be a Godly Christian under his tutelage."

My voice grows gruff as I speak the next words, "He's got a wasting disease. He's dying, but he lives each day like he's gonna live a hundred more. Every time I see him, I think it'll be the last."

"I'm sorry to hear that," she says.

I wipe the sweat trickling down the back of my neck as I struggle to tell her about the amazing man. "The burning desire McNelly instills in ever' Ranger is to make Texas a safe place to live."

Up ahead I see a cluster of buildings. I can't remember the name of this settlement, something like Bee Town, but they have a general store/post office and a blacksmith's shop.

"Miz Stokes, I need to ride ahead and buy some supplies. I'll catch up with you down the road."

I put my knees into the dun horse and gallop on. Dolly tries to race after me, but wisely Esther tugs the little mare back. We have a long way to go yet.

The one-street town quietly bakes under the sun. The only person I see is a fat man chewing tobacco, sitting on the porch in front of the post office. A hand-whittled pair of crutches lean against the wall next to him. Then I notice the man has only one leg. I reckon he's a war veteran; he's the right age. This country is hard on a man who is a limb short.

I dismount in front of the mercantile and tie Chief to the hitching rail. A fancy sign in red and gold paint declares the establishment to be Rothsteins. Everything looks quiet enough, but I never know when I might encounter someone with an ax to grind.

When I walk into the general store a bell on the door announces me. The room is packed to the ceiling with everything from kerosene lanterns to #9 wash tubs. I pull off my hat to wipe the sweatband and smooth back my hair with my hand.

"Hello there, I'm Yacob Rothstein. How may I serve you?"

I scan the room but can't spot the speaker. Behind the counter a man wearing a skullcap stacks ten-pound nail kegs. The heavy accent helps me place the skullcap-wearing Jewish owner from Germany. The store's only light source comes from the large front window, and it takes a moment for my eyes to adjust from the bright sunlight.

I'd spent a lot of the morning thinking about outfitting the woman and the new horse. She'll need a war bag for the new pony—some oats, and a fence tool. With the fence tool she can pick the little horse's hooves, hammer and pull a nail, and if need be, cut a wire. I see a small set of spurs, a bandana, and a quirt. As I stand over the glass case filled with handkerchiefs and gloves, hunting a good pair of leather gloves small enough to fit her hands, a young woman comes in.

"I'm Rachael Rothstein, sir, how may I help you?"

"I'm looking for a sturdy pair of work gloves for a woman."

I see the pretty young woman bristle and glance at her husband. In this country, many a man mistreats his woman, using her like a slave.

"We're ridin' into brush country, and the cloth gloves she's wearing won't hold up more than a day. I want to surprise her," I add, ducking my head with what I hope is the proper amount of modesty a sweetheart might have.

Rachael smiles at me. "I have just the thing—calfskin, very durable." She opens the case, removing several pairs and setting them out on top of the glass. She displays a black pair, a natural brown pair, and a white pair. I try to guess which ones Esther would like best, and I chose the black ones because they will show less dirt.

"Could you add two ropes to that pile?"

I wonder if I should provide Esther with a sidearm. From her reaction to the gunplay, I can't imagine her shooting anyone, so I drop the idea. After I get everything I can think of, I reach into the pickle barrel and pull out four big dill pickles, then I see the buggy pass the store. Mariah Jane stirs on the seat and then drops back to sleep. So I add a dozen sticks of peppermint and a sack of soda crackers.

The shopkeeper says, "Did I just see a buggy with a woman and two children pass?" I walk to the door and look down the street after the buggy.

"I believe you did," I say in a measured tone, the hairs on the back of my neck rising. "Did you know 'em?" What interest could a storekeeper this far north of the Strip want with Esther Stokes and two children?

The shopkeeper shakes his head. "Just yesterday, a stout fellow was in here asking if I'd seen a lone woman with two youngsters."

"A husband?" I ask cautiously.

Rachael responds, "If so, heaven help her. The smell of whiskey lingered strong about him, and it was morning."

I pull out my silver peso coin cut into the five-pointed star, and Yacob's eyes widen. "What did this feller look like?" I ask, "I'll keep an eye open for him."

"Strong as a bull. Thick lips, round face. Not tall. Mean. Unhappy."

"Anglo?" I stare hard into the man's pale blue eyes.

The shopkeeper nods.

"Armed?"

Rachael speaks up, "Two pistols and a rifle."

"Did you see what he was riding?"

The shopkeeper shakes his head and looks to his wife who also shakes her head.

"Did you notice which way he headed?"

Rachael responds, "Toward Austin, I believe."

As I finish, the shopkeeper adds, "I just butchered a hen, and for two bits, I'd let you have a nice half-chicken, just ready for roasting."

"Sounds good," I say, my mouth watering at the thought. It's been a while since I've had chicken. Although Hilda's pot roast last night had tasted mighty fine. Anything not jerked venison or beef was a treat.

The shopkeeper wraps the chicken in butcher paper and then totals the bill. I pay him, reseat my hat, and step out into the sunlight, a burlap bag in one hand and the other resting on the Colt. But the street remains quiet.

As I set Chief at a gentle trot to catch up with the buggy, I can't help but wonder who would be tracking Esther Stokes. Maybe it was some other woman and two children. I hope this won't complicate things.

Last night I'd thought about how to explain keeping company with the widow. We could say I'd come to look over her place to see if I wanted to buy it—but who'd believe I had the cash? I wasn't exactly the picture of prosperity with my threadbare shirt sleeves.

We could say I was her suitor, but I knew she wouldn't be happy with that explanation. She would have to pretend she cared for me and then when the work was finished, she'd have to go through the pretense of breaking off with me. Suffering the neighbors' undeserved sympathies would be too much to endure. So, saying I was a suitor would never do.

We could say I was working for her, but who'd believe she had the cash to pay me? She could barely afford to keep Tomás.

What if we said I was to be her partner? We could say I was running some cattle on her land and splitting any profits with her. That might do. That might do nicely if it rained and her place got a little more grass.

As I near the buggy, I see Billy stretch and yawn. The first words out of his mouth are, "I'm hungry."

Riding up next to the buggy, I nod my head at her as Esther opens the basket beneath her feet and pulls out a cold biscuit and bacon. She passes one to Billy, which he eagerly eats.

"Where'd you go, Uncle C. W.?"

Pointing to Mariah Jane, the widow puts her finger to her mouth in a "keep silent" gesture, but the damage is done. Mariah Jane lifts her sleepy eyes and rubs her face.

"I need to stop at Ole Egypt pretty soon, Miz Stokes."

I can see that Esther wishes they had stopped in town. For a lady, an outhouse is preferable to a bush anytime. Trying to divert the little girl's mind, I ask, "Could you eat a bite first?"

The little girl takes a biscuit from Esther's hand.

"Can I ride the black mare when we're finished eating?" Billy asks.

"You'll have to ask Mr. Wallace."

Mariah Jane speaks up, "But he told us she's yours. Auntie Hilda said that mare is a courtin' gift."

Esther blushes. I realize explanations might not be necessary with these two loudmouths around. "Mr. Wallace isn't courting me."

"Then why's he coming with us, if he ain't sweet on you?"

"He looks at you with calf eyes," Billy adds.

My presence will undoubtedly start the neighborhood gossips. I throw the two new hemp ropes and the small burlap bundle behind the buggy seat and they land with a thud.

"Miz Stokes and me share the propitious opportunity of being partners."

Billy is obviously not interested in explanations. His mind is fixed on one thing. "Could I ride Chief this afternoon?" Billy begs. "The buck should be out of him."

From my boyhood, I remember that desperate feeling of wanting to try out a new mount. "I don't mind, if Miz Stokes says you can."

"Pleeease," he begs her.

She nods affirmatively.

"And can I ride the mare?" Mariah Jane asks hopefully.

Esther looks to me askance.

"I'll tell you in a minute. Just keep driving," I say. I bend down and untie the mare's lead from the back of the buggy. After I snub her tight, swing my left leg over Chief's head to where both of my legs are on the same side of the big dun horse. Then placing my left leg in the mare's stirrup, I put my weight onto her saddle. The girth is tight and the saddle doesn't shift. Next, I swing my right foot over her back.

Billy asks, "Hey, how'd you switch from the big dun to the little mare so fast?"

Mariah Jane adds, "You didn't even touch the ground. Or stop."

Esther scolds, "We could have stopped."

"That was dandy, Uncle C. W.," Billy says. "Can you learn me how to do it?"

"Could you teach me how? Please." Esther automatically corrects the boy.

"When you're closer to growed, Billy, and your legs are longer, I will."

I throw Chief's reins to Billy before galloping the small black mare up the road. I pull her to a sharp stop, then back her up. Dropping the reins onto her neck, I urge the mare forward into a trot and begin to control her with my legs only. She is bonny. She moves to the left four steps and then to the right eight. While she is still on the move, I swing my left leg over her rump, off her right side, touching the ground, then do a flying mount. She never bucks or acts as if anything odd is happening. Then I rein her around and come back to the buggy at a brisk walk. She is five gaited and smooth as a silk suit.

"She's a fine Meskin mare, well-trained, responsive. You kids can ride if you don't ill use 'em—runnin' and such nonsense. Let 'em graze by the side of the road, then you can trot 'em back to the buggy."

As I swing off the mare, the kids tumble from the buggy before Esther pulls it to a stop.

"Run to the brush," Esther encourages, and the two children scamper off. "Watch for snakes," she cautions.

When they return, I remind the children again, "Don't let the buggy get out of sight." Then I lift my Henry out of the saddle scabbard and lay it on the buggy floor at Miz Stokes's feet next to the scattergun. I hold the horses' heads as the children mount. Chief snorts as Billy grips the reins.

"Loosen up on him, boy, he's tender a' mouth." I warn. "Don't kick 'im. He'll leave you in the dirt! He can start out like a jackrabbit. Just lean forward and he'll git up and go."

Billy nods eagerly.

The buggy tips down as I step up. I suddenly feel nervous as I settle in the seat when Esther snaps the reins and the buggy moves forward. It's silly, I know, but she smells clean, a pleasant earthy fragrance that reminds me how female she is, and I wonder if she can smell me. I have not been alone with a girl since I was about fifteen. Even last night Hilda and James waited just inside the screen door, but out here on the road there is no one but the children, and I turn around to see that the children are about a quarter a mile back letting the horses graze, just as I'd suggested.

I wonder if I should tell her about the feller asking after a woman with two children. I decide not to. Perhaps that feller was looking for someone else. But I knew it wouldn't hurt to keep my eyes open.

The children trot up to the buggy and let the horses begin to eat again. Chief pulls at the summer shoots of wild oats that grow along the roadside. Just beyond the road, the vegetation is thick with black brush and catclaw broken by the occasional oak mott. I know when we round the bend up ahead the children will be out of sight, but I can hear them laughing and chatting merrily. Their voices fade in and out with the wind.

I wrap my gloved hands loosely around hers to take the reins from her. As my large hands dwarf hers, she self-consciously slips her hands from under mine. Trying not to notice the intimacy of this act, I turn to intently watch the children. They are ranch-raised; I suppose they'll be safe and savvy even if I'm not around. I cluck Dolly into a faster walk. We need to make time. The hours rapidly tick by, bringing us ever closer to the full moon.

"Would you like a biscuit?" Esther asks, breaking the spell of my musings.

When my attention shifts back to her, I squirm uncomfortably. We both sit hugging our side of the narrow buggy.

"Yes, ma'am."

Esther pulls out a biscuit and splits it in half with her thumb, then layers on several slices of cold bacon. She reaches to take the reins back from me, but I shake my head no and transfer both reins to my left hand. I know constantly driving is a strain.

From under the seat she pulls out the Mason jar of water. Unscrewing the top, she rests it on her knee for me to reach whenever I want it.

As I eat, we crest a small rise. Esther gazes intently at the low range of hills and up toward the distant sheer rock escarpment on our left. The vivid green color contrasts with the gray rocks and blues of the sky. I know the San Marcos River runs near the base of the bare mountain wall. I can see a thicket of trees that might be cottonwood.

She smiles. "It is a wonderful sight to see! I'm so grateful for my new spectacles. I'd forgotten what long distances looked like."

I study her face, then smile. "They look right handsome too."

She ducks her head with embarrassment.

"Things in your life will get better. Together, we'll uncover this ring of criminals and bring them to justice. When the Strip is safe . . . when criminal activity is halted, surely a rancher will come and buy your place."

"Yes," she agrees, "things do appear to be working out nicely."

CHAPTER
TWENTY-TWO

"I feel guilty bein' this close to home and not stoppin' to check on Ma." My deep voice breaks the silence, startling her.

"How close are we?" Esther asks.

"Day's hard ride through the backcountry, but that means two days, comin' and goin', and no tellin' how many killin's might happen down your way in that time." I study the large puffy clouds building in the western sky over the escarpment. I can't help but think that if the weather turns bad and the roads muddy up, we might be delayed anyway.

Joyous laughter precedes the children. The two siblings trot the horses past the buggy up to where the road takes a bend. Billy turns in the saddle and waves. Esther waves back.

The graceful horses stretch their long-muscled necks down to nip on the long grasses that grow by the ungrazed roadside. Poor Dolly, pulling the buggy, plods on, not getting an afternoon snack.

"They're good children, aren't they?" Esther stows the Mason jar back under the seat.

"I savvy Indians much better than . . . " I was going to say women and kids, so I break off. Truth be told, kids and Indians scare me. But good women really do, too.

"They're fine young'uns," I finish lamely.

Mariah Jane waves as the buggy pulls beyond where the two horses graze. Esther smiles and calls, "Pull up your bonnet, Missy, or you'll get brown as a pinto bean and freckled as a Plymouth Rock hen . . . "

"And then you'll never get a boyfriend," Billy taunts.

"I don't want a boyfriend," Mariah Jane spits back. "I'm sick of boys. We got too many of 'em at home. I want a beautiful horse, like this one. One I can ride ever' day, anywhere I want to go."

The children's arguing voices drifts away as the buggy rounds the bend.

"Don't lose sight of the buggy," I warn in a loud voice.

From fifty yards behind us, Billy hollers with assurance, "We can see you through the trees."

It is an unwritten Texas code that admonishes strangers to keep out of each other's business, but I know I have to violate the code again.

"I know it's none a' my business," I blurt out, "but how many acres you got for sale?"

She laughs a bitter laugh, "I have no secrets from you, Mr. Wallace."

I feel ashamed knowing she refers to my searching her home. But it isn't as if I had another choice.

I bluster, "I meant no offense to your privacy." I'd already broken so many rules of the code: not introducing myself, rummaging through her things, shooting a man without warning, what was one more violation? I feel so flustered. I had misled her and she knew it. I had wronged her, but for the right reason. Once again, she has snubbed my tongue to my teeth, and I can't say a thing. How did she do that?

"I'm sorry," she says. "I know I shouldn't be bitter. I've forgiven you, but I'm still trying to forget." After a brief pause, she says, "I'm the proud owner of one hundred seventy-five pasture acres, used to be thirty in cultivation. Now it lies fallow. There's six in bluff and rocks."

I laugh. "My ma says we grow more rocks than corn kernels. She's built stone fences almost all the way around our place, and there's still more rocks."

"They do seem to sprout out of nowhere," she agrees.

Leaving the other horses behind causes Dolly to slow her gait. Flicking the reins to encourage the mare to pick up her pace, my bare forearm brushes Esther's. Because of the heat, I had loosened my shirt cuffs and rolled my sleeves up to three-quarter length. She starts at the touch and pulls closer to her side of the buggy. The blond hair on my forearm glistens in the sunlight and the old white scars from being bound tightly around the wrist contrast strongly with my tan. I catch her staring at the scars. I reckon I should have left my sleeves buttoned, but it is awful hot.

I decide to distract her. "There's a granite mountain called Enchanted Rock north of our place, and Ma says ever' night it takes a walk and leaves a trail of rocks so it can find its way home."

"You must get your whimsy from her," Esther says.

"If whimsy is a good thang, I got it from her."

From the corner of my eye, I see her studying my face, so I stare intently into the distance between Dolly's forward pointed ears. Esther seems to be waiting for me to say something else, so I add, "She acted as both ma and pa to me . . . always loving me, in spite of everything."

Just as Esther opens her mouth, and I know she's going to ask what I meant, a loud wail rends the air.

"Ooowee!"

I quickly pull the left rein to turn the buggy around. At the same time, I apply the long black whip to Dolly's rump and the startled mare takes off with a jerk.

The children are nowhere in sight. My heart pounds like Indian war drums. Esther leans forward in the buggy, as if she can make it go faster. It lurches and rocks over the rough road. The screaming intensifies. What is happening? Where are the children?

Images of savage Indians hauling them off by the hair, or bandits lassoing them from their horses, flash through my mind. How can we ever face Inez? Why had we let them go off alone?

Suddenly Chief, riderless, bursts around the corner, running at full speed. I whistle sharply and the big dun slides to a stop. The horse drops his head and crops the grass in between the wagon ruts as if nothing has happened as the buggy whirls past.

Mariah Jane flaps both heels into the black mare's sides, rounding the bend. I don't slow Dolly's pace, so Mariah Jane circles the buggy and gallops up next to us.

"He's bawlin'—I reckon he's hurt bad."

Billy sits sobbing in the middle of the road a half-mile back from where we had last seen him.

"Oh, Lord," Esther prays, "please help him!"

"Why, that little dickens!" I mutter. "He rode in the opposite direction!"

"He was trying to stand up in the saddle," Mariah Jane confesses. "I told him not to, but he never listens to me. Your sins always catch up with you," she intones with a shake of her head.

"Hush! Mariah Jane," Esther hollers as Mariah Jane gallops next to us. "Don't talk that way. He may be hurt badly."

The little girl ducks her head with shame.

How can it take so long to go a half-mile? I wonder.

Shoving the reins into Esther hands, I spring from the moving buggy like steam from a train whistle, sprinting the last few feet to Billy. By the time she halts the buggy and climbs down, I sit cross-legged in the road holding the boy in my arms.

Billy sobs uncontrollably. With the collar of my shirt, I wipe the little boy's tears. "I know it hurts, powerful bad, Billy. Yer arm's broke clear through."

From the unnatural bend in the boy's forearm, it is broken all right.

"I want my mama!" Billy wails.

Biting her bottom lip, Mariah Jane sniffles.

As I pull my beaded leather pouch from my pants pocket, I continue to talk softly, "I got a magical potion here given to me by a great medicine man of the Noconi."

I crumple the dried leaves in my hand.

Billy's chin quivers as he wails and whimpers.

"It's awful bitter, but after you swaller it, I'll chant the song that helps it work, and we'll ask Jesus to heal you."

Spitting on the leaves resting in the palm of my hand, I roll the mixture up into a tight little ball. Humming the eerie tune of healing my adoptive father taught me, my voice rises and falls as I sing-say Lipan Apache words. I wave my empty palm in front of Billy's eyes and as Billy watches my empty palm, I suddenly push the ball of dried weeds down his throat with my forefinger, the way a farmer doctors a sick calf.

Turning, Esther runs to the buggy and pulls out the glass jar of water. As Billy gags on the bitter pill, she unscrews the lid and shoves the jar toward me. I lean the boy's head way back and massage his thin throat and chest.

Continuing to chant, I stop my massage and take the jar, holding it up to the boy's lips. Billy takes a long drink. When he's finished, I hand the jar back to Esther.

"Intervene on behalf of this boy, Jesus," she prays. "Ease his pain and heal this hurt as only you can. Amen."

As Esther turns to walk back to the buggy, a flash of lightning splits the air and a boom of thunder rapidly follows.

I glance toward the Northwest. In all the excitement, I hadn't noticed the black clouds boiling. The wind abruptly blows swirling dust and leaves around us.

As I continue to chant and rock the boy, Billy's eyes drop shut.

"Tie Chief to the buggy, then get in, Esther," I say quietly, almost still singing.

The shock of hearing me call her by her given name seems to rivet her to the spot for an instant, but stinging drops of rain bring her to her senses.

After she climbs into the buggy, I place the little boy into her arms. I can see that in that instant, she realizes Billy is not sleeping, but is drugged.

I crawl up into the buggy. "I've got to set that arm pretty quick. But we've got to git out of this weather. In a few minutes I think the windows of heaven are going to fling open. If I'm not mistaken, there's an abandoned adobe—really a *jacales,* near here." I had noted it on our way up to Austin and wondered why some squatter hadn't found it.

Jacales are nothing more than huts made of mud and brush. It wouldn't keep out much water. But I suppose it's better than nothing.

Because I set the mare in a trot, Esther must concentrate to keep Billy from bouncing out of her lap. As if to never let us out of her sight again, Mariah Jane keeps the black mare close to the side of the buggy.

The sky turns ominously black and the temperature drops rapidly. With another dramatic thunderclap, the drops of rain increase intensity. Soon cold drops pour down in a steady rhythm. The rhythm turns into a cacophony, blowing sheets of water and debris across the road around us. At least it isn't hail.

Esther shivers and shouts over the weather, "I hope you can find the place. It's getting dark fast."

The structure sits a good hundred yards off the road between two big sycamore trees. It had been visible as we traveled north, but I'm not sure what it will look like as we head south. Something catches my eye and I glance back. The overgrown path I'd been looking for appears. I wheel the buggy off the main trail, but Dolly balks at the rough track. With a quick snap, I lay the buggy whip across her rump, and with a lurch and jump she complies. Finally, after we reach the top over a small ravine, I see the tiny rock building. It looks better than I'd remembered, about sixteen feet wide and twelve feet deep, and made of rock instead of mud. I can't see any windows. The gap on the south side that serves as an entryway didn't have a covering, but the rain blows from the north, so if the roof is good, it should be fairly dry. I hope so, because we are soaked clear through and Esther is having trouble controlling her tremors.

With her teeth chattering together, she says, "The warmth is draining out of his thin body. The last thing he needs is a chill."

When I stop the buggy, I motion for Esther to stay put. I disappear into the cabin and a second later reappear.

"Never can tell who lives in an abandoned cabin," I holler over the howl of the wind as I take Billy from her arms. "Once I happened in on a bobcat with kits. I'll never be that dumb again. There's no door, but we'll make do."

Esther grabs as much of our gear as she can and hauls it into the dark building. I lay Billy on the dirt floor next to the crude fireplace that stands opposite the door. I strike a sulfur-tipped match and toss it into the back of the pile of leaves and kindling.

"Thank goodness for Texas hospitality," she indicates the dried wood in the fireplace, ready to be lit.

"The only thing I hate about a fire that's already laid is the varmints that sometimes crawl out," I say as I kick at the wood that is not burning with my boot. "So, keep your eyes open for snakes or spiders."

But as the flames leap high, and light creeps throughout the room, nothing slithers out. Mariah Jane enters, looking like a drowned rat. I think I see tears mingled among the raindrops streaking her face.

As Esther drops her load of blankets and bags, she says to me, "You tend to Billy and the fire. Mariah Jane and I'll tend the animals."

I nod as I reposition the boy onto a blanket.

When Esther steps back out into the cold rain, Mariah Jane follows, and I hear the widow say, "I'll unsaddle. You get the feed."

Lightning flashes; thunder cracks.

Through the open doorway, I watch Esther fumble, probably with numbed fingers, at the buckles on Chief's saddle. Breast collar, martingale, surcingle, and girth. She lifts the heavy tack from the horse's back and, piece by piece, carries it into the cabin, dumping it in the corner.

Through the door, I see the little girl struggling to remove the bridle from the black mare's head. Whenever the thunder booms, the mare raises her head, eyes rolling in fear, revealing white. I settle the little boy in preparation of going to help her, but before I can, Esther reaches up and slips the bridle off the animal and the feedbag on. The mare quiets some as she began to chew oats.

Mariah Jane crawls under the mare's belly, buckling the right-front hobble and the left-rear hobble. The mare nervously lifts her rear foot in protest. I worry that the child might be kicked, but Mariah Jane is obviously horse savvy, and the mare finally submits.

I pull a Bowie knife from the top of my boot as I step back out into the rain to cut splints for Billy's arm. As I disappear behind the cabin, Esther turns back to her work, removing the heavy saddle from the mare's back. When she enters the room carrying the second heavy saddle, Billy begins moaning.

As she rushes back outside to get me, she bumps into my chest. I steady her by grabbing her arms. In my left hand, I carry three straight sticks.

"The boy's moaning."

She smells like cedar, I think. The icy rain vaporizes as steam rises off her warm clothing and skin, radiating toward me. I marvel at my desire to wrap my arms around her. I duck my head and look away, when I realize her wet thin dress clings to her body.

She notices my gaze and her cheeks turn red as she pulls the soaked material from her chest. She rushes back toward the buggy into the dim gray light.

I can see she trembles uncontrollably now. The cold rain has chilled us all thoroughly. Her lips are blue.

"Go on in," she yells to Mariah Jane. "Help Mr. Wallace." The little girl enters the cabin and kneels next to her brother.

Finally, Esther finishes and enters the dry cabin where the willow-thin, wet girl and I lean over a sick little boy.

CHAPTER
TWENTY-THREE

"**C**an I help you?" Esther asks.

"Yes, ma'am," I respond. "Make us some hot coffee."

Realizing I didn't really need her help, she quickly set the pot to boil and starts preparations for supper.

"There's a half chicken in the burlap bag over there." Without a word, she quickly turns and goes to work setting the meat on a spit, placing the coffee pot over flames.

I tear strips of cloth to use to tie the splints against the break, then I set his arm with a gentle tug. Only one bone is broken and it seems to snap back into place nicely.

Billy groans.

I direct his sister, "Put your finger here," as I tie the knots.

Esther slices a half-link of Brother Matthew's sausage into the skillet. Soon the smell of meat cooking fills the room. When she hears my stomach growl, Esther makes eye contact with me and smiles. As the sausage cooks, she lays out our bed rolls and makes up two beds. Thank goodness most of the bedding remained dry. The tiny cabin feels very cramped with Billy laid out in the center.

The chaotic storm continues to rage through the open doorway, but the small room remains dry. When I reach a stopping place in tending the boy, I hammer my heavy oiled cloth slicker into the lintel over the threshold with my fence tool. The little room quickly warms. Then I tie a rope onto one of the nails that sticks out of the wall and run the line across the room to the fireplace. Placing a colorful Mexican blanket Miz Hindes sent with the children across the rope, I divide the room.

"You girls git out of them clothes. I'll watch supper. The last thing we need is to catch cold."

Esther starts to object, but then realizes this is not a good time for arguments or inappropriate modesty. She and Mariah Jane step behind the drapery.

As I pour a bit of water over the sausage and add some dried herbs, dried onion, and corn, I hear her say to Mariah Jane, "Don't you wish we had one of Mrs. Matthews's fluffy towels so we could dry our hair? But we'll have to make do."

I turn the chicken on the spit, fat drips into the fire, raising flashes of flame and sending an amazing smell throughout the little room. I glance up and see Miz Stokes's shapely shadow on the wall. Shielding herself with another garment, she pulls the wet garment over her head. I duck my head in embarrassment. I shouldn't have been watching . . . even if it is just a shadow.

Esther says, "The rain seeped through one side of the carpetbag. I hope it will dry by morning."

I can't resist glancing at the shadow again. She softly instructs the girl, "Unbraid your hair, Mariah Jane, wring it out and fan it across your back so it can dry."

"I'm still dripping wet," the little girl whines.

"We have our warm nighties, and Mr. Wallace cleverly fixed a door, so the room is growing warmer. The stickiness will soon go away. God has provided this lovely cabin for us. I can smell the good food."

"But Billy . . . "

Esther's quiet voice interrupts.

"Billy will be just fine. Mr. Wallace is taking good care of him."

CHAPTER TWENTY-THREE

"Soup's on, anytime," I say. "I toasted some of Miss Hilda's good biscuits."

Trying to maintain modesty, the widow slides the blanket that hangs on the rope back from the fire another foot, careful to keep most of their side of the room in the dark.

"Sit here," Esther instructs the child, "near the fire on one of the unfolded blankets."

After the little girl sits down in the shadows, I hand Esther a steaming tin mug of sausage soup, which she in turn hands to Mariah Jane.

"I'm a pretty good soup maker," I brag. "I cut the sausage into chunks. Look how it floats in that thin clear broth. I also added some dried corn, onions, and peas, and a pinch of salt and sugar."

"It looks delicious, doesn't it?" Esther asks the shivering girl. "The warm liquid will soon warm our insides."

Mariah Jane quickly downs her soup and a skillet-warmed biscuit. Then the child lies down next to the wall. I hear the youngster's sobs. Rhythmically Esther pats her back, and soon the sobs are replaced by the deep breathing of sleep.

With my thumb, I bore a hole into a biscuit and fill it with honey. Handing it to Esther, I can't stop from smiling. "Billy'll be sore tomorrow, and I reckon he won't be standin' up in the saddle for a month or so."

Esther chuckles. "Experience is a hard teacher."

We sit in companionable silence, warmed by the dancing flames of the fire, listening to its pop and crackle accented by the thunder, wind, and rain from the storm outside.

I lean against the rough rock wall with my right leg stretched out straight. My bent left leg feels like a mountain in the cramped room. After eating, I pick my teeth with the wooden end of a sulfur match, until I realized my mother would scold me for not being couth.

She sure looks pretty in the firelight. I feel my insides twisting. A man could just sit and stare at her big brown eyes forever, but I don't think it advisable. If I'm not careful, she'll be chewing into me with her sharp tongue and teeth again—and I'd deserve every bite. I shouldn't have let the youngsters go off like that.

Mrs. Jobe Stokes certainly has spunk. She isn't a flirt or fainter, and I appreciate that. Her thick brown hair fans around her shoulders like a picture frame. I wonder what it would feel like to put my fingers through it. I pull my earlobe and bite my lip, hard. I need to change the direction of my thinking. Bachelor's thoughts can be dangerous.

"Where does your family live, Miz Stokes?"

She stares into the fire. "My mother and two brothers died of influenza when I was six. My brother, Clyde, died at Vicksburg in '63. My pa's health broke then, and he never really recovered. He died in '69. My only living sister resides in Hannibal, Missouri. I haven't seen her in eight years. But we try to correspond regularly. And by regularly, I mean twice a year."

I rub the sprouting whiskers on my chin. "How 'bout the late Mr. Stokes's family?"

"Both his parents are dead. He has one no-account stepbrother that I've not heard from in five years. As far as I know, his stepmother still lives in Dallas. She remarried several months after the older Mr. Stokes died. She didn't come to Jobe's funeral, and she hasn't answered any of my letters. She squandered all the money that had been left to provide for Jobe, so she probably feels guilty. I doubt I shall ever hear from her again."

"You'd be surprised how few criminals feel guilty, ma'am."

She laughs. "I probably would. How about you, Mr. Wallace? Where does your family live?"

"My ma lives in Kendall County on my ranch."

"Alone?" Esther asks.

"There are hired hands, but yes, she's alone."

"It must be hard on her, having you gone all the time."

"It is. But she's a remarkable lady. She's been through tough thangs. I hope I have an ounce of her faith and strength. She does a good job of managin' the place and half the country, besides."

I smile and she laughs.

"She sounds lovely," Esther says. "I'd like to meet her sometime."

Unexpectedly, the fire crackles and sputters, and without thinking

I grab my rifle and spring to the side of the door. Force of habit. A mesquite log breaks and sparks, then settles into the growing bed of coals. Feeling foolish, I nudge the glowing wood back into the flames with the sole of my boot. My strong reactions have saved my life on many occasions. But I can see my swift actions have upset her.

The shopkeeper's words about someone looking for a woman and two children bothers me, setting my nerves on edge. Did Tomás report that she left the farm, and had the rider of the nicked shoe horse followed her up here? Was she the next to be killed at the full moon?

With some chagrin I say, "Never know who might drop in on this place expecting it to be empty, just like we did."

I reckon she thinks I'm dangerous. Grinning sheepishly, I acknowledge the fire with a nod of my head. "You never know. Force of habit, I guess." I decide to distract her. "When I rode acrost your place, I didn't see any livestock."

"I have almost a hundred hens."

"Yes, ma a'm, I saw them, but I mean cows, hogs, or sheep."

"Cows and sheep are too hard for me to take care of. I had several head of cattle, but they were stolen last summer, so I decided to butcher the last cow last August rather than have her stolen."

I gather my courage. The plan has been growing in my mind since I met her. I have long been thinking about quitting the Rangers. I am ready to settle down. She seems a pleasant companion—strong and healthy. She needs someone to care for her. So, perhaps foolishly, I decide to declare my attraction and let the cards fall where they may. I reckon most marriages in Texas have an element of convenience to them.

"Miz Stokes, I greatly admire your courage and compassion. It's obvious you're a fine Christian woman. The more time I spend with you, the fonder of you I grow."

My words make her turn her face away. She says softly but with a prickly tone, "Thank you for your kind words, sir. I don't want you to think I'm soliciting your affections."

I admit quietly, "No, ma'am, but I think you're gaining 'em without soliciting 'em."

She turns back to face me. "I do not want your interest, Mr. Wallace."

"I reckon." Biting the bullet, I determine to have my say, so I continue, "I know I couldn't be more different from your late husband, and I could never hope to take his place, but I'm a man with two hundred cows, a thousand sheep, and four thousand acres of Hill Country. I need an excuse to stop Rangerin' and settle down and raise a family. You're a woman who's got no family, and if I'm right in my assumption, you're broke. Think on it, Miz Stokes, we might make a right fine partnership—a practical marriage of convenience."

The anger that springs onto her countenance surprises me. Then she says, "How dare you say such things! If and when I get married, Mr. Wallace, it won't be because I want to form a partnership, or a marriage of convenience. I've had plenty of opportunity for that. The only reason I'll marry is for love. There are plenty of offers of convenience. But I'll marry character, not convenience."

We sit in silence with the fire crackling between us. I know I've made a mistake. Thought about things from my perspective, not hers. This courting thing is not easy. How stringent, adamant, and upset she becomes by my proposition. I'd taken her for a sensible, practical woman. Anyone could see this would be a good solution to her problems, but it is obvious she is offended and doesn't want my affections. I'm too old to suffer through puppy love, or any kind of love, for that matter. Of course, she wouldn't want to marry a violent rolling stone like me, no matter how charming I might try to be. She is used to much better educated fellows than me. I realize I've set my sights too high. She is too good for me. I just need to get this assignment over. Arrest the man on the horse with the nicked shoe and then go home.

"Good night, ma'am." With that, I turn over and settle down to sleep.

CHAPTER
TWENTY-FOUR

"**H**ello, the house!"

I spring behind the wall beside the doorway, pistol in hand. The oiled cloth blocks my view and I don't want to move it, for fear of drawing fire.

Sleepily, Esther sits up, no doubt wondering where she is, because I'm having the same reaction.

Instinctively, I crouch while simultaneously motioning with my free hand for her to stay back and down. Both children remain sound asleep. It is just growing light outside.

"Hello, the house," the call comes again.

Slowly, I move the oiled cloth open an inch with the barrel of my gun. Through the dim gray light, I see dark shadows under the oak trees.

"Esther, are you in there?"

She starts when she hears her name. "Who could know we're here?" she whispers.

"Who are you?" I holler out.

"I'm lookin' for Esther Stokes and my little brother and sister."

Sitting up and rubbing the sleep from her eyes, Mariah Jane asks, "What's happening?"

"Albert?" Esther calls.

"Who's in there with you, Esther?" Albert asks.

I pull the slicker off the door, and we can see Albert Hindes approaching, leading his horse and Dolly. Esther, still wearing her nightgown, pulls the blanket up over her chest.

Albert pokes his head into the tiny room. When he sees me, he spits, "What the hell are you doing with him?"

"Watch your language, sir," I growl. Albert is armed with two shooters, slung low on his hips and tied down. I don't worry too much about them; he has always been a lousy shot. His hands ball into fists that rest akimbo on his waist in a defiant manner. But the last thing I want to do is tangle with Albert. I also fear more gunplay will send Esther over the brink before we even get to our mission. And I'd hate not being able to complete our mission.

Billy and Mariah Jane are both wide awake now.

"I'd like an answer, Esther," Albert demands.

Obviously sleep still fogs her brain. She looks at me as if to ask what story we had agreed on.

"Don't you know who he is and what he's done?" Albert asks. "I don't like Billy and Mariah Jane running around the country with the likes of him."

In her confusion, Esther's mouth flies open to protest, but no words come out.

"And what are you doin' naked in front of a stranger?"

"I'm not naked," she stammers as she pulls the blanket higher.

"Wanton, with your love-tousled hair tumbling about your shoulders. Settin' a terrible example for them kids."

She reaches up to tame her hair back with a twist.

I step into the doorway, forcing Albert to step back outside. Albert is a stout little bull only five feet, nine inches or so, but still, it was a risky move on my part. Now I'm face-to-face with him and his guns. And Albert has always been a powder keg, going off willy-nilly without reason or warning.

CHAPTER TWENTY-FOUR

"Watch what you say to the lady, Albert," I warn in a firm but quiet voice.

"I'm not sure she is a lady—she doesn't seem to be the lady I thought she was, or she wouldn't be sittin' there in her drawers. What do you think her holier-than-thou dead husband would say if he was alive and caught you two shackin' up together?"

I wish she hadn't heard that remark, but the way he hollers, I know she does.

Esther comes to the door. She has thrown on a dress and curled her hair into a knot at the base of her neck.

Albert dances around like a banty rooster pointing his finger at her. "First, you promised my ma you'd leave them children with her sister in Castroville. Then you run off with a liar and womanizer like C. W. Wallace and drag them children with you."

"That's enough, Albert," I say. "We'll settle this man to man, over behind them trees."

"I'm not goin' anywhere with a back-shooter like you." Albert's face flushes red. "But I've heard enough! You kids, git up and git in that buggy. Don't waste time gittin' dressed and don't back talk me or you'll regret it!

"And you, Esther Stokes," he continues, "are a fool!"

Albert pulls his pistol and aims it at me, "Stay back."

I lift the barrel of my Colt into the air in a sign of surrender. "I'm not gonna shoot you, Albert."

Although the wounds with Albert are old, I find them raw as the day they were first inflicted. I wish I could say some magic words and change things between us, but it would take both of us wanting the same thing, and Albert never seems to give me a chance.

Albert spins on his heels and stomps over to hitch the buggy. Mariah Jane, still in her nightie, dutifully gathers up their things and heads outside. Billy whimpering, his arm in a red bandana sling I'd had made for him, follows Albert.

Albert roughly shoves the children into the rig, then he climbs in.

He lays the whip harshly against poor Dolly's rump. The buggy, with Albert's horse tied behind, surges forward and heads south at a gallop before we can say a word of farewell to the children. I am grateful Albert hadn't noticed the broken arm and started a war over it.

When Esther turns toward me, she demands, "What was that all about?"

With her rejection last night still stinging, I spout, "I guess your suitor is jealous."

I whistle loudly and Chief hobbles into the clearing. I enter the little stone house and lift my tack. As I bridle the gelding, Esther rails at me. "He is not my suitor—he's my neighbor. And his anger wasn't directed solely toward me!"

"It's over," I mutter, "just forget it. Let's get on with the work at hand."

"You may be able to forget it," Esther says, tears welling in her eyes, "but I can't. That man brings me mail and takes my eggs to market. If he refuses to do that, I'll be in big trouble."

"I'm sorry, Mrs. Stokes." After I threw my saddle onto Chief's back, I couldn't resist the temptation to lay my head against it. It seems as if everything I do irritates her. This day is not starting out well. Of course, encounters with Albert always create a sore on my soul that never seem to heal.

"The wound between Albert and me is an old one, and it never seems to scab," I say.

Turmoil and pain reflect in her soft brown eyes.

I continue, "I'll try to put this straight for you when we've finished what we need to do."

I set my jaw, and she seems to know she'd have to content herself with that for now.

"You want breakfast?" she asks.

I nod. "We'd best eat now 'cause we got a long hard day of riding. Without that buggy, we can take the Escarpment Indian trail, stop at my place tonight, and be there in half the time."

She turns back to the cabin, builds up the fire, and begins to cook breakfast.

I can't believe I put her into such a compromising position. I should have slept outside in the rain. With Albert's big mouth, word of the sleeping arrangements in the little cabin would be all over South Texas in no time. Her reputation would be ruined, and it's my fault. Even with the rain, I should have bedded down outside. Then everything would have been all right.

I decide then and there to get this job done and then get out of her life.

CHAPTER
TWENTY-FIVE

lbert laid the whip heavily on the pony. She was lathered already and running as fast as her short legs could go. He'd been whipping her, without mercy, for two miles. The pony was wheezing and stumbling, but Albert didn't stop lashing her.

"Stop, Albert, stop!" Mariah Jane pleaded. "You're killing her."

"You're making me kill her. You should have done what Ma told ya. You're gonna make me late fer thangs I need to do."

Suddenly the pony stumbled to her knees and the buggy lurched.

"Ride your horse, Albert," Mariah begged. "Billy and I can drive Dolly home."

Billy added, "We'll go right home."

Albert seemed to contemplate their request. Finally, he pulled the rig to a stop.

"You go to Aunt Helen's and wait for me. I'll be there shortly. I have business in San Antonio."

"You gonna buy another new bull?"

"Keep your nose out of my business, Little Miss, or I just might cut it off."

CHAPTER
TWENTY-SIX

AUGUST 12, 1877

Waxing Crescent Moon

"**M**r. Wallace, I don't know how much longer I can hold on. I haven't ridden astride since I was a child."

It is the first complaint I've heard her utter. I'd set a brutal pace. Even with the black mare's easy gait, every bone in her body probably felt beaten and broken. We had followed Ranger push regimen, walking our animals a mile, trotting two, and then galloping a mile before settling back into a walk. Twice, we dismounted for ten minutes' rest. The first time, she promptly scooted behind a rock and vomited her breakfast. The second time, her legs looked so wobbly she could barely walk. In one day, we'd come almost thirty miles.

But the country gets rougher as we wind into the hills, and there will be no trotting or galloping from here to my home.

"I pray we stop soon . . . or that God will let me die."

The last thing I need is her losing her seat and breaking something. The sun, still bright and warm, lights the winding rocky path we follow that take us higher and higher into the Balcones Escarpment. At times the trail disappears, but I read the mysterious sign laid by Indians long ago through the rocks, cedar, and pear cactus.

The strike of horseshoes on rocks and the occasional songs of mockingbirds become the only prominent sounds. I know the rhythm of the horses' gaits can be mesmerizing and monotonous, hypnotizing a rider into a stupor. I also know if I can distract her, she might be able to last a while longer.

"People often ask me why I use a girth and a surcingle. I just smile and know they've never ridden over a rough trail like this. If the girth breaks, I can count on the surcingle to hold that saddle on tight 'til I can stop and make repairs."

As we top a particularly precarious precipice, I realize my tack fact didn't really offer her comfort or stimulation. I am no good at small talk. I try to think of what would comfort her. Then it comes to me. I remembered her cooking eggs and humming hymns. I remember her singing at the Matthews' house.

The rhythm of the horses' gait mimics the rhythm of the common-time hymns. So I began to whistle the tune of "Shall We Gather at the River." When she starts humming, I take up the refrain of the hymn, singing. Esther softly joins in, easily following my lead. Verse after verse, we sing on until hoarse, and I had sung every common-time hymn I know. But when I quit singing, she sings softly on . . . hymns I'd never heard.

Even after the sun sets, we keep following a single-file trail. Finally, a good two hours after dark, we cross a stone fence about two feet high, and I know I am home. Coming home is always good. I think about how it will be on the day I come home to stay. I hope it won't be in a pine box.

"Keep your eyes open for a little lady hauling rocks," I say.

"It's dark," Esther said. "What little lady would haul rocks after dark?"

"My ma built this fence. She always claims she can't die until she's run fence around a hundred acres. She works on it ever' day."

CHAPTER TWENTY-SIX

Esther doesn't respond. I reckon she didn't hear me or is too tired to answer.

Several dogs bark. From the two-story stone house, a door flies open, and silhouetted against the lighted doorway, we can see a thin woman.

I whistle three sharp notes that have long been a family signal that all is well, and the woman's hands spring to her cheeks. I throw my long leg over Chief's head and land on the run, wrapping the lanky woman in a warm embrace. She lovingly places both of her hands on my cheeks. Then she wraps her arms around my neck and pounds my back.

"Come in the house, boy, come in the house."

Releasing her, I come over to help Esther off her horse. I know the widow would have fallen if I hadn't held her.

"Ma," I say, "this is Mrs. Esther Stokes."

"Come in this house, Missy. Come in the house. Leave the horses and the boys'll get 'em."

I can see Esther is having trouble walking. I think about scooping her up and carrying her into the house, but neither of us is ready for that fight. So, I put my arm around her waist and give her something to lean on.

As I lead Esther into the solidly built two-story stone house, four young Mexican ranch hands come out of the barn, rubbing sleep out of their eyes, and take our horses away.

The smell of fresh-baked bread rolls out the door, causing my stomach to gurgle. Inside, the ceiling is low, barely five inches above my head. At the end of the room stands the cold and clean fireplace made of round river rocks that has a wooden cross cemented above the thick mesquite mantel. A lit kerosene lamp rests there. To the side of the fireplace there's a rocking chair and quilting frame with a partially done kaleidoscope quilt. Situated in the center of the room is a settee covered in a black and white cowhide. An open rolltop desk nestles against the far wall, and a spinet piano is located opposite it. A braided rag rug covers the center of the rough-hewn wood planked floor. In my eyes, it is the most homey and handsome room I've ever been in. Every time I come home, I wonder why I don't have sense enough to stay.

"Have ya eaten?" Ma asks as she pulls back the oilcloth covering the table to reveal a myriad of prepared food—cornbread, pickled beets, fried chicken, beans. Each morning, she cooks enough for an army of hired men and visitors. Nothing ever goes to waste. Leftovers became food for dogs, hogs, and chickens . . . or neighbors who have less. Mama sends food to folks for miles around.

I shake my head no. "Ma, Miz Stokes is done in. Can you put her to bed while I fix her a plate of supper? Then you can take it up to her."

I wonder if Esther can lift her feet to climb the narrow, well-worn staircase. As used to the saddle as I am, this has been a hard ride for me. Esther looks as if she might burst into tears, but she doesn't, although I see a single tear leak out of her eye, which she quickly pushes away. She is made of stern stuff.

As my mother grabs Esther's hand and leads her up the stairs, I hear Ma say, "You'll find a chamber pot and a pitcher of drinking water there. I'll have Nels bring up a bucket of warm washing water for you. These two rooms belonged to his sisters. They're very seldom used nowadays." The hinge on the door squeaks open. "Take the south room, it'll have the best breeze this time of year. Don't worry about your privacy. Nels's room is downstairs."

Downstairs, a young hired hand sets her carpetbag and my saddlebag inside the front door. I grab hers and climb the stairs, my boots thundering on the wooden steps.

Esther stands, as if lost, in the room that has windows on three sides. Light summer quilts I don't recognize cover the two double beds, but my mother is as handy with a needle as she is with a rock. Green gingham curtains lift in the breeze.

"I brung your bag," I announce as I walk in and place the carpetbag on the nearest bed. Then I lead Esther by the shoulders to the south bed and gently push her down. When she doesn't move, I bend down on one knee and unlace her boots.

"You shouldn't . . . " Esther protests.

At my impropriety, I see the alarm in her eyes, so as if dealing with a flighty colt, I say, "Carmen came in and is heating up supper for us. She'll bring it up in a minute."

When I finish removing the boots, Ma enters the room and says, "Nels, you go on and wash up. I'll help the lady and be down in a minute."

As I go downstairs, I hear Ma say, "I can see you're plumb tuckered out, Missy, but I'm glad to see my boy in the company of a lady. Nels is like a dog with a bone; once he starts workin' on somethin', he don't want to let it go 'til it's done. He should've noted he was wearin' you to a frazzle."

"Tenacity is a quality I admire," Esther mutters.

I know I'd pushed her to the limit, but resting here will be much better than sleeping on the rock-hard ground. This rest will also allow me a visit, even though brief, with Ma.

I see Carmen carrying a bucket of hot water toward the stairs as I go to my old room and throw my saddlebags on the bed. The room looks the same. Then my nose pulls me toward the kitchen where a young woman stands at the stove warming beans and tortillas. My favorite! After Carmen goes up, Ma comes down the stairs and sits at the table. She folds her hands in her lap. The bone structure of her hands is plainly visible, along with age spots, knuckles swollen with arthritis. Her nails are short and not well manicured. They are the hands of a hard worker. I grab her frail-looking hands and gently squeeze them. I am happy just to be with her.

Carmen comes back in and puts the beans and tortillas on the table. Between bites I state the obvious, "It's good to be home, Ma."

From force of habit, Ma smiles tight-lipped so the empty slot in her bottom gum won't be revealed. I can't believe how much I love her and how grateful I am to have her in my life. I also can't believe how she's aged. I didn't think it'd been that long since I'd seen her. But then I calculated, it must have been before All Saint's Day.

She pats my chest and I know she reciprocates my feelings. "It's good to have you home, Nels. It always is."

"What do you think of her, Ma?"

"Is she in your custody?"

Between bites, I answer, "No, Ma. She's the widow of Reverend Jobe Stokes. She's helping me find a feller."

"A no-good feller?"

"I suspect so," I say with my mouth full.

She pauses. "Do you love her?"

I swallow, "I think I could, but we've got an ordeal to go through."

Ma nods slowly. "A trial."

"I hope not much of one."

Ma concluded, "But you've got to go through it. Ever'body goes through the fire, if they want to come out gold." She pats my cheek and I grab her hand and kiss it. "I'll pray for you, boy. I'll pray hard for you and the girl, both. And I'll pack you a good load of victuals for you and your animals."

"We'll be leaving just before first light."

"I'll be up."

My night is short, but restful. I'm safe here. Before I know it, Ma knocks at my door with a lamp in her hand, "Time to get up, son. You'd best commence the scout."

As I enter the living room, Esther comes down the stairs carrying her bag. She wears a split skirt made of heavy denim that my ma must have dug up from my sister's things.

"Nels, I've outfitted Miz Stokes with those long john pants.

Esther shuts her eyes with humiliation.

Ma doesn't notice and continues, "While they may be hot, they'll pad her thighs from the saddle, and the skirt'll protect her modesty. She's got sores already that'll bear watching."

I chuckle to myself, as I can just imagine her wanting me to check the saddle sores on her thighs. I duck my head so she won't see my amusement. Then I head out to check on the horses. The boys have everything well in hand.

When I come back in, Ma has set a full breakfast of eggs, ham, pancakes, and milk. Esther eats sparingly. She explains, "Yesterday, I didn't do so well on a full stomach."

Ma pats Esther's hand sympathetically. "Someday I'll tell you about the time I was in the Runaway Scrape from San'tanna. Ridin' hard is hard on man as well as beast. I had two babies, and my man was headed to meet with Jim Bowie. You'd be surprised what a body can do when you have to."

Outside the window, I can see the setting moon glowing fat but lopsided; otherwise, it is still pitch-black outside. In four or five days, that moon will be full, and we have an appointment at Cantina La Paloma. I just hope this is the hardest part of our journey.

Ma says, "You've not had time to really appreciate my hospitality. But Nels says you've urgent business down south."

Esther re-pinned the hair that has tumbled from its braided crown. "Yes, ma'am, unfortunately we do."

"I know better than to ask questions when Nels is Rangerin', but I get the burden for him somethin' terrible and I pray and pray for him. The Lord has brought him through a lot a' scrapes. He'll watch out for you. Will you watch out for him, Miz Stokes? I'll pray for you both."

Standing in the soft glow of the lamp light, I realize although my ma's face is etched with years of pains and trials, most of all, sweet joy reflects in her eyes. She is a woman longing to protect her boy, and a mother incapable of doing so.

When I say goodbye to her, she reaches up to pat me on both cheeks, holding my face between her hands; then she stands on her toes and kisses me quickly on the lips.

Mrs. Stokes obviously isn't sure what to say, so she hugs the older woman. Then realizing what she wants to say, she turns back, "I never had a mother to worry about me. I appreciate your prayers. Thank you for your hospitality."

As we walk to our horses, I say, "I hope you slept well."

"Like the dead," Esther responds. "You get any rest?"

"I always sleep good at home."

I help Esther mount the little black mare, then I mount Chief. Ma lays her hand on my leg. "I'm always glad to see you, boy. And I'll be happy when you come home to stay."

It seems odd to hear myself referred to as a boy. I obviously left boyhood long ago. But, somehow, it is comforting.

As we start out, Esther can't suppress a groan.

"It gets easier," I say sympathetically.

"It does, Missy," Ma calls out to us.

As the sun peeks up, we ride out of the yard and down a stone fence line that leads past a plowed cornfield. Startled by our horses, a deer, white tail waving like a flag, bounds out of the field and leaps over the knee-high rock wall.

Down in the pecan bottom by the creek, I point to a little log house that can barely be seen in the dim light.

"I was born there. My ma lived there until we built that other home for her."

"It's a lovely home."

"It's all her doing. She taught all us kids how to stack and cement the rocks, but she made it a home. She says it's getting too big for her to take care of, but when all the girls come home with their chil'ren it seems awful small. She threatens to move back to that little log house all the time."

I didn't add that she always said she'd move there when I brought back a bride.

"No doubt God has blessed your family."

"We moved about some when we were young—looking for good grass and water, but we always came back here. This is home."

When we ride past another stone fence, the country grows wild. We're forced to pick our way around the thick black brush and mesquite.

"Slow down, Mr. Wallace."

The brush is tall enough that occasionally she loses sight of me, so Esther kicks the black mare up until the animal's nose touches Chief's tail. Chief is not happy about it, and occasionally his ears flatten against his neck.

"I'll keep talkin'," I say. "That-a-way you can follow the sound of my voice if you start to drift."

I glance back and see her shift in the saddle, no doubt trying to find a comfortable spot that doesn't exist. I decided to distract her, "When the Comanches would come raidin' they'd always lose us in this brush."

"I can see why," she swats at the cloud of annoying gnats swarming her face.

"We had a hole dug in the floor of that log house so Ma could open the trap and plop us kids in. We called it the Glory Hole. When we started gettin' too big, she had us boys dig it out until Uncle Von convinced her the cabin was gonna cave in. When we finally got too big for the hole, they put a rifle in our hands and had us help. That's why that old house doesn't have windows—just rifle slits."

"How many children are in your family?"

"Nine—three boys and six girls. Five of the girls are still living. I'm the only living son."

Shame washes over me. I don't really want to tell her the whole story of my greatest failure. But if I don't, I supposed she will hear it from Albert one day. But I dread the day she hears the story, because her opinion of me is low already.

"I wish I had brothers and sisters," she confesses. "I suppose they are a great comfort to you."

I can't bear to tell her what a neglectful brother I've been.

"You mother is lovely. Tell me about her. As the children would say, you are a right fine weaver of tales."

I smile. "I miss them, too." I don't add I hope they're fine, but I know Albert's temper, and I worry that he is taking out his wrath on them. I hope the fear of Inez will keep him in check.

The brush thins and the black rocks begin again. The rocks turn to boulders, and the path leads sharply upward again. Soon we are climbing knolls where the views are breathtaking. Below us, a forest of hardwood oak and mesquite, softwood sycamore, and cottonwood form a canopy as far as the eye can see. A hundred different shades of green dot this landscape, broken only by a few dark-gray boulders. The path is not evident. But Chief knows the way, although I have not traveled here in three or four years.

"My parents married when they were sixteen, and with a promise of free land, like many God-fearing folks, they headed to Texas from Tennessee. Mexico owned this land then, and they promised settlers if they became good Catholics and learned Spanish, that they could be Mexican citizens with all the rights and privileges that citizenship conferred. Mexico was hoping these new settlers would help drive the Indians out.

"So my folks got baptized into the Catholic Church in Nacogdoches, then headed south. They found a nice piece of land in Matagorda County and began to homestead. But there was no one there to teach 'em Spanish nor any priest to provide Catholic services, so they continued to speak English, and they congregated for worship with other ex-Americans. When the Mexican government became upset that the settlers weren't living up to their part of the bargain, they raised their demands, including more and more taxes. My folks moved to Gonzales County still hoping to fulfill the government's requirements. But you know the rest of the tale. War came because people felt they had tried to live up to the standards Mexico required, but that Mexico hadn't lived up to its end of the bargain."

"It seems like there is always war."

"Nature of man; way of the fallen world."

Mourning doves called to their mates. Thank goodness, the sky, filled with heavy navy-blue clouds that shifted and changed with the winds aloft, blocked most of the harsh sun. The occasional shade made the ride easier than yesterday.

Esther says, "If we were able to sit and rest, I would enjoy imagining animals in the cloud shapes. Look! There's a dog's face and a turtle."

I look up in the direction her finger points. I know she's trying to make the best of a hard situation.

"Hoy! I do see the dog, but the turtle looks more like a bumblebee to me."

But by afternoon the clouds have burned off, and again the sun blisters our noses in spite of our wide-brimmed hats. We cover over twenty miles of extremely rough terrain. Uphill, downhill, around boulders, across creeks, through thickets of brush, into meadows.

Midafternoon, during one of our stops, Esther says, "The purple mountain laurels are blooming late. Isn't their smell luscious?"

All I could smell was the load Chief just dumped.

Sweat drizzles down my back and chest. I know I must stink like horse, but then she probably does too. I bet those long johns itch unbearably and she is ready to shed them.

We remount and ride on. Tomorrow we'll reach Uvalde. The next day, we'll reach her ranch, and the next night would be the full moon. I didn't like to contemplate what would happen if we failed our mission.

Last night's rest seems ages ago.

"Do you have friends near here?" I finally ask as the sun touches the mountaintop.

I see her jump and I realize my voice startled her. We haven't spoken more than three words in hours. I am too used to riding alone, and I supposed she's used to being alone, too.

"I don't know where we are," she confesses.

"Bandera County. Let's stop for the night. There's good water up ahead and the weather'll be pleasant enough to sleep in the open tonight." I don't add, if we stop somewhere else, we'll have to explain ourselves. Being polite might cost us precious time that would cause our adventure to fail.

"Up ahead, behind some boulders is a nice protected hollow with huge rock walls all around. A kind of a fortress."

I reined Chief toward a large granite formation, picking and weaving behind a gray boulder that comes up to Chief's withers. As the trail ascends steeply, the breeze seems to stop. The black mare follows closely behind Chief, her nose occasionally touching my leg. The bird calls diminish. The huffing of the horses and the clicks of their hooves on the rocks become the only sound.

Then the footfalls become drowned out with a soft but prolonged rumbling. I know that sound. Water falling.

Finally, we round a boulder that hides a tiny hollow about forty feet wide with a clear stream running north to east. On the north end, creek water falls about four feet into a lovely twelve-foot pond. The sound of the falling water is soothing and restful. Ancient live oak trees rim the clearing's edge, and cypress trees line the pond bank. Ungrazed grasses, hock high on the horses, promise the animals a good evening's supper. No one has been here for a long time.

I stop and swing off Chief.

With a prayer of thanksgiving on her lips, Esther pulls the mare to a stop and slips to the ground, clinging to the stirrup with her hands to hold herself upright.

I rush to her side, "Let me help you, ma'am."

She pushes me away and bends to loosen the girth, "I can do this. I always try to tend to my animals before I worry about my own comfort."

"You'll make a good Ranger, then."

As she pulls the saddle off the mare's sweat-soaked back and lets it fall to the ground, the mare sidesteps, crushing Esther's foot. "Lordy!" she gasps in pain. Then she laughs. "And I thought all feeling was lost in that foot."

I easily pick up her saddle and carry it near a burnt-out fire ring. Then as I turn, she commences to buckle the hobbles on her mare.

I admit, "I've been stomped on so many times, it's a wonder I can walk."

"I don't think anything's broken, but she bruised my feelings."

I laugh. "You should name that mare Trail-Eater. She does a good job."

Esther mutters, "I wonder what my backside would feel like with a horse that did a bad job?"

I turn away so she won't see my smile.

"How about just plain Trail."

While I unsaddle and hobble Chief, she gathers sticks and drops them into the fire ring. She isn't any more talkative than I, but I can't stop whistling a jaunty tune I learned when I'd camped here as a boy. This place holds a lot of memories for me.

"Good 'nough," I say. "If you want a bath, the best skinny-dippin' hole in Texas is up behind those rocks. It's worth the climb, and it'll help your muscles not stiffen up so much." I add, "I'll make supper."

She climbs the rough dirt and rock trail up between giant rounded rocks as the sun drops behind us, casting long shadows over the clear-flowing emerald-colored water. At the top, I know she'll find a nice green pool about eight feet deep with two-foot catfish swimming on the bottom. At the back of the pool, more water tumbles off a six-foot ledge, creating a peaceful melody. I'd forgotten to ask her if she could swim. Many women folk didn't.

I commence getting supper together.

In this dell, it'll be pitch dark in twenty minutes, I think. *I'd best hurry if I'm gonna get everything done.*

"Miz Stokes! Supper's ready."

When she doesn't respond, I start up the rocky trail. I wonder if something has happened to her; perhaps the water is too deep. It's almost dark now, so I won't get near enough to see her nakedness, but perhaps she can't hear me over the tumble of the water.

"Miz Stokes!"

"Yes," she answers, her voice high and startled. Then I realize she's fallen asleep.

"Supper's ready."

"I'll be right down," she hollers back.

Back down in the clearing, I pull some of the tortillas Ma sent with us and warm them in the skillet. Finally, Esther stumbles into the camp, "The trail is difficult to follow in the dark, even though the moon's rising."

Even with the warm night, I see her shudder. The words are unspoken between us. Soon the moon will wax full. What will happen then? Will we be in time to stop the murders and thieving the Castilian and Tomás promised to commit?

CHAPTER
TWENTY-SEVEN

AUGUST 15, 1877

◑ *1st Quarter Moon*

A s Esther sinks down on the pallet I'd made for her, the smell of coffee hangs in the air.

"This is an amazing place," she says, "The bath felt wonderful."

"I've camped here ever' chance I got since I was a small fry. Folks are startin' to fence the range. I know I won't always have access to it. But it's one spot on earth I love."

Holding the hot metal cup, hunger suddenly overwhelms me. The flames of the fire create shadows that dance on the rock walls of our little "room." The rocks create shade during the day and never get hot, so the temperature remains cooler than it'd be if we were out in the open. They also block most of the wind, and the smoke curls straight up. The trickle of the creek, the quiet popping of the fire, and the occasional stomp of horse combine to create a gentle sweet feel to the evening.

When she takes a bite of the warmed tortilla wrapped around a slice of beef fajita meat, she says, "I've never tasted anything so wonderful." Then she adds, "Your mother is so prodigious."

I'm not sure what prodigious is, but Esther's tone indicates it is something good. Even in the dim light, she is disarming. All day long it's been niggling me to tell her about Jesse. I want to talk to her, but it is difficult for me. The story does not paint me in a positive light. There are probably twenty fellers for every gal in Texas. Many with finer qualities than me. I wondered if I can tell her about myself without offending her. And I wonder if I can ask questions about her without seeming too nosey.

"My ma is amazing, but I haven't always treated her so well." I take a deep breath. "I figure there's somethin' you need to know before this journey's over. I'm bettin' you'll hear Albert's side sooner or later," I say quietly, "but I dread tellin' ya because after what Albert said yesterday mornin', ya think so badly of me already."

"My curiosity is piqued."

"But I don't want to keep any secrets from ya." I take a deep, shuddering breath.

If I have any hope of working smoothly with her, this has to happen. My greatest shame must be brought to light. *Confession is good for the soul*, I remind myself. But I dread telling her. The firelight dances in her big brown eyes. Since I've known her, I've watched them change from guarded to trusting and I hate to see them return to loathing. But she deserves to know the story, and she deserves to know the story from me.

"This was where we spent the first night."

She looks confused.

Continuing to stare into the fire, I take another deep breath and begin, "When I was four, I was taken captive by Lipan-Apaches. By their way of thinkin' it wasn't kidnapping; I was simply replacing those children who had been killed in the wars. I wasn't a slave, like many who were taken, so over the years I forgot most of my white upbringin'. But when I was twelve the Rangers rescued me and brought me home. In their world I was a twelve-year-old child returned, but among The People, twelve is an adult. Child or man, I didn't know what I was supposed to be."

She had probably heard of captive children, for there were hundreds of us, but I know it is rare to meet one. By the expression on her face, I know she will find this story hard to take. I find it hard to tell.

"I never knew my earthly father, but my Apache adoptive father was very good to me. Comin' back among white folks was very difficult for me. I didn't remember being white. I thought like Apache. I couldn't read or write, and when I started school, I had to sit with the little chil'run instead of the boys like Albert."

The old humiliation washes over me.

"I didn't take to the discipline of schoolin'. The only thang I liked was the girls. The romance of my upbringin' and my braided long hair drew girls to me like bees to flowers.

"I was anxious to prove my manhood, and for weeks, one girl, Matilda, a blonde-haired blue-eyed devil, led me to believe she would oblige me. Anglo mating and marriage is not the same among the tribes. So, I waited for a chance to be alone with her, not realizing it was different here."

I pause then say, "I didn't know Albert Hindes thought of Matilda as his girl."

Across from the flickering firelight Esther fingers the hem of her dress. When she doesn't say anything, I drop my gaze and continue.

"The Apache skills I excelled at with The People counted for nothin' in white society. Stealing ponies and killing enemies are not virtues among Christian folk. Even after they cut my hair, those Christian folks stared and pointed at me constantly. They figured they could trim my rough edges and I'd gee/haw with them, but they knew where I'd been, and who I was. I hardened my heart toward white society even more. I didn't fit in."

I slap at a mosquito that buzzes around my ears. It grows so quiet I only hear the water falling and the hobbled horses chewing. I sift dirt from hand-to-hand. Then I throw it down and brush my hands on my pants.

"I remembered little about my first four years, but I did remember my ma, and the love I had for her. When I came back, she tried to explain her God to me, but I didn't understand. Thangs she called bad, thangs she said were sin, seemed normal to me. I couldn't comprehend how God could become man and how one man could die for all. It all seemed stupid."

I glance at Esther and it unnerves me when I find her eyes riveted to me.

"I certainly never remembered having an older brother." I can't stop my hint of a smile, but I hope my moustaches shield most of my emotions. "I don't rightly know when Jesse came along, but in my mind none of these people were my tribe. I never thought of Jesse like a brother, but more like a rival."

I shifted on the pallet, bringing my leg up like a mountain. "One day Jesse came to me and said I was playing the fool. . . that Matilda was only flirting with me to gain Albert Hindes's affections." Staring into the flickering blue and orange blaze, I realize I've only told this part of the story to my ma and the cap'n. Esther is such a gentle woman; how would she ever understand? I take a deep breath and began to speak as if in a trance.

"There was a party. I was very quarrelsome under some stolen liquor. Jesse told me I was a fool for refusing to be part of the family. I thought of myself as Apache, although I knew I couldn't go back to the Apache because I had been traded for some ponies, cows, and peace. Jesse said I was a double-minded man and a fool if I didn't choose a true path. Anger burned in my heart toward Jesse, mostly because he was right, and figured out my secret. In a flash of anger, I picked up a hatchet and hurled it with all my might. Jesse turned and looked at me with rabbit eyes before the hatchet took off the top part of his head. Blood flew everywhere, but none hit me."

Esther can't stop herself from gasping in horror.

"I congratulated myself on such a clean kill. Even though my own brother lay on the ground, kilt so quick, he ne'er twitched, anger still burned in my heart toward him. I felt glad I kilt him. He was not of The People. Not of my people, or so I told myself."

Esther bit her lip. It surprises me that instead of revulsion, I think I see pity or compassion in her expression.

She speaks quietly, "Your horrible act of violence obviously cost you dearly. But something caused you to change."

Unable to muster a full voice, I whisper, "Just like Cain, I left Jesse there to rot, got on my horse, and rode back to the party. I ate and danced and laughed as if nothin' had happened. A rider came in and I heard him tell my ma that the body of my brother had been mutilated by Indians."

Taking a deep breath, I wring my hands, then run them across my face before I continue. "But my heart tore at me. Hearing those words, the killin' vengeance drained out of me as I watched my ma's face twist in pain. I had not meant to hurt her. It wasn't her fault. She suffered so many tragedies in her life.

"I carried the guilt and horror of what I did for three days as neighbors plotted war on the Kickapoos who were the only tribe in the area. Jesse's face kept loomin' in front of me when I tried to sleep. He was tryin' to tell me somethin', but before he could speak, the top of his head would fly off."

The worst of the story is almost over, and I feel my voice grow stronger. "The whole community gathered to our place at dawn on Easter mornin'. They were armed like a posse, but sounded like a war party. Even in those days, poor folks with everything to lose were willing to risk their lives for each other. There were no preachers back then, but my ma brought out her Bible. She stood and spoke about Jesus's death, resurrection, and his love for us. She said we should love our fellow man and pray for them. And how revenge is an un-Christian thang. Now as I look back, I realize she was speakin' to the posse—but at the time, it was like God spoke right to my heart.

"Suddenly I understood God's great sacrifice for our sin and iniquity. I knew the only crime Jesse had done me was revealin' my fickle heart. I thought he was tryin' to humiliate me, but he wasn't. He loved me enough to risk our friendship, our brotherhood, fer a time, so I might see my own foolishness. He wasn't pokin' fun at me or calling me an Injun; he was telling me the truth. I was a selfish fool. I sat down and cried like a nursling."

After downing the last of my coffee, I continue. "For this mortal lifetime I'll not share earthly love with my brother. Although I know we shall meet in heaven."

I take another breath, hoping to stop the quaking in my voice.

"He loved me, and I kilt him."

The firelight reflects anguish on the sharp planes of her face. We sit in silence for a long while.

Finally, Esther speaks, "I know about violence. My husband was cut down in the middle of the road. He left to ride his circuit one day, and I never saw him again. He lay, who knows how long, bleeding to death from being slashed with a knife. I longed for vengeance on Jobe's slayers. I've prayed for justice, but God seems to be withholding even that from me."

She leans closer to the fire. I can see her trembling, lost in thought.

"The likelihood of anyone ever catching Jobe's killer is so remote."

Unfortunately, I have to concur. I want to offer her comfort, but I can't think of how. It seems so long ago that Jesse died, yet to me it is just like yesterday. I know the same is true for her concerning the death of her husband.

"I was following the Indian code where wrongs are settled with violence. This code is one reason folks call Indians uncivil savages. I suddenly realized God has a different code. I begun to cry. I didn't feel embarrassed to be cryin' in front of all those folks, 'cause the Holy Ghost swept o'er me to confront me of all my sin—big and little. Then like peace flowin' from a cool stream in the desert, I knew Jesus died for me and that he forgave me. I understood that God created me for a purpose. He had allowed me to live an Indian life for a reason that was beyond my understanding. My guilt lifted.

"My ma offered an altar call and I walked to the front of that posse and told what I done to Jesse. How my rejection of God's love played a part in killing an innocent Jesus, and I had kilt his namesake, Jesse, by committin' the sin of anger and murder. I begged folks to ask forgiveness for their sins, and twelve men converted that day. When I finished speakin', none of 'em believed I kilt Jesse. They thought I was simply usin' proper elocution techniques. After I persisted in my story, they thought I was crazy, until I asked 'em to remember that the hatchet found near the body was one Ike Johnson had made for my pa in San 'toneya.

"The posse was stunned as the truth sank into their hearts. Vengeance wasn't due the Indians. It was due me. But one day, I'll be face-to-face with Jesse and Jesus and I'll say thank you to both of 'em for lovin' me enough to die and change my life."

I reach over to throw another log onto the fire.

"When I looked up, instead of the shame I expected to see in my ma's eyes, for the first time I could remember, I saw pride. She's quite a gal. Although she'd lost Jesse, she'd regained me.

"She stood up and proclaimed since she and God had forgiven me, that they all should forgive me—and much to my amazement, they agreed. Back then, the frontier was a rougher, stranger place than it is now. Men often did thangs, dishonorable thangs, just to survive. Nothing more was said about my punishment, because each of those men had done thangs they weren't proud of. Of course, probably none of those thangs they'd done was as bad as killing their brother, but they'd oft' times done cruel and evil acts."

Esther whispers, "I know that's true. The mourners' bench at Jobe's revivals were often filled with sorrowful people who regretted their lawless actions. Life would be simpler if people inquired of the Lord before acting in haste, needing to repent at leisure."

"Someone said my actions were accidental, and there was no lawman to disagree. But I knew in my heart it weren't so. I vowed never to kill in anger or vengeance again." I take a deep breath. "I wanted to vow I'd never kill again, but times in Texas are too violent, so I knew I would probably have to break that vow in protecting that which God committed into my care. Instead, I vowed, if possible, I would never kill a man without allowin' him time to understand Jesus's sacrifice so he could repent for his sin. Shootin' that saddle thief south of Austin grieved my principles more than you knew. It haunts me like a sin to have done it that way.

"I prayed long and hard. Now that I was a new creature, how could I kill? God said, 'Vengeance is mine,' but at times he told his chil'run to go into the land and leave not one person alive. I fasted seven days, beggin' God to show me what to do. That's when neighbors came askin' Ma to give their eleven-year-old son a Christian burial with a Bible reading. The boy'd been kilt by banditos the night before as he checked the stock's water."

Esther leans her chin on her bent knees. "Almost everyone I know has been affected by random violence."

"I joined Texas Ranger Company D, and those good men helped me understand who I am. Years later, the cap'n saw the change in me as the Word sank into my heart. When Gov'ner Coke asked the cap'n to raise a special battalion, the cap'n pressed me to join him. He said he needed me to bring a balance to the lawlessness in South Texas. The blood of a bad man never atones for the innocent blood he's spilled.

"Brave and true men have to protect the frontier—I cain't be a man and a Christian if I turn my back and leave the task of meting out justice for vigilantes with the same type of vengeance I once held in my heart. Good men must stand in the gap, or evil will win."

I can't help but think of a fifteen-year-old girl hiding in an out-house watching evil devils slaughter her family. I wonder what type of evil we will encounter at the Cantina la Paloma.

Esther smiles a sad smile at me, her features softened by the bright moonlight that has risen above the rocks surrounding us. The moon grows brighter and rounder each day. As its light filters through the live oak boughs creating dancing patterns across the ground, a jolt of anticipation shoots through me, reminding me of the promise of more violence in the future. I just hope I can keep Esther out of it.

When she doesn't say anything more—I don't know if I was hoping for words of comfort and reconciliation, or an expression of her repulsion—I realize she is tired. No, exhausted is a more appropriate term. So I stand up.

As I climb up the trail to "the bathtub," she speaks, "Every now and then, as I sleep, Jobe's face comes before me in my dreams. Then he tells me everything is fine. But it doesn't stop the hurt in my heart."

I am about halfway up the trail when I turn to her and say, "Takin' a life is a most terrible thang. It rends your heart forever." I listen for a reply, but all I hear is crickets and the pop of the fire. When I get to the top of the climb, I call, "Good night, Miz Stokes. Sleep well."

CHAPTER
TWENTY-EIGHT

○ *Waxing Gibbous Moon*

In the early morning light, I watch Esther sleep. She looks so pretty with the golden rays of sun streaming through the trees, her hand under her cheek, her brow smooth and her lips not frozen in a frown.

From the moment I had first seen her, I thought, *I could fall in love with a woman like this.* But when did I truly come to care about her? I don't know—probably when she ran down the road screaming I was a murderer. I hated shooting that brazen villain in front of them, but it was the only way I could think to protect her and the children.

I do love her. I could spend the rest of my life with her, but I know I can never have her. She is so different from me. She buffaloes me. I'm not sure how she will handle my confession from last night. It is a hard story. A repulsive story. But it is my story.

When she awakens I will know what she thinks, if her expression remains guarded. I can't stop the half smile sneaking onto my face.

She does not have a poker face—almost every thought telegraphs directly to her countenance.

An impossible task lays ahead of us. I'm not sure she realizes what she's gotten herself into. We have to swim the Rio Grande, try to blend in at this cantina, try to learn their plans, then I will follow the criminals and try to prevent them from committing a murder, and she will have to make her way home by herself. How to keep her safe troubles me. I can't fault her courage. She certainly has sand—grit. But I also know she needs rest, or she could break. I've been pushing her pretty hard, and so far, she hasn't complained much.

The sun is well up when Esther wakes up. Soft sunlight rays filter through the leaves. The air is still and starting to heat up. The soothing sound of falling water competes with the buzz of insects. She stretches and groans as she tries to straighten out the kinks in her body.

As I bend over Trail's hind hoof checking the shoe and cleaning the manure from the frog, I surreptitiously watch her. Chief sleeps standing on three feet, his hip slumped and his left hindfoot cocked.

"Good morning." She sits up and reaches back to braid her hair. She had fanned it out to dry last night, and it lay in ripples down her back.

"I'm becoming a slug-a-bed. I've slept the morning away." She hides behind her hand as she yawns.

"You needed rest. Because of our shortcut, we're ahead of schedule." I don't add, now I just have to determine what to do next. I hand her a cup of coffee. "I figger we'll head to the city of shade trees, Uvalde. It's not as far as we rode yesterday."

I can tell she is grateful for that.

Sitting down, I pick up my cup of coffee, enjoying the quiet fellowship of a righteous woman and the gentle morning songs of the birds as they hunt for the cicadas.

She asks, "What was it like to camp here as a four-year-old child, wrested away from your parents and in the company of people whose language you couldn't understand?" She shudders. "You must have been terrified."

"I don't remember it much." I remember being hungry, and getting harsh beatings by the women whenever I stole food. I remember my new father scooping me up and teaching me the ways of The People. I rub the whiskers on my jaw to rid myself of the unpleasant memories. My stubble reminds me how much my blond beard perplexed the whole tribe, one of the happy memories.

"It's good to rest," she says, bringing me back to the present.

She must have known by my answer that I don't want to talk about it, because she kindly changed the subject. "Have you thought of what you'll do when this is over?" I ask her.

She shakes her head no. I know she hasn't let herself think that far ahead.

"If this plays out like I think it will, you won't have a hired man. He'll be jailed or hung." I pour myself another cup of coffee. "Me, I'm gonna go home. Quit Rangerin'. Get me a brindle cat and train it to ride around on my shoulders all day long like Ole Sam Houston. I'm gonna get me a yeller dog, a big dog. The cat'll purr all day and the dog'll thump its tail on the porch. Then I'll sit in my rocking chair on that porch and whittle sling shots for all the little boys and girls I'm gonna have. And I'll pick out pecans and eat 'em all. Well, maybe I'll save enough to make a pie. Then I'll eat the whole pie and get fat. I'm gonna go fishin' ever' day and eat vegetables—no more dried venison or beef, ever. Except fajitas and a Sunday roast. And I might sleep 'til noon. And I'll go swimming ever' day, maybe even in the winter."

Esther laughs, and the sound is music to my ears. I've always heard that expression, but never knew what it meant until now. I know I will act the fool just to get her to laugh again and again.

"Sounds good to me, but someone will have to grow those vegetables and cook them."

I stretch my long legs out in front of me and sip on that scalding-hot coffee. "I reckon I'll have to think on that problem when I've got some time. But right now, we need to make some plans."

"They say man plans and God laughs."

"That is the truth, but we'd better try."

I feel more at ease with her now that she knows about my horrible past, or perhaps it is because our rigorous ordeal is nearing the end.

"I've been thinkin' on what we want to say to folks. I think it'll be best if we don't disclose our real purpose."

She nods.

"Have you given it some thought?"

"My place needs cows, and you have cows that need a place."

"Works for me. We're going to ride through Uvalde about noon today. I thought we'd stop by the bank and café and see what the word on the street is. I'd like to palaver with Parrot, if I can find him. And," I hesitate, "since we're partners, I might as well tell ya ever'thang—I want to check on King Fisher's whereabouts. You said the Spaniard was talking about 'the king,' and the Ross girl said one fellow was wearing striped chaps, and King Fisher wears tiger-skin chaps—black and orange stripes. She said another wore flour-sack pants and that could be Tomás. But there are three or four other fellers and we've no idea who they are."

From her expression she suddenly understands what I'm trying to say. "But you don't know what to do with me while you're nosing around. . ."

I smile at her. "You're a good partner, Miz Stokes."

"I'll shop for supplies, then I'll do what every respectable widow does." She laughs again, and I love the sound of it. "I'll go visiting."

"I reckon we can be at your place for a full day before we have to head to the cantina."

"I'd like that. It seems like I've been gone a long time. I wonder if I'll have a single chicken, cornstalk, or bedsheet left." She repeats the words of my mother, "I reckon we'd best be on the scout."

I stand up, slap my hat onto the seat of my pants to clean them off, then plop it on my head. I reach over, grab her hand, help her stand up. "Let's get it done."

We pack up and mount. As I bid goodbye to one of my favorite spots on Earth, I wonder if I'll ever be back.

Soon the trail wanders out of the rocks and onto the plain. The constant clink of the horse hooves on rock silences as the soil transitions into a rich black loam. The horses delight in stopping to occasionally nip at the thick knee-high grass. Small trail ruts turn into the double ruts of a wagon trail; the wagon trail turns into a well-worn road, and by early afternoon we see the tall pecan trees of Uvalde.

As we enter the good-sized town, a dog comes barking at us, causing Trail-Eater to side step, but Esther rides her like a professional. As we head down Getty Street past the stately homes, Esther asks, "Should we separate?"

"Nah," I answer. "We're partners now. I'll drop you at the mercantile and meet you at the bank at four."

A dozen people carry on their commerce when the street changes from houses to the two-storied brick buildings of downtown businesses. I nod and tip my hat. Occasionally passers-by call a greeting. Mr. Miller looks surprised when he realizes who rides the horse next to Chief.

"It'll be all over town in an hour now," Esther whispers under her breath. "His wife tends to talk."

"That's fine," I say. "Maybe gossip will distract folks enough that they don't think about what we're really doin'."

Judging by the buggies parked at the hitching posts, the mercantile is doing a brisk business. Esther leans over and whispers, "I just can't face all those folks right now. I'm going to Mrs. Blake's. If you need me, it's the small house with all the flowers next to the Methodist-Episcopal Church on Oak Street. I'll come back here after three, when the crowd lessens."

She puts her heels into the little black mare, and they prance down the street at a rapid pace. I decide to skip the store too. I head down the alley to the livery to leave Chief for a good rubdown and some oats. Then I walk across the street to the back door of the saddler's.

As I open the door a little brass bell rings. The sharp smell of leather and horse liniment washes over me. New saddles form an aisle up to the counter. On the walls behind the counter hang buckets holding bull whips, ropes, quirts, spurs, bits, halters, and head stalls. Over in the back corner by the cold potbelly stove sit five ladder-back chairs. Three of them are occupied by cowboys chewing tobacco and braiding rawhide ropes.

One older man, Josiah Young, rises and comes over to shake my hand. I recognize him as a man who rode with the Rangers in the fifties.

"Glad to see ya, Preacher. I got a message for you from Parrot. He said if you got into town today, he wants you to come to Mrs. Gilliam's party tonight."

I contemplate this information. What is Parrot thinking? We don't have time for party going. There must be something he wants me to learn or see.

"I hope you got a string tie and a top hat, Preacher. It's no hoe-down; it's a fancy-dress thang. That negra opera sanger from New Orlins is here. She sangs real purty." I gently shake the old man's arthritic hand and thank him.

Stepping onto the boardwalk, I cogitate what Parrot could have for me. I head to the barbershop. I always seem to pick up a good piece of gossip there, and I did need a shave and haircut.

A barber in a white coat sweeps hair off the wooden floor. Only one of the three barber chairs is filled. I freeze momentarily when I realize the occupant of the center chair, whose face is covered in warm towels, wears tiger-skin leggings. I know of only one man in Texas who wears those orange-and-black striped chaps: King Fisher. The gal-leg spurs dangling off his fancy patent-leather pointed-toe boots leave no doubt in my mind that this is the infamous pistolero.

I sit down in the chair near the door and lean back. "Trim me up, George."

"You in town for the Gilliam soiree tonight?"

I nod as the barber lathers my neck.

"That Miz Gilliam is determined to erase Uvalde's reputation as a lawless Western town."

The other barber queries his customer, too, "You goin', King?"

The young man pulls the towels off his face and throws them into the basket. "Wouldn't miss it. I like rich girls when they're all dressed up and smelling sweet."

About twenty-five, dark, handsome, and cocky, King winks at the barber and throws him two bits. The barber catches it and slips it into his white coat pocket as King turns to leave.

The barber asks, "See ya tomorrow?"

King preens in the mirror. "No. Not tomorrow. I'm heading to Mexico early in the morning. I'm hoping to get some cattle." The brass bell on top of the door tinkles as Fisher shoves open the door and leaves.

I don't think he ever looked my way. I relax and meditate on this fortuitous information. So, King Fisher is going to Mexico for cattle. I suddenly wonder how Esther and I can wrangle some fancy-dress clothes.

The stroll to the Widow Blake's modest single-story wooden house is about six blocks. Trail-Eater stands tied to the picket fence out front. Mrs. Blake and Esther shell peas as they rock on the porch. I doff my hat to the ladies and continue walking by in case Esther doesn't want to be seen in my company, but Esther calls out to me. "Mr. Wallace, come meet my friend, Mrs. Blake."

I remove my hat and walk up to the porch that badly needs painting. The elderly lady with soft features and white hair ringing her face smiles at me and offers her shriveled hand. She giggles like a schoolgirl when I bow over her hand with the finesse of a proper Southern gentlemen.

"My dear Esther was telling me how kind you've been to her and how you're helping her out."

I slap my hat against my dusty pants. "I'm trying, ma'am. But she probably didn't mention how she's helpin' me too. But we have a dilemma now."

Esther looks quizzically at me.

"We've been invited to a fancy-dress party tonight."

"Oh, how exciting," Mrs. Blake softly claps her hands together. "Mrs. Gilliam's opera soiree. She's raising funds to build a proper opera house on the town square. Believe it or not, I remember when I was young and inclined to courting."

Esther begins to protest, "Mr. Wallace, I can't go. I have nothing appropriate to wear."

"Nonsense," Mrs. Blake interrupts. "I have a closet full of things. An elegant dress is always fashionable. We can rip lace from one gown to lengthen another."

Esther protests strongly, "I thought we were going home tonight."

Mrs. Blake stands. "Cinderella will be ready at seven, Mr. Wallace. Can you remove her things from the horse? She'll be staying the night. And can you tend that horse for her?"

I grin like a kid in a candy store. I can't help it. This lady is a dandy. I shove my hat back on my head. "Thank you, ma'am, I'll see you ladies at seven."

What an interesting twist this day has brought. Once again, I'd have to remember how to comport myself in polite company. I've had more contact with civilized folks in the last ten days than I've had in the last ten years. Wouldn't the boys back at camp hurrah me if they knew?

Mrs. Blake grabs Esther's hand, "Come on, dearie, we have work to do."

I remove Esther's carpetbag from Trail's back and place it on the front porch. I figure I'd better see to myself now.

The only place I can think of to get fancy dress clothes is from the undertaker. It is the fashion to dress up dead criminals and pose them in the store window. I hoped they might have clothing to fit me. So I head back to the barbershop, because the barber is also the undertaker.

CHAPTER
TWENTY-NINE

As the shadows deepen, I remove my borrowed black beaver top hat and step up on Mrs. Blake's low-roofed porch. I feel pretty stupid—naked. It is the first time in years I haven't carried a sidearm. The haberdasher did give me a walking stick. I guess if worse comes to worst, I can beat someone with it—but it won't stop a bullet, and it sure won't fire one.

I hope no one realizes I'm in the formal suit the undertaker uses for deceased criminals. He rented it to me for four bits.

With great flare, Mrs. Blake stands back and leads Esther by hand out onto the porch. In the golden light of the lamps, I survey my partner in amazement at Mrs. Blake's handiwork. I think about the trembling, grim-faced woman I'd met almost fifteen days ago. Esther doesn't look anything like that woman. She looks beautiful, and young. Her dark eyes sparkle in the lamplight.

Before I can say anything, Mrs. Blake announces, "She'll pass. No one will be jealous because her dress is the most stylish, but no one will snob her and think her a back-brush hick."

The dress looks amazing—a black beaded gauze thing with a satin under shift. Mrs. Blake has obviously pulled out an ancient corset and laced Esther up. The corset pulls curves into Esther's figure that I didn't know she had. The shift accents those curves in a stunning way. The low scooped neck reveals more cleavage than the young woman has probably ever revealed before, but it is not indecent, and it is definitely alluring. An inch-round cameo on a black velvet ribbon hangs around Esther's throat. Although only three-quarters length, the sleeves don't look inappropriate when Esther pulls on the elbow-length black gloves.

I hear Mrs. Blake whisper, "Remember, dear, with a corset, you must take frequent shallow breaths instead of slow deep ones."

Mrs. Blake confides to me, "It took five curling irons, two 'rats' of wadded hair, a bottle of homemade glue, dozens of pins, and a handful of ribbons to get that hairdo. I used to be good at this, when my daughters lived at home, before the war. Have I lost my touch?"

"Lovely, she looks lovely," I reply.

Two small black feathers poke into Esther's hair just where the hair gathers into three long ringlets cascading over her left shoulder. The hair is puffed around so it frames her face.

Mrs. Blake drops into one of the porch rocking chairs, obviously tired.

Esther demands, "You must stop, Mrs. Blake, you're wearing yourself out. We're all done."

"Nonsense," the older woman says, "it feels good to be tired."

Esther turns to thank Mrs. Blake, but the older woman holds up a hand in protest. "I should thank you, my dear, for putting up with an old woman's fiddling. I'm sure the hairstyle is dated, but it suits you, and I had fun doing it."

"I definitely feel like Cinderella going to the ball."

The older woman reaches up and pats the younger on the cheek. "You certainly are, my dear."

"I've not been to a fancy-dress party in years, and I'm surprised I'm this excited and nervous."

I bite my tongue rather than mention that I've never been to a fancy-dress party.

Mrs. Blake's eyes twinkle. "Cinderella caught a prince—maybe you can too."

Esther demurely looks away.

"You look beautiful, my dear."

"She does," I echo, as I run my finger beneath the white cravat tied around my throat. I imagine it last served to cover the wound of a hangman's noose. I've waxed my moustaches straight out to the sides and I hope it looks debonair instead of dumb. But it feels dumb. I also feel stupid carrying this silver-headed walking stick instead of a Colt. I really don't know what I'm supposed to do with it. Am I supposed to tap it on the ground as I take a step, or just carry it around under my arm? I am definitely a fish out of water, here, floundering around for air.

"I don't have a buggy. Do you mind walking?" I ask.

Esther shakes her head no, and her little ringlets bounce up and down. As I hold out my arm to her, Mrs. Blake hands her a little black beaded purse.

"Your handkerchief, my dear."

Whispering, "Thank you," Esther bends over and hugs the tiny older woman, murmuring in her ear, "Does my carriage turn into a pumpkin at midnight?"

Mrs. Blake laughs. "Mine turns into one about nine-thirty, but yours probably won't turn until after midnight." She places Esther's hand back on my arm. "Have a good time, young folks."

And, in the growing dark, arm in arm, we begin to stroll down the tree-lined street. To have Esther's arm entwined with mine makes me feel humbled and proud at the same time—an odd feeling. And I decide to carry the stick under my arm. I should have just left the darned thing at Mrs. Blake's.

Every window in the stately two- and three-story homes lining Getty Street glows with sparkling golden light. Happy voices drift through the air as people walk toward the event. Torches light the way. Dozens of horses and buggies stand by the curb. Then I see what I've been look-ing for: Parrot's picture-taking wagon. As I lead Esther up the brick walk, I notice people's inquisitive stares. So much for remaining anon-ymous. Small-town curiosity would have tongues wagging in no time.

Mrs. Gilliam's large mullioned windows stand open to catch the occasional breeze, but mostly it is hot. The twenty-foot oblong parlor and adjoining twenty-foot dining room hold about fifty chairs, set up in rows. I guide Esther to a chair in the back by the kitchen door. Once she is seated, I go to the punch bowl in the sunroom to procure her a cup of punch.

A dapper gentleman setting up a box camera on a tripod ap-proaches me. "Sir, step aside or I may take your photo."

I smile and move. Mr. Parrot lights the potassium chlorate flash powder and snaps the picture. Few would recognize him as the griz-zled old Parrot I know him to usually be. His hair is slicked back with a sweet pomade you can smell across the room.

"Good to see you, Mr. Parrot. May I pour you a cup of punch?"

"I'd be much obliged," Parrot answers.

I dipped the heavy sterling silver ladle into the large silver punch bowl and bring up the sugary, ruby-red liquid. I hand the cup to Parrot.

The large walnut table with two tall candles that send smoke curl-ing up to the high ceiling is laden with tasty petit fours and candies.

"Your lady is very beautiful," Parrot says.

"Yes, she is," I agree, "and brave."

"She may need to be," Parrot says. "Cantina la Paloma is a rough place . . . populated with scallywags, ladies of the night, and banditos."

Obviously, the captain has gotten word to Parrot about our mission.

"You've been there?"

"Too many times," Parrot admits. "But I cain't be there for you. Lieutenant Robinson is in town. As soon as this party is over, I've got to talk to him. I'll get back as fast as I can."

I immediately regret involving Esther. If only I spoke more Span-ish, she wouldn't have to go. But I need her to go in case she can pick up vital information.

The large room fills with people and the discordant sounds of a stringed quartet tuning their instruments. Our hostess gives Parrot a "do your job" look, but before he moves off, he says under his breath, "I'm trailing King. If I can, I'll head out to her ranch late tonight and camp just past that western hill."

Extending my hand toward Parrot, I smile and nod. "In the mornin' we'll be right behind you. Watch out for her hired man, Tomás. He's in on this somehow."

I turned and freeze. Standing to my left is King Fisher, and he has probably heard everything I said.

Fisher examines me up and down. "Don't I know you?"

Still wondering how much the cowboy has heard, I extend my hand but not my name. "Today we were in the barbershop together." I neglect to mention our encounter at the Menger.

As King Fisher still puzzles over me, I pick up two cups of punch, nod at Fisher, and walk toward Esther, knowing the pistolero's eyes follow my every step.

I hope that our encounter at the Menger bar was not memorable. My hair had been long and dirty. My face covered in hair.

Across the room, in the corner, wearing a tuxedo, stands Calvert Johnston, a Negro brush scout who served with me in the Rangers for years. I am surprised to see the strong young man also dressed in evening wear. He looks right handsome, not the dusty *caballero* I am used to seeing. Apparently he is just as uncomfortable as I feel in his starched white shirt. The hostess opens the dining room door, and out steps a beautiful woman with creamed coffee-colored skin, wearing a stylish purple gown that swishes about her legs when she moves.

I lift my glass in acknowledgement to Calvert.

The hostess tings a spoon on a crystal glass, and the room falls silent.

"Ladies and Gentlemen, it is my great pleasure to present Mrs. Marva Le Lune Johnston. She has performed before crown heads of state throughout Europe and in opera houses from New York City to San Francisco. Please welcome Mrs. Johnston singing 'The Queen of the Night' from Mozart's *The Magic Flute*."

Mrs. Johnston? Obviously, Calvert had gotten married . . . and married well.

When the violins and piano begin to play, it is as if the room holds its breath. The powerful opening music shakes the beveled glass in the windows. I can see folks sitting outside on blankets on the grass.

As the soprano sings the intricate song that sounds as if birds are singing, Esther's expression becomes rapturous.

I'd like to think I'm having trouble focusing on the music because the lyric is in a foreign language, but King Fisher keeps glancing at Esther and me. As the singer moves from song to song, I find most of the tunes long and boring. I try to turn my face into shadows. No doubt the lady has an amazing voice, but why can't she sing something in English? "Turkey in the Straw" or "The Schottische" are much more to my liking. Like when I'm hunting, I discipline myself not to fidget, but the suit is itchy, and I can't help but think of the fellers who had worn it before me. I can see why they only wore it once themselves. I wonder if it has fleas or lice. Then I hope I don't end up wearing this suit posed in a coffin that's propped up against a storefront.

To distract myself, I begin working out the time schedule to get to Cantina la Paloma. When the woman finishes singing, relief washes over me, and I politely applaud. At the intermission, I shake hands with several civic leaders, eat some of the fancy fixings, and introduce Esther to several of the society matrons, but my heart is already crossing the Rio Grande.

Although I cordially mingle with the crowd, it becomes obvious to Esther that something is wrong. She keeps casting anxious glances in my direction as I try to be charming. But King Fisher, who sits in the third row of chairs, keeps turning around and following us with his eyes. Esther places her hand on my arm and squeezes. I want to reassure her, so I turn and smile at her, whispering, "Having a good time?"

She nods and gives me a shaky smile. "It's wonderful."

As I study her, I could have sworn sparks flew between us. I know she doesn't intend for them to, but they do. She looks away, demurely dropping her chin toward her chest.

"Cap'n McNelly's wife loves entertainments like this," I say, trying to diffuse what just occurred, but she knows I am just trying to make idle conversation.

After the intermission, the program resumes with a patriotic recitation by three young sisters accompanied by their mother on the violin, and then their brother performs a juggling act, throwing horseshoes into the air and causing the audience to gasp as they come perilously close to the crystals on the chandelier. Mrs. Marva Le Lune Johnston concludes the program with Beethoven's "Ode to Joy."

Glancing down at the polished oak floor, Esther whispers. "You're being watched by that man with the dark hair."

I lift her chin with my hand, my gaze riveted to hers. "You're a good partner, Miz Esther Stokes. I got him in sight." The intimate act of touching her face seems to stop time. I wish, for a brief moment, that I could hold my hand there forever. But the room erupts in thunderous applause and the spell breaks.

Our hostess stands up. "I want to thank y'all for attending and remind you that money is being raised to erect a real entertainment venue—an Opera House with a dragon gargoyle weathervane on top of the corner turret and two hundred seats. It'll be a venue that brings world-class talent to Uvalde and showcases the downtown square. It will attract people to the area for years. My husband, standing there by the door, is catching money in his hat. Be as generous as you can."

When the entertainment completes, everyone stands, applauding; then they slowly began their exodus. Esther slips her hand between my side and my arm. I place my hand on top of hers and squeeze it. It feels right to have her hand there.

Suddenly, King Fisher approaches us. Esther steps behind me, perhaps finding the man's piercing eyes unnerving.

"Are you Esther Stokes?"

"Mrs. Jobe Stokes," she responds frostily.

"I heard you want to sell your place."

I can see this catches her off guard. Of course, she wants to sell, but to him? She stutters, "I've found a partner to run cows on my place, so I don't have to sell the land, unless I'm offered top dollar."

King Fisher warns, "Lots of rustlers out that way, ma'am. Bad things happen out in the Strip. I'd watch out if I were you." Then he turns and walks away.

That sounds like a threat to me. All I have to defend her is a stick, and I'd even left that by the door with that silly hat. It makes me want to slug the guy, even though I know it would serve no purpose. It might actually spoil any chance of making things right, but it doesn't stop me from wanting to beat him senseless. I clinch my jaw so tightly my teeth hurt. I remind myself that our mission is justice, not vengeance or a duel of honor. The war against lawlessness can only be won with patience and perseverance. But if the opportunity ever arises, I'll gladly duke it out with that fellow.

At least he's unarmed, too. So, I don't think the danger is immediate. But I will have to watch her back.

Angrily, Esther turns to me and demands, "Was that man threatening me? Who is he? How does he know me?"

I tilt my head and smile gently at her. "Madam, you have just met the infamous, notorious King Fisher."

She still trembles as we thank our hostess and drop a couple of dollars in the hat. Walking on the yards toward Mrs. Blake's home, we hear various voices spilling out the open windows, laughing, and calling good night. The cicadas hum. In the distance ring the clopping of hooves on cobblestones and the jingle of trace chains. We walk in silence. The almost-full moon has risen above the horizon and is beginning to light everything around us. She clings to my arm over the uneven ground. Suddenly, in a very dark spot where the limbs above us are thick, I stop and spin her around to face me. I move my face so close to hers that I can smell the cloves on her breath. I want to see if we are being watched, and sure enough, a fellow leading a horse stops when we do.

"Please don't cry out," I put my hand behind her head and draw her close enough to whisper in her ear. Hugging her this close, I wonder if she can smell the bay rum on my neck. "We're being followed."

She tries to glance around, but I hold her head tightly to my cheek.

"What should we do, Mr. Wallace?" She whispers back, and I hear the panic in her voice.

"This little interlude is letting me get a bead on this fellow."

"Oh," she says with a breathy voice. "You don't have your pistol."

Then I quickly kiss her tenderly. Her lips feel warm. "We'll be all right."

I can feel her chest rising and falling.

"He's leading a horse and staying back in the shadows." I laugh loudly, startling her. I bend her head back and tenderly kiss her along her jaw and up to her ear. She leans into me. Her breath makes me shiver, and I realize I am not breathing.

I whisper into her hair, "I want you to slap me hard and yell at me for making an indecent suggestion. Then I'll see you to Mrs. Blake's door. In an hour, be ready to ride. Be ready," I insist. "I'll be back to get you in an hour or so."

She takes as deep a breath as the corset allows and gives a barely discernible nod. Then she whispers, "Should I strike you now?"

I squeeze her tightly to my body.

She speaks loudly enough that the follower can hear. "Please, Mr. Wallace, stop! How dare you! Unhand me! Let me go! I won't stand for this type of behavior. It's indecent. Let me go!"

But I don't let her go, so she slaps me. Her gloved hand doesn't make much noise or sting, but I whip my head around as if it had been a wallop. I let go, bend over frozen for a moment, studying the bushes behind me.

We hear laughter coming from under another tree where the watcher waits. She turns and begins striding toward Mrs. Blake's house as fast as the tight straight skirt will let her. I stand for a second, then start after her, calling loudly, "I'm sorry, Miz Stokes, it won't happen again. You're just so beautiful I couldn't help myself." I run backwards in front of her so I can look behind us. I grab her arm and continue to quietly plead with her. I spin her sideways, like in a dance, and we peer into the darkness. But the watcher has mounted and ridden away. Between the clops of hooves, we hear him chuckling all the way down the street.

When we arrive at Mrs. Blake's front porch, I grab Esther's hand and squeeze. "Just go in and I'll sit here on the porch mooning after you for a few minutes to make sure he doesn't come back around. Change and pack. Make your explanations to your hostess, then shut out all the lights and come out the back door."

"I'll be ready in thirty-forty minutes," Esther answers as she slips through the door.

"I'll bring Chief and Trail." Through the window, I see her wake Mrs. Blake, who snoozes in the rocking chair next to the unlit fireplace.

Within two hours, under a bright rising moon, we ford the shallow rocky Nueces River to cross into the Strip—and head at a trot toward her ranch.

CHAPTER
THIRTY

○ *Great Moon*

It is the middle of the night when we get to her ranch. Probably a little before two. Although dark, from high overhead, the almost-full moon casts enough light to plainly see cactus, startled deer, and javelinas.

On top of the hill, we find Parrot's wagon, with him sleeping underneath. As we approach, he sits up and growls, "Who goes there," no doubt with a weapon aimed at our bellies.

"Go back to sleep." I picket Trail and Chief. "I'm gonna see the lady home."

Before Esther and I approach her house, the two of us study the little homestead from the top of the hill where I'd first watched her days ago. There is no activity.

"Go down on foot, Esther. Stay in the open until you feel safe so I can cover you with my long gun."

The dog begins to bark, and we see Tomás come out of the barn. Things must have been fine, because after a few minutes' palaver, she enters the house. I see the light flare in the window.

About an hour passes, and a figure appears from the barn, his moon shadow stretching across the yard. Tomás, with a loaded flour sack slung over his shoulder and his hat in hand, steps across the yard and onto her porch.

"What's goin' on, you reckon?"

Startled, I whirl around to find Parrot creeping up behind me. How that man moves so quietly, I'll never know.

Esther comes out of the house hooking her wire-rimmed glasses behind her ears. It looks as if she washed the glue out of her hair because it lifts in the breeze. I can't hear what they are saying, but she nods and goes back into the house. Then the hired man walks toward Mexico. We watch until he disappears into the brush.

Parrot buckles on his holster, and says, "Follerin' him through the heavily wooded area in the dark will be near impossible, but I reckon I'm up to the challenge." Then Parrot takes off on foot after the hired man. "I'll be back after I'm sure he's head'n to Mexico."

After waiting twenty minutes to be sure Tomás doesn't double back, I mount and ride down the hill leading Trail-Eater. Esther's dog, Worthless, barks incessantly.

The moon drops into the western sky and the great light begins to darken, but I can see Esther dressed in work clothes—a sensible dark skirt and a white shirtwaist. The light inside illuminates her silhouette as she steps out onto the porch to greet me. "It's really true," the sadness apparent in her voice. "Tomás says he's going to Mexico for a week."

"Each of us has free will," I respond quietly, hoping to console her.

"But after spending so much time with Jobe—seeing his goodness, you'd think Tomás would choose good instead of evil, life instead of death."

"It's the mystery of grace. It's available to everyone, but not everyone wants it."

I understand her disappointment. I have felt the same disappointment in people over the years. I lead the horses over to the corral and remove the tack, throwing it onto the rail. Then I walk back to Esther's house. I doff my hat and sit down in a chair she has on the porch. "I figure we're about two hours from Eagle Pass and we can sneak across near the cantina. I aim to stop these fellers if they prove to be the ones plotting another massacre."

"We can warn the ranch they're targeting, can't we?"

"We'll do what we can. What we have to, I reckon. Right now, we should rest and be ready to push the fight to them tonight."

She looks exhausted.

"I'm ready," she says, trying to convince herself. "It's just my house that's a mess."

"Get some sleep. When the sun rises, we'll do some chores, because we don't have to leave 'til late afternoon. So you have plenty of time to rest and catch up on some chores."

"That'll be fine," she says. "Would you like some breakfast now?"

I sheepishly confess, "While we were waitin' up on the hill, Parrot built a campfire a ways back, 'n brought me a couple a' eggs. They were delicious. He told me to tell you thank you. He stole 'em from your hens."

"I'm so sorry. I should have—"

I cut her off mid-sentence, "Now don't go apologizin' for needin' rest. We got a busy evenin' ahead of us. I'm gonna sit here and catch a nap, then me 'n Parrot are goin' to work out a plan." The dark circles under her eyes appear more pronounced today. The rough travel, late nights, and worry are telling on her.

"Fine."

"Take the mornin' to rest and do what you need to do," I repeat as I lean the chair back on two legs against the wall. Repeatedly, I slap my hat against my pant leg in hopes of diminishing the dust, then I pick up my rifle and lay it across my lap. I settle the hat back on my head, pulling it down to cover my eyes to block the remaining light of the moon as I conclude, "Parrot took off to try and follow Tomás, so I'm going to sit here and rest 'til the sun's high in the sky and he's back. You'd be wise to do the same."

THIRTY-ONE

The streets of the Mexican border town Piedras Negras were just waking up as Tomás crossed the river. His wife, a bitter old woman, lived here with four living children in a house made of mud and sticks. He wasn't sure they were his offspring. He gave his wife all the money Señora Stokes gave him. But the money the general gave him he kept in a Mason jar buried beneath a boulder twenty paces southeast from the windmill on Stokes's farm. When it all was done, the general had promised that little homestead would be his.

With the property in his possession, he could find a pretty, sweet young woman who was eager to have a home and garden of her own. They could live a happy life. She would be strong enough to do most of the work. Perhaps he could make enough money running goats to hire a boy to live in the barn and do the rest of the work, but that boy must not be handsome enough or old enough to interest the pretty young woman of the house. With two women he would have two families, and he would be the patron.

CHAPTER THIRTY-ONE

Then he could sit on the porch, play his guitar, and drink tequila. It would be a good life.

But before his dream could come true there was work to do. He did not resent the work. Yes, it was hard, but that's why it was work. As he cut gringos' throats, he always remembered they were invaders. This country should belong to him.

THIRTY-TWO

Puffy clouds cover the early morning sky, as Esther wanders out into the yard to check the chickens and look at the progress in the garden. She bends to pull some weeds. Because I know washing is on her agenda, I walk across the yard to the water pump, where I fill the big black washtub. I start a fire and set the pot to boil.

When Esther comes back to the cabin from the garden, she says, "I do need to sweep the house and do laundry. We have a partly sunny sky with a light wind, so the clouds will burn off by noon. A good day for fast drying."

The smell of mesquite wood smoke drifts toward her.

"Did Tomás set the pot to boil before he left?"

"No, ma'am, I did. This time a year it doesn't take long for clothing to turn ripe. I ran out of clean clothes a good while ago," I admit, "and I don't need the criminals smelling me before they see me."

I throw my dark clothes into the huge pot of bubbling water. A swatch of blue denim washes to the top. Esther picks up the large wooden paddle and pushes it back down and under. The fire is getting low, so I walk over to the wood pile to split more kindling.

The crack of metal against wood reverberates throughout the valley. It has been a long time since I split kindling and I feel seldom-used muscles tighten.

With the paddle, she scoops out the scalding material. After a scrub of lye soap, she vigorously rubs a garment back and forth over the ribbed metal washboard. She waves her scalding hands into the air to cool them. One at a time, she washes her new dress, then my two shirts. Her hands grow rough and red from moving in and out of the hot lye water as she handles the articles of clothing, tossing them into the rinse pot one by one until the wash pot is empty.

While the clothes hang on the line to dry, she goes into the house and brings out her ironing board and two cast iron irons. After setting the board on level ground, she undoes the catch on the top of the irons. Grabbing the fire tongs, she fishes into the flames for several good-sized coals to put inside each iron. It will take a bit for the irons to heat evenly. As the lids on the irons clang closed, I fondly remembered that familiar sound and how many times I'd watched my mother and sisters perform the same tasks. It seems long ago, and I wonder if this type of daily chore will ever become routine in my life again. A sense of doom hangs over me. But then it always does when I walk into an evil situation.

I sight in my pistol and let five bullets fly in rapid succession, knocking a circle into the corral post. The noise shatters the silence, causing a covey of doves to fly out of the brush and setting the chickens squawking.

"Clean clothes are such a blessing," Esther calls across the yard, not even flinching.

She glances at the sun; then I do too. It will soon be lunchtime. I can't keep my eyes off her. When she wanders over the rough ground back toward the garden, I can't resist following her. The summer smells of the freshly turned earth assaults our senses. The okra plants grow shoulder high, sending their fingers up to the sky. She begins snapping off the long pods.

"Okra!" She holds up her prize.

"I do love okra," I answer back. "Fried, boiled, baked . . . any way."

I enjoy watching her work. She gathers up the edges of the apron tied around her waist to catch the vegetables she collects. She seems tireless. As I sit on the porch cleaning my weapons, I worry about the evening. I know it's a sin to worry. But it's hard not to when you're headed into unknown danger.

By noon Esther has a full meal of fresh vegetables ready for me. She pulls the table out onto the porch, in the shade and away from the warm stove.

"You said you like vegetables, Mr. Wallace. I hope you get your fill today."

I don't mention that this might be our last meal.

"I'll never get tired of vegetables. Now all I need is that dog's happy tail thumping and a cat purring on my shoulder."

She laughs. "Worthless has no tail, so you'll get no sound from him."

I find myself eating with gusto. She is a good cook. The only thing I could have wished for was a little butter instead of lard, and a big brown yeast roll.

She laments, "Looking at the neat, recently hoed rows in the garden, I know Tomás's hand worked that soil. I find it so hard to think of him as a murderer. Maybe, just maybe, I imagined or misinterpreted this whole thing."

I know tonight she will find out differently. That feller is a poisonous snake. She would find out whether all her efforts were in vain, if this mad race had been for nothing, or if the neighbors' lives would be saved. I have seen the gruesome work of these men at the Ross Ranch, the Saldaña's, and the Müeller's. I just hope we stop them for good before other names are added to that list.

Esther believes in the goodness of men, but I know how ruthless these men are. If they catch us, we will never see Texas again.

But even as she picks at the dark collard green leaves on her plate, she whispers the phrase *"assesinato sangriento,"* so in her gut, she knows what's at stake.

I begin praying everything will go well. But I've been on enough of these "fact-finding" missions to know that things don't always go as expected. Finally, in the end, I keep praying, "Have mercy on us, most merciful Father."

The Mexican government frowns on Texas Rangers "invading" their country. Although just a stone's throw across a river, Mexico is very different from Texas. People are less likely to forgive and forget, turn the other cheek. An eye for an eye is the rule. The law there says guilty until proven innocent. But I know a greased palm can smooth the way with most *alcaldes*. Here in Texas, graft is a bad thing—a bribe, a payoff. In Mexico, it's just good business, a necessary tax.

Late in the afternoon, when the shadows lengthen but the heat of the day still remains, I bring the saddled horses up to the house.

"I guess we'd best be on the scout, Miz Stokes, if we're gonna get across that river before dark."

She steps out of the door carrying the large black Mexican shawl— *rebozo*—she would use to hide her identity. Her hair, braided into two long braids, lay across her breast in front of her shoulders, almost to her waist. Although she tries to mask her jittery nerves, her unease transfers to Trail because the mare dances and sidesteps as Esther tries to mount. Reaching down to grab hold of the bridle, I whisper, "Whoa, little girl, whoa, now. Steady." When Esther looks back at me, I can tell she thinks I am talking to her, not the horse.

As soon as Esther is well seated, I mount, and we head south toward Mexico at a reluctant walk. I wish I had something fine and jolly to say, but I don't. Every step leads us toward danger. She can't resist looking back at her little homestead and whispering, "I wonder if I'll ever see it again."

I'm not fool-hearted enough to tell her that she will, because the odds are against it.

CHAPTER
THIRTY-THREE

AUGUST 23, 1877
○ *Full Moon*

From atop a sandy knoll, a quarter-mile away, we look down at the silver ribbon of the Rio Grande River. In places, tall cottonwood and short salt cedar trees block our view of the snaking water. But in other places, we have a clear view of Mexico. Occasional flashes of late afternoon sunlight glitter off the lazy-looking river that's about forty feet across from bank to bank.

We picket our horses on the Texas side; no need to be accused of invading Mexico. The Mexican government can take a dim view of *Norte Americanos* entering their country. I figure if we walk in, we could just say we'd come to meet someone. And we have. The plan is to sneak in and out on foot as quietly as possible.

"All we have to do is identify the men, and if possible, the target. Then I will set up an ambush and pick them up before they do another dastardly deed."

I hold her elbow as we start down the sandy hill. She shivers with anticipation, and if truth be told, I am anxious too. In a few minutes we will wade across into old Mexico. The efforts of the last twenty-eight days will culminate tonight when we go to the Cantina La Paloma to locate that voice she heard so long ago. Would she remember what he sounded like? Would we find the horse with the nicked shoe, or had the shoe been replaced?

We stop at the river's bank on the Texas side. Up close, the river looks wider. Unlike the Frio and Nueces Rivers, which flow clear and clean, this water runs red and muddy and appears to have an easy, slow current. We can't see the bottom, but it's bound to be shallow. People wade it every day, don't they? That's where they get the name *wetbacks*.

Sitting on the sandy bank, I pull off my boots. She giggles when she sees my big toe poking through a hole in my sock.

She chastises me. "That sock wasn't in the laundry, or I would have darned it."

I hadn't deliberately withheld it. I'd been wearing it and just forgot. "Been meanin' to fix that myself," I say, with red heat creeping up my neck.

She sits down and unlaces her boots. I take a long strip of leather and tie it through my boot loops. She ties her laces together. Next, I lash together my gunbelt around and around the carbine. I roll up my pant legs to my knees. My legs are hairy and pale, in contrast to the tan of my arms. The blond hair on my legs glisten in the dying sun. When I take off my shirt, I see her study the white scars dotting my torso.

I mutter, "'Scuse me, Esther," for it is truly indecent to be undressed this way. Then I wrap my shirt around the guns. I reckon I'll have to tell her how I got them scars one day.

If she wonders about the scars, she doesn't ask.

She stands up and pulls the back of her skirt up between her legs, tucking the end into the front of her skirt's waist band. This time it is her turn to be embarrassed as she bares her legs up to her knees. She is quite the contrast to the elegant lady of last night.

I want to continue to stare at her bared legs, but I know she wouldn't appreciate it, so instead, I look into her eyes with a grave compassion.

"You're a brave woman, Esther Stokes. I appreciate you partnerin' with me."

"Let's get it done," she says brusquely.

"I don't want you riskin' yerself needlessly."

"I'll be careful."

"I'll give you a handgun when we get acrost. But remember to conceal the weapon, as best you can, by your side. If someone official approaches, throw it away from you. Don't be caught with it if you can help it."

The river's water feels warm on the surface as I step in, but the soft sandy bottom is cool. I take one step and then another. The water swirls around my ankles, then my calves. It becomes colder as I wade farther into the Rio Grande River. But I am hot, and the cold feels nice.

Then the sand under my feet turns to pebbles and my feet are tender, causing me to bite my lip to keep from whining about it.

As I turn to her, the river bottom suddenly disappears beneath my feet. I flap my free arm trying to keep the weapons and my head above the water, but before I can regain some footing, the muddy river water slips over my head, filling my open mouth and choking me. The current rips the carbine and pistols from my hand, lost forever. I struggle to the surface just in time to see Esther tumble under the water. I grab for her flailing hand, but it disappears through my fingers.

I lunge for her but only sink back beneath the surface myself. My feet reach for the bottom, but there is nothing but the flowing current's tug.

I dive toward her, swimming with all my might. The current and the boots around my neck, now filled with water, make it difficult to swim. Vainly, I reach for her, but she is lost in the swirling eddies as they drag us downstream at a rapid speed. Her skirts would be lead weights.

The current yanks me, so my head slips under water again, and something like a branch hits me from behind. I thrash at it, but it eludes my grasp. Finally, my head bobs above water and I spit out as much river as I can before I gasp in air. I try to tread water, to catch my breath and orient myself, but the current is too strong and continues to tow me downstream, jerking me once again below the surface. It is impossible to negotiate the roiling water.

Esther, Esther, where is Esther?

My head bobs in and out of the water. I try not to fight against the current. The murky liquid enters my nasal passages, causing me to panic. As I go back under, I failed to get a breath. Suddenly, I need to breathe—have to breathe! If I can't breathe air, I will breathe water and drown. Finally, my head breaks the surface again. I sputter desperately for air. I can't get enough. I roll on my back and try to float with the river.

As I kick with the current, searching for her, I spy her heavy mane loose and flowing out around her, jerking her head downstream. I realize the water has ripped apart the braids of her hair. I grab for the mass of floating hair but it slips through my fingers before I can hold it. Her skirt, loosened from the waist band, is filled with air and bobs on the surface, but I can't see her head. I know the skirt is entangling her arms and legs, possibly even her head.

Suddenly I realize she is drowning.

I flap and flail as I sink beneath the water again. The murky water rapidly sweeps us downstream. We are powerless. Helplessness washes over me. With intense pain ripping my lungs, my leg muscles knot, and I know it is hopeless. I surrender to drowning. *God help us,* I think. Soon it will all be over for us. Parrot will have to catch Tomás and the Castilian by himself, or the murders in South Texas will continue. At least the pain in my head and lungs will end, and I will be with Jesse and my Pa. I quit struggling and give in to the water.

The river begins to shallow out. My feet skid along the bottom, scraping against rock, I bend my knees and kick away from the cold bottom.

Where is Esther? I don't know if she is dead or alive. Is she upstream or downstream? I can almost stand but keep stepping into eddy holes. I quit struggling and concentrate on finding my footing as I stumble toward the nearest bank.

When my head is clear of the torrent I frantically survey the surface of the water, but she doesn't bob up. She's been down too long. No one can stay underwater that long and live. Desperation washes over me. I have killed her.

Devastation and overwhelming loss get the better of me and I gulp, not just for air but with the threat of sobs. My feet drag against the ground, so I stand and wade against the current. The water is shoulder deep, then chest deep, and finally it is waist deep. My feet touch mud and water plants grab at my calves. Instinctively, I seek the hard surface of the bank. The river seems to be shallowing out. The current is slower.

I struggle to the shoreline. I have to find her body. In a hope against hope, I run along the bank. Perhaps I can grab her and bring her to shore before the pressure in her lungs builds and builds and she breathes in water and is gone forever. Surely, she hasn't come this far just to drown. Have I lost her forever?

Then, just over my shoulder, I see the floating skirt. Behind me she swirls in a weak whirlpool. I briefly catch a glimpse of her head bobbing just upstream from me. Is she alive? I wade out as she floats my way.

Spitting and gasping, she flutters her arms in the air as she tries to establish her footing. She is alive!

Relief floods over me. I wade toward her, grab her hair and then her arm, and I pull with a supernatural strength, landing her like a fish. Her fingers constrict around mine. She tries to kick her feet to help me, but the heavy skirt binds her legs tightly. Then the skirt flows out and wraps around my legs, too.

The unnatural touch of the water in her lungs has left her pale and her lips blue. She gulps at the air and water spews out her nose.

"Slow down, Esther," I drag her to the bank. "I've got you. You're all right. Relax, you're safe."

When we are out of the water, I scoop her up in my arms and carry her up the sandy bank. I fall back onto the sand but don't let go of her. As she pants for breath, I turn her over my leg and pound her back with a flat hand.

Dirty water and lunch spew from her mouth as she vomits. Tears fills her eyes as violent coughing spasms rack her body.

I hold her forehead as she retches again. When she finishes vomiting, I cover the effluvium with sand, then wipe her mouth with a blue bandanna I always carry in my back pocket. Miraculously that cloth square remained in place. Then, as if she were a child, I pick her up and carry her farther from the river. She begins to sob.

A hundred emotions wash over me—for the first time in a long time I had seen a different future for myself. I've dreamed different dreams. She is those dreams. I want to see those dreams fulfilled.

I still cradle her in my arms. I'm shirtless. As her warm tears trickle down her cheeks, they fall on my chest. I continue to hold her and stroke her stringy wet hair.

"I didn't know the water would be so swift," I apologize.

I feel her shudder.

"I almost got you kilt."

Wrapping my arms around her feels good . . . too good. I know if she were in her right mind, she would struggle against me, prim and proper, but I hold her firmly, and it is nice. Then suddenly she feebly shoves against me.

"Don't fight, Esther. Just sit easy a minute, git your wind back. Rest."

"I don't want to sit easy," she stammers. But she doesn't have the strength to contend against me. She falls back against my bare shoulder and cries more. From her desperate sobs, I know she is crying about more than the river. I suspect she has not cried in a long time. Maybe she'd never even mourned her husband, and she certainly had no time to cry about Tomás's betrayal.

The sun sinks lower, sending scarlet fingers up into the sky.

She struggles against me, but I croon, "Let me comfort you, Esther."

Incredulously, she jerks her head up and looks into my face. I know my eyes are full of emotion. I glance away.

"Let me take care of you—"

She shoves me away. "I can't believe you're pressing your suit now! I almost died, and you're proposing again?"

I know a thousand venomous phrases spring to her mind, but before she can open her mouth, I grab her hand and say, "Forgive me. I was wrong to say that now."

She jerks her hand out of mine. "Yes, you were, Mr. Wallace. Don't ever say anything like that to me again."

I study the setting sun. "I cain't promise you I won't, Esther." I take a deep breath and exhale it, my chest muscles rising and falling, the pain of the water still there. "I'll let it rest for as long as I can."

Gritting her teeth, she glares at me. "If I marry again, it won't be to a violent rolling-stone, saddle-tramp policeman, no matter how reformed, handsome, and well-fixed he is. No matter how good his arms feel."

I try to hide my grin behind my hand. She thinks I'm handsome, well-fixed, and reformed. Maybe I have a shot.

She sits up and looks across the river. Then she clutches her face. "My glasses!" She struggles to her feet, then runs to the river, searching the bank, "I've lost my glasses!"

I follow her.

"They're gone, Esther. We'll get you another pair."

She glares at me, "You don't understand. Without them I can't see beyond that *arroyo*," she points across the river. "I can't afford another trip to Austin to replace them, and I don't have money to spare."

She sits down on the bank, holding her head in her hands. I think she might cry again, but she doesn't.

"I loved those glasses. They literally changed my outlook on life. Things were so much better since I had them. So much for earthly possessions."

"We also lost our firearms," I admit as I troop up and down the shore looking for the things we've lost. I find the boots she'd tied together and hung around her neck, snagged in a branch. Farther down, I find my ripped and torn shirt.

Without the guns, how can we defend ourselves? How could we go on and accomplish our mission? Can we find the Castilian general? Can we stop cattle from being rustled? And, more importantly, can we prevent some family from being murdered? We have lost everything. Should we quit? God had brought Esther back into my care. Did I have the right to put her in danger again?

"One thing we haven't lost," I admit, "is our lives. And when I was in the middle of that river, I thought we were done for sure." I retrieved her lace rebozo that was snagged on some cattails and put it at her feet. "You were just supposed to cross the river, and figure out who is plotting murder. We can telegraph the governor and say that we failed… let the Ranger company handle the problems. Or," I add, "you could just go home now."

She glances up at me. She looks as miserable as I feel. Being this near death, her silence is not at all awkward.

With my bare feet I kick a pit into the sand beside her and click two flint rocks together, building a small fire out of a handful of dry sticks that won't smoke too much.

She looks at her skirt, lifts her head, and quietly says, "Look, the river has dyed my dress an ugly brown, and it is the first new dress I've had in five years."

The small flames, combined with the warmth of the air and dying sun, are enough to begin to dry her clothes and hair.

"I'm sorry I don't have a coffee pot or anything to eat, Esther."

She looks up at me, again. "It's fine. Let's just go on and get this over with," she mumbles. "The river seems less deep here. Let's just cross and get this done."

"We are acrost."

"Good thing," she says, "because I don't know how to swim."

THIRTY-FOUR

Running her fingers through her almost-dry hair, Esther tries to pull out the tangles. When smooth, she braids it into two braids, wrapping the long Mexican rebozo over her head and then around over her shoulder. "Do I look enough like a Mexican that suspicions won't be aroused?"

She did not, but I'm not about to tell her that. First of all, she stands a foot taller than any Mexican woman I'd ever seen.

We head up the hill, slipping from salt cedar bush to bush. It grows dark as we work our way toward the town. Trekking over the rough ground, composed of powdery white caliche dust and silver dollar–sized round river rocks, is not easy, especially barefooted. At least Esther has shoes, but I have to reach out to keep her from slipping several times. Once, when pebbles tumble down a slight incline, I grab for her elbow, but she rights herself before I can help her. I don't have the guts to insist she hold my arm. I wish she wouldn't bite my head off every time I try to do something nice for her.

From the top of the hill, we see the quiet little town. A dust devil kicks up sand, lifting a chicken and causing it to squawk as it scurries across the narrow dirt street. The small tornado reminds me that the last time I saw a whirlwind was at the Ross Ranch. My life has certainly been tornadic since then.

I point. "I count fifteen *jacales* and a couple of pier and beam buildings. Most folks around here live on little *ranchitos* outside of town. Downtown is those three brick buildings and the adobe Catholic Church."

She pouts. "I can't see a thing."

Minute by minute, the light fades as we walk closer toward the town. In the distance, the light disappears below the chalk cliffs, casting long spectral shadows. Even with the hot breeze, Esther shivers. I wonder how much is nerves, and how much is being damp. The earth spins, time passes, and soon the moon will rise, bathing everything in bright white light.

"The second building is Cantina La Paloma," I point out the white board and batten building with peeling paint, even though I realize she can't see it.

Esther squints into the distance. I grab her arm and point her fingers toward it.

"Good, it's pier and beam."

"Why good?"

"Those tall cedar posts buried in the ground, and heavy beams laid on the posts, keep the flooring built on top of that clear of any flood water. There's a decent crawl space underneath it. Beside the church and downtown buildings, it's probably the most expensive structure in town."

"Corruption pays, righteousness costs everything. Especially my glasses," she whines.

I don't know what to say to that. Obviously, she is on a well-earned self-pity tear, so I figure it best to keep my mouth closed.

"Parrot said we should be able to see the bar and gaming tables from that eastern window." A faint yellow lamplight glow comes from the distant windows.

She buries her drawn and pale face in her hands. Then she looks up and confesses, "Now that the time's come, I don't know if I can do it, Mr. Wallace."

"Only eighteen days ago you stood behind the barn door listening to a European Spaniard talk about murdering your neighbors. You traveled almost three hundred miles to prevent a murder, and what we find in that bar will tell you if it was all worth it."

"Yes, but if Tomás's there, then I'll know I've been living with a horrible person who could have murdered me at any time."

She exhales the breath she's been unconsciously holding. That causes her to cough uncontrollably, expelling remnants of river water from her lungs. She clutches at her chest as if it still aches.

"Are you all right?"

She nods and smiles weakly. "I'm fine, Mr. Wallace," she assures me. "I just want all this to be over."

"Me, too."

"I want to be angry with you, but I'm not. I just need to get this done."

"Remember, we're spies here, not soldiers. We'll eyeball the fellers—maybe you can pick up a few hints about when and where this action's gonna' take place—and then when they cross the river, I'll trail 'em and put an end to this."

"I hope I'll be home, safe in bed, before dawn."

I touch her cheek with the back of my hand. She doesn't pull away, and I take that as a good sign. Then I start down the incline toward the Mexican bar.

"If we git separated, we'll meet back at the sandbar near the river below the bluff."

When she doesn't respond, I touch her arm and gently push her around to face me.

"Esther, don't go crossin' that river without me, under any circumstances."

"Before I step foot back into that watery grave, I'll sit there waiting for you for weeks, if necessary."

Closer now, the sounds of life reach our ears—a rooster crows his final farewell to the day; random dogs bark and another answers; a burro brays; and Spanish phrases drift from jacales. Uncertain of exactly how to get where we need to be, we wander south on the narrow paths that form nonexistent streets, hiding behind build-ings and stick and cactus fences as best we can. Esther does a pretty good job of blending in, but I am another issue. It's hard to hide a tall skinny cowboy with tender feet in a town where the average man stands less than five foot nine.

A brown dog, tailed curled up over his back, appears out of no-where and trails after us as raucous laughter drifts on the breeze and touches our ears. By the sad melodic harmonies of a guitar that filters through the thin board walls, I know we've found Cantina la Paloma.

From behind a cow shed, I mouth the words "this is it" and point to a side of the building that is almost totally dark.

A bright yellow glow pours out of the cantina's windows, casting eerie shapes across the rough ground. Dark, shadowy figures occa-sionally move across the light.

Esther comes close to me and I put my mouth near her ear and whisper, "Stay out of the light as much as possible. You probably won't even have to point out the man. If Tomás's there, I'll recognize him, and they'll probably be sitting together."

I look left and then right and can see no one, so I step across the open space between the cowshed and the cantina. Another dog barks in the distance. I slip into the shadows and freeze.

A *vaquero*, with heavy silver spurs jingling, comes out the back door and down the wooden steps. Although his wide-brimmed black hat shields his face, I can't help but wonder if it is *him*, the man with the nick-shoed horse. My heart pounds so hard I wonder if Esther can hear it all the way over at the cowshed. I lift my hand, palm toward her. She recognizes my signal to stop and she holds her position.

As the vaquero disappears into the outhouse, the door creaks.

I motion Esther forward. I see her take a deep breath, gather her skirt, and try to cross the open gap quietly, but the crunch of the pea-sized gravel under her feet sounds enormously loud to my ears. I watch her as she tries to lighten her step by tiptoeing and at the same time lengthening her stride. Tiptoeing in boots is no easy task. Finally, she makes it. She moves next to me, pressing her back against the roughhewn outer wall of the cantina.

The outhouse is so close to where we stand we can hear the man inside humming the guitar's tune.

We round the building's corner and stand in the shadows. Esther is so close to me I feel her knees shaking. I've heard people talk about being so afraid their knees knock together—but I've never known it to happen. Usually I'm so busy acting and reacting I don't have time to be afraid. Esther doubles over, covering her mouth, and I realize she is trying to cough or throw up again. She takes deep breaths and seems to calm down.

Suddenly my eyes fix on the horizon. The moon begins peeking over the cliff. It first appears as a blood-red fiery frown, then ever so slowly it inches up over the earth's edge. It makes me think of the passage in the Book of the Revelation of John, where it says the moon will be blood red at the end of the world. I hope this isn't the end of the world for us.

Finally, the man exits the outhouse and heads back toward the cantina. He drunkenly fumbles with his trousers and gunbelt, all thumbs with the buckles.

I can't keep my eyes off the rising moon. It glows orange on the edge of the horizon as it begins to creep up. Within minutes it becomes a huge yellow ball. Finally, the lunar disc turns milk white and a steady light begins to shine like a spotlight, illuminating our shadowy hiding place, until we are fully visible in the night.

The vaquero stops abruptly only feet from us. He totters in a haze, fully visible in the moonlight, and we are fully visible to him. All three of us hold our breath. With pursed lips he finally speaks.

"*Siguiente*," he burps and stumbles back toward the cantina entrance.

"He says, 'next,'" offers Esther.

"Yeah, I got that." Again, I move us around the southern corner of the building, back into the shadows, but near the eastern window.

Relieved to be in the only remnant of darkness around the box and strip building, out of the glare of the fast-rising moon, I grab and squeeze Esther's hand. She squeezes mine back.

The lamplight pouring out of the cantina catches Esther's eyes, and they flash yellow.

Someone inside is speaking rapid Spanish when she holds up her hand and nods. She has found the man behind the barn.

I bend down and she whispers into my ear, "We should stop raiding when the moon is so bright."

Another voice says in English, "The moon makes the work easier." The voice catches my ear—could it be King Fisher? If so, Captain McNelly will be relieved to know we finally have something concrete on which to charge and hold Fisher.

Then the Castilian speaks again. Esther translates, "The moon makes it easier for us to be recognized. The Ranger will be looking for us."

A second English speaker says, "That's why we mustn't leave anyone behind who can recognize us."

Instinctively Esther lifts her hand to cover her mouth but not before she whimpers loudly. That last voice is extremely familiar. *It can't be,* I think. I place my left hand onto the windowsill and rise up to peer into the smoky room.

My heart sinks. It just can't be true! But there sits Albert Hindes at a table with the Spaniard in a wide-brimmed sombrero, Tomás, and King Fisher, wearing his tiger-skin chaps.

When I glance at Esther, a tear rolls down her face. I wipe it away with my thumb. I wonder if that tear means she is in love with Albert.

From inside, I hear King Fisher say, "Did you just hear something outside?"

Albert says, "No, but I thought I saw something."

Suddenly, the sounds of chairs scraping across the floor and footfalls coming toward the window register in my mind. I shove her shoulder downward and point to the ground. She drops down and wisely rolls into the small space under the pier-and-beam building.

Glasses clink and more footsteps pound on the floor, then someone smoking a cheroot leans out the window.

I don't have many options at hand. I need to draw their attention away from Esther. Thinking quickly, on my tender feet, as if drunk, I stumble toward the outhouse, my moon shadow dancing before me, looking long and exaggerated, like a macabre *Dia de los Muertos* puppet. I sing, softly off key, a bawdy lyric about swimming with bow-legged women.

"Hey, gringo!" King Fisher calls out the window.

I know I can't run. Even if I was on horseback, they'd catch me in no time. The best I can do is hide. I don't stop, or turn around, hoping they'll forget about me. I step into the outhouse wondering if I'm not locking myself in a prison. It doesn't escape my memory that this pursuit started because of a girl in an outhouse. I pull open the outhouse door, and it creaks loudly. I slam it shut. It springs back open before I close it again and swing down the latch.

I hear a voice I think belongs to King Fisher say in English, "Find out who that is."

My pulse throbs in my throat. Through the little moon cut in the door, I watch three men burst out of the cantina entrance, down the steps, and approach the outhouse with their pistols drawn. So much about them forgetting me. I can't help but think about a fifteen-year-old near Frio City who through the cutout in an outhouse door watched her family slaughtered by these criminals a month ago.

I know I'm in a fine mess now. I debate whether I should come out swinging. I am afraid if I do, Esther will think it her duty to come to my rescue. I hope she has sense enough to stay hidden. It will do no good for her to be discovered. There is nothing else she can do for the time being but wait.

With humor touching his voice, the Castilian general says something in Spanish. Tomás laughs.

The next few minutes seem to move in a snail's pace. Albert pounds on the door, "Come out with your hands up."

"Give a feller a second," I call in a slurred voice.

"If you don't come out, we'll shoot through the door," Albert says.

"I got no gun." *Or any way to defend myself, except with my fists.* I open the door and twist and roll, still hoping they'll think I'm drunk. But before I move far, Albert hits me over the head with the butt of his six-shooter. Silver stars burst in my head. I crumple face down to the ground, waves of pain rolling through me. With the toe of his boot, Albert kicks me and rolls me over. He swears softly as he realizes who I am.

"This feller ain't no drunkard. Hell, he don't even drink."

"Who is he?" the Spaniard asks in heavily accented English.

"The señora's partner." Tomás answers.

"He ain't nobody's partner," Albert spits. "He's a little McNelly."

"*Que?*" the Spaniard asks.

"A Ranger," Albert spits. "A damn Texas Ranger."

"This ees not Tejas," the Spaniard says in heavily accented English. "Keel him and be done wit it."

"Find out what he's doin' here first," King Fisher hollers from the window. "And if anyone knows he's here."

Albert kicks me again. Pain ricochets through me as I feel a rib crack. When I try to move, I can't stop the moan escaping my lips. Before I can steel myself, Albert viciously kicks me in the stomach. Air explodes out of me. Desperately gasping for air, I hear the Spaniard repeat his demand.

"Keel him and be done. This is Mehico."

Then the man in the tiger-skinned chaps appears outside.

"Don't kill him. Look. He ain't got no boots. Bind his hands and feet and lock him in that storage shack until we can interrogate him."

Tomás pulled his rope belt out of his white flour sack pants and bends to bind my hands. To no avail, I kick at Albert as the stout man grabs me by my hair.

"He don't have no gun."

"He's smart," Fisher says. "He has no authority here. He would hang if he killed someone here."

Then Tomás and Albert reach under my arms, dragging me away from the cantina. Painfully, my bare feet scrape across the rocky soil. I want to cry out, but I force myself to relax, realizing it is better if they think I'm unconscious. I allow myself to be dead weight in hopes of finding the right moment to surprise them by twisting and springing to action.

Soon we are in the brush. I try to surreptitiously observe where we were going. But quickly I am lost in the cenizo, white brush, and salt cedar bushes.

"Will we still go on the raid, *El Rey*?" Tomás asks in broken English.

"Probably not until we find out what the Ranger is doing here."

"Will we keel him?"

"This is a dangerous country. He might have an accident."

"Maybe he quit the Rangers to go into business with la señora."

Albert laughs, "He may not currently be on the payroll, but once a Ranger, always a Ranger . . . and why else would he be here?"

Tomás shrugs his shoulders exaggeratedly, "Maybe he likes tequila or señoritas. Señora Stokes has a cold heart. She is only concerned with herself. She would never see the needs of a man."

Albert says, "Before her husband died, she sang and smiled. But once he was dead, the light went out of her. He was her God. She has no other. She pretends to follow the God of her husband, but in truth, her husband was her god. I'm glad that sanctimonious preacher is gone. He thought he was God's gift to mankind, always poking his nose where it didn't belong. Bad talkin' folks who just want to get ahead in this world."

Tomás continues, "The *Padre* knew of our alliance. He knew we were driving the cattle across the river. I did not think he had spoken of it to her, but he must have, since she brought the *rinches*."

Albert says, "You are an idiot."

"I had to kill the padre because he sent me away for using the tequila and stealing the cows. Now the señora must die too."

Albert says, "Make her death look like an accident, Tomás, or those idiots from Austin will be down here in a flash." Punctuating the words with more vicious kicks to my body, Albert continues, "So, she wants to trade one preacher for another. Esther would be better off with a real man, like me, instead of some self-righteous do-gooder, like this. I could teach her how to really live and have fun."

When Albert kicks me again, I feel another rib break and know I'm in danger of blacking out. I had hoped that by not fighting back, they would do less damage to me. But I should have remembered how cruel Albert could be. I reach for dirt to fling into Albert's eyes, but he slams a boot onto my fist before the task can be completed. The sound of bones snapping fills the air, and I can't stop from screaming. Then Albert kicks me in the face, and I feel a bottom tooth pop out. Before I black out, I hear Albert say, "This is for the grief you caused me with Matilda."

CHAPTER
THIRTY-FIVE

I wake with a start. It is dark. I don't know how far they dragged me, because somewhere in between the cantina and here, I passed out.

I think my own moaning wakes me. If town is near, it lies silent except for the distant braying of a donkey. My left eye is swollen shut and my right eye can't focus well. I shut it, hoping there's dirt in it that will clear if I keep it shut. My left hand throbs, and I am having trouble breathing. The slightest movement sends violent waves of pain through me. I could swear even my hair hurt. How long have I been out? Is this the same night—if so, it feels endless. I wonder what has happened to Esther. Did they find her? If not, would she be able to find help? Has Mr. Parrot come back? Does he know what has happened? How will they find me?

I have been an arrogant fool for leading her here—especially after I lost my weapons in the river. Just a bit of spying. And now I've probably killed us both. I'd deliberately walked into mean fights before, but this was supposed to be easy. Just hide near the building, listen to the voices, figure out who she overheard, then walk back to Texas.

What an idiot I've been. I should have just left her home and tracked Tomás. I'd be no worse off, and she'd be much better off.

A rooster crows, signaling approximately an hour before dawn, an hour before I can hope Parrot will be able to find tracks to follow me. After the escapade of almost drowning in the Rio Grande, I didn't think I'd ever want water again, but my mouth is caked with caliche dust and the smelly bandana tied around my mouth holds the dust firmly in place. I try to sit up, but my limbs are numb from being bound together. My head swirls. My feet are full of cactus thorns. My stomach rumbles. I hear a strange sound, and I realize it is me, whimpering and groaning.

The wind gusts dust up from the ground and blows it through the cracks in the building. This day would be a hot one. The wind is already warm. In the distance, a challenging rooster crows, accompanied by occasional dog barks and horse whinnies. I am not far from town. Finally, the first rays of the sun light the eastern sky. Through cracks in the plank door, sunlight streams in long thin rays, causing dust motes to dance on the rays of light. Time is short for me to try to escape. They will be back from their raid shortly and want to deal with me.

When I open my good eye, I can see I'm in a small dark shed about four feet by four feet. It is built out of ill-fitting planks of wood that run vertically about eight feet tall, set directly onto the dirt. The building has four corner posts ringed by cross braces about four feet off the ground. Each board held in place with two nails on the bottom, two nails on the center support and two nails on the top support. Tiny shafts of light shoot through old nail holes in the rusting, repurposed roof. The light shaft angles change with the moving sun and the passing of time.

My head throbs. As the day heats, the wind increases. It buffets the salt cedars, causing their long shadows to wriggle across the cracks in the walls. I realize just how hard the wind is blowing when the only sound I hear is the shed creaking under the strain. The sound eddies from no particular direction. Then disappointment washes over me as I realize town might be farther away than I originally thought. The wind could have blown the sounds to me.

A mourning dove calls to her mate, but it sounds like a death knell. I know I'm hurt badly. Blood still drips from my head and who knows where else.

A horrible screech rips the quiet as the wind blows a branch across the corrugated tin roof. At last, when that wind gust subsides, I imagine I hear someone calling.

I try to respond, calling out that I'm locked in the building, but the sound I make with the gag in my mouth comes out like a growling dog.

Then I hear her voice nearer. "Nels," she whispers, "are you in there?"

I groan again.

It is Esther. I don't know whether to be happy she's tracked me, or afraid she'll get caught. I hear her frantically searching for a way into the building. Then I hear her jiggle a lock. I know she doesn't have any tools to break a lock or pry the door off the hinges. She isn't tall enough to climb onto the roof to search for a hole. I hope she realizes the only thing to do is go find Parrot. The only way anyone could get in is to dig under.

She disappears for a while, or maybe I black out again. Then I hear it. Esther viciously attacking the chalky dirt, digging into the hard-packed soil as she grunts with the effort.

Sweat forms on my upper lip. Then it drips down my brow and back. I drift in and out of consciousness as the sun tracks higher in the sky. By mid-afternoon, the sun on the tin roof will cause the temperature to rise well over the hundred-degree mark. By late afternoon, without water, I doubted anyone could survive in here for long.

I am having difficulty breathing. I suspect my nose is broken, and the broken ribs and the rag in my mouth prohibit me from sucking in air.

I struggle to sit up again. My muffled groans stop her digging. "Nels," she cries, "is that you? Can you answer me?"

She begins to speak, "Your mother told me you never quit." I hear the catch in her voice. "I want to quit. I know you want to quit. I need to quit. I know you need to quit. But I'm not going to quit. And I know you're not going to quit. Your mother is praying for us. We are going to get out of here. We are going to meet Mr. Parrot, and we are going to go home."

Her words make me want to smile. That's my girl. Nothing is too hard for her. God has certainly picked the right partner for me.

The hole is finally big enough for her to look under the building. Through my one good eye, I see her cheek resting on the ground, peering under the boards. She is a sight! Dirt on her face, hair straggling everywhere. But I worry that her hole is too narrow and the building too dark for her to see inside. With a huge effort and an "uumph," I twist around to let her see I am here. She sees the movement and reaches her hand under to touch my face. I wish she could have pulled the bandana out of my mouth and given me a drink of water.

After finding me, she assaults the ground with renewed vigor. Unladylike, she grunts with the effort. Stretching a broken pick-ax up under the border of the shed, she is able to use the edge of the building as leverage. Huge chunks of earth fall away.

"Ouch," she cries out when the pick slips, and her elbow bangs into the building.

The way I am lying causes my side to go numb. I hope that means I'll stop feeling the gravel digging into my flesh and my broken rib.

With a broken pitcher shard Esther scoops away the chalky ground. Finally, she realizes she can now crawl under the building's edge. She eases her body under the frame.

The darkness must have left her momentarily blinded because she pauses in the cramped space. When she finally speaks, she says, "It's so hot and musty in here."

I want to laugh, but I don't have the energy.

"Nels?" she whispers.

She reaches out and touches my face. Her hand feels cool on my fevered brow. My long legs and bare feet stretch all the way across the floor. Even though by now her eyes have somewhat adjusted, the empty nail holes in the ceiling don't provide much light.

"Now that I'm inside, I should be able to dislodge some of the boards." She scoots on her bottom back toward the hole she's made.

She grabs the two inside braces of the building. At the same time, she seems to gather the entire force of her will, and then she kicks at the base of the boards. The nails squeak. She kicks it again, and the nails groan and give way.

Standing, she moves to the center support. She braces herself again, and lifting her skirt to a very indecent height, she kicks with all of her might. The rusty nails reluctantly give way with a squeak. Light pours in, shattering the darkness.

Then she turns and sees me. At the sight, she cries out in fright. "Oh, God! Heal his broken body."

She helps me sit up, which sends pins and needles shooting through me. I can't stop my head from lolling against my chest as if it's broken. She wipes at the blood on the left side of my face that has crusted where it trickled down until the gag in my mouth stopped its flow. I try again to open my left eye, but it is hopelessly swollen closed. Fresh blood oozes from my nose and ear. I guess sitting up has knocked something loose again. My shirt is gone. Then I realize they used it to keep the gag in my mouth.

"Oh God, oh God," she cries out. "Please don't let him be dead."

I don't think I'm dead . . . I just want to be, especially when the unbelievably sharp pains hit me again. She sits down next to me and tries to tenderly pull my body into her lap. I whimper like a puppy. She places her palm flat on my chest and feels the ragged rise and fall.

"Thank you, oh thank you, God."

As fast as her swollen fingers can move, she unties the knot that binds the gag into place. When she pulls the gag out of my mouth, I croak, "Esther?"

"Don't talk just yet," she whispers. I nod. She strokes the blood-matted hair back from my forehead.

"They really beat you up. Are you hurt bad?" she asks.

"Not good," I growl.

It is then that I see her hands are bleeding, the nails broken back to the quick. Red blisters adorn her palms. I realize all she has done to get to this point.

With my head resting on her knee, she touches my bruised rib, then she rolls me over enough that she can reach behind me to untie my hands. The ropes are too tight, the knots too set. It is impossible to undo them with her torn fingers. "Your hands will have to wait until I stop your head wound from bleeding."

She continues to murmur in a comforting tone. "No telling how much blood you've already lost. All I have is the nasty Rio Grande-soaked hem of my petticoat."

I hear the garment rip. Then I feel her wrap it around my head. Pulling her shirtwaist out of her waist band, she bites and tears the hem of her blouse. Tearing the material cross-grain proves difficult; she can't do it.

"Knife," I whisper.

She looks at my feet where I usually carry my blade and realizes I have no boots to hold the knife.

I croak, "Pants."

Esther reaches into the pocket of my pants, her face twisting with embarrassment because of the intimacy of the act. Finally, she extracts the small five-inch onyx-handled knife that McNelly gave me back in his office. She tries to pry it open, but finds she no longer has any fingernails.

"Hold it behind me, I'll do it."

She positions the knife so I can reach it.

With garbled speech I apologize, "My hands are sorta numb,"

Realizing how swollen and mangled my left hand is, she holds my right hand in hers and with her right hand guides the knife into place. The well-oiled tool springs open. Quickly, she slips it between the harsh horse-hair rope and saws back and forth until the taut cords split. I groan as my hands spring apart.

She picks up my right hand and begins to rub the life back into it. I bite my lip to keep from crying out as the tingling darts of throbbing pain seem to override the agony in other parts of my body. The skin around my wrists is raw and torn. She massages the palm of my right hand and each finger but, thank God, she doesn't touch my left hand.

"Thank you," I sigh.

"Hush now," she says.

I close my stinging eye as I flex the muscles in my upper arms and chest. Sweat pours down my face. When the effort proves too great, I fall back into her lap, exhausted and almost comatose. She uses the knife to slice away the bottom portion of her blouse. Then gently, she wraps it around my wounded hand.

"I'm really afraid," she admits. "I need to know how badly you're hurt, because I'll probably just wound you more when I move you. But we're not gonna quit until we get back to Texas."

The ache washes over me again. Then my breathing becomes even and I realize I am dozing on and off. She rolls the rebozo and slips it under my head. I croak out the words, "Don't leave me, Esther."

"No water, but I've got a raw egg I want you to eat."

As a form of acquiescence, I faintly nod.

She exits through the small hole in the back wall of the shed.

I stir when she slips back in.

"This'll taste horrible, but it'll give you some strength."

With one hand she strokes my bristled cheek and with the other she pokes her thumb through the egg's shell. Tipping the egg up, she eases open my jaw. It feels broken, but I guess it isn't because it works well enough when I open my mouth. The egg slides down my throat. To stop me from gagging, she pets my bristly neck, like I had done Billy's, but I eagerly swallow the slimy mass. It is wonderful, cool and moist. Then I sigh.

"I love you, Esther Stokes," I whisper, "you're something special to come after me."

She stills my speech by placing a cool finger on my lips. I realize she doesn't want to hear my declaration of love. But then she holds her hand to her ear. I can't be sure, with the wind as high as it is and the ringing in my ears, but it sounds like horses and riders in the distance.

Albert has come back!

THIRTY-SIX

"Just burn the place down. They'll never find him. All that will be left is charred bones."

The horses churn up a cloud of dust that washes over the shed, filtering in through the cracks and nail holes. Thank goodness Esther decided to kick out the board on the back side of the building. No one seems aware of her presence yet.

"Sí, señor," I hear Tomás say. Esther puts her hand over my mouth and I realize I am groaning. "But the general wanted to know what *el rinche* knows."

Horses stir and leather squeaks. Even through my broken nose, I smell the strong odor of kerosene.

"Light it," Albert says. "As dry as that wood is, it'll go in a flash. We'll have a drink and come back to scatter the ashes and bones."

"What about the señor's horse?" Tomás asks.

"We'll have to ride the river to find it."

"Perhaps I could have it? It is a very fine *caballo*."

"That horse attracts a lot of attention. It's evidence that could link you to the Ranger's murder."

"Then it's best," Tomás agrees sadly. "This fine horse must be destroyed. Or perhaps I could take it far into Mexico and sell it."

Albert snarls, "Perhaps *I* could take it far into Mexico and sell it."

Tomás acquiesces, "As you wish, señor."

"Light the fire—we have work to do."

"Shouldn't we check on him?"

"Are you afraid he ran away?" Albert asks with a laugh.

Esther makes eye contact with me when she hears the strike of the match. I had heard it too. The faint acrid odor of burning seeps under the door. Then the horses nervously stomp as the flames take hold of the kerosene-soaked wood. With every pop and crack of the fire, my fear grows. I wonder if I can move. I do not want to burn to death.

She whispers, "We dare not exit until the riders are gone."

I nod then whispered, "But we dare not stay, either."

Within seconds, sparks and ashes swirl around the tiny room. The heat and smoke become overwhelming. She lifts the edge of her skirt and pushes it up against her mouth and nose.

Finally, I hear Albert say, "He's cooked. Let's get out of here."

Black smoke billows into the tiny space. I struggle to stand, but the best I can do is crawl. Esther tugs me toward the back of the building and the three-foot hole she's made.

By this time, the fire scorches us both. Dropping sparks singe our skin. With superhuman effort, she pulls my right arm over her shoulders and stands, lifting me to my unsteady feet. She shoves me toward the hole under the four-foot-high wall brace and I fall out of the building coughing. She scrambles out and drags me from danger as flames, with a whoosh, engulf the shed.

Using her hands, she snuffs out her smoldering skirt and hair.

"They'll be back," I croak.

She pulls me into the shade of the brush about forty yards from the shed. "You rest and let me worry about things for a while. Rest, I'll be back in a minute."

Here the river runs northwest to southeast. I get my bearings and point east over the rough terrain. I whisper, "Parrot should be by the river."

CHAPTER THIRTY-SIX

"It's imperative we get the horses." She doesn't add that there was no way I can walk out of Mexico. But she knows it, and so do I. The horses remain on the Texas side—so she has no option but to cross that river. I wonder if she can cross it without being seen, and without drowning.

As rapidly as she can, she walks away. I hear her praying, "Oh, God, please let that river be close, and don't let them come looking for him until I get back."

My voice comes out raspy and weak as I call out, "Better break branches every few feet so you can find your way back."

She stops and turns back to me. Of course, she realizes by leaving such a plain trail, she is marking a path for anyone who wants to follow it.

Without further acknowledgement she says, "I can just follow the smoke." Then she disappears into the brush.

Sweat pours down my back as I try to crawl, but the effort proves too much. I decide I am better hiding in the shade than fainting out in the open. The building collapses with a whoosh.

The next thing I remember is a hawk flying overhead, screaming. I jump. I can still hear the crackle of the fire, but the roar has died down. By sun time, at least an hour has passed, so I must have fallen asleep. Albert would be back soon.

CHAPTER
THIRTY-SEVEN

An unusual irregular clacking rhythm catches my attention. I shift my head, trying to pick up the sound more clearly. With each passing second, it grows louder. Then I recognize it. A herd of longhorn cattle is trailing nearby. Minutes pass before I see the legs through the undergrowth as they pass by. I had heard them a good quarter-mile away. Their longhorns knock together as they walk, and the calves frantically bellowing for their mothers.

The dust of their hooves swirl into the air, catching in the wind like little cyclones. The shrill whistle of a ranchman splits the air followed by his "hup, hup."

The herd moves to the west. They are so close I smell the manure. I suspect these are stolen Texas beef. Within a few hours, they will be rendered to hide and meat, and some poor Texan's family will do without next winter.

So, Albert and Tomás probably accomplished their lethal deed last night. Had they killed an innocent family? It appears that we have made a mess of everything and failed in our mission. It is no consolation, but if we can get out alive and testify about what we know, it might be enough to curb crime for a while.

I know if I don't get farther away from here, Albert and Tomás will come back to kick through the ashes, sifting to find evidence that I'd perished. Upon finding no bones, they will come looking for me. I can't run. My tracks are evident. I can't even move much, so unless some miracle happens, I'll be dead again.

I need to give Albert as wide a berth as possible.

I find a dried mesquite bean and suck it, hoping the sickly sweet taste will put moisture in my mouth and stop the grumbling of my empty stomach, but it only makes me feel queasy. I struggle to my knees, then grab the trunk of a mesquite tree and try to stand. I take three or four steps before I fall, huffing and puffing. I know I have to try again. It is doubly hard without boots. But I marshal my strength, take as deep a breath as possible, grabbing the rough bark of the neighboring mesquite tree as I pull myself up. I take two steps, then I black out again.

The next thing I know, the full force of the afternoon sun reflects off the white bluff beside me. The light ricochets everywhere, leaving very few shadows. I am tied in place, astride a horse, my hands bound to the horn and my legs bound to the stirrups, but I don't remember how I got here. Had Albert found me? Or had Esther?

I squint through my good eye, trying to see what is happening. The horse's hooves clop loudly against the fist-sized rounded river rock. Every step jars my sore jaw and jerks my broken ribs. Then I realize we are crossing the river.

Waves of gratitude roll over me as I recognize Parrot's grimy hat sits on the fellow riding the horse in front of me. On the north side of the river, mercifully, Parrot stops the horses and unties me. But when Parrot pulls me off the horse, I black out again.

When I wake up, I am sitting on crumbled caliche rocks, leaning against the twenty-foot-tall bluff.

"Thanks to yer lady, yer back in Texas, Preacher. She's gone to get your mounts."

Parrot opens a can of peach halves with his knife. He stabs one of the gold beauties with his knife and lifts it to my lips. I swallow it whole. Parrot sticks another, but I shake my head no. I'm not sure my stomach can take it, and I can't imagine retching in my condition.

"Maybe you can eat another in a minute."

We hear the soft nicker of a horse. Parrot lays a pistol in my lap before he disappears into the brush. I don't know if I have the strength to lift the .45, but I put my palm on the grip and my finger on the trigger. Every bone and muscle in my body screams.

Esther breaks though the wall of brush, riding Trail and leading Chief. The animals tug at the reins, pulling Esther toward the bluff. I think, *she's headed for disaster if she doesn't get control of those beasts.* I wish I could get up to help her, but I collapse with the effort.

I whistle two soft notes and Chief hears me. He steps ahead of Esther, but she pulls him back, then realizing it is me, she wisely lets him go. The big dun comes into the shadow of the cliff and nuzzles at my bare foot. He snorts when he smells the blood.

"Steady," I whisper, and he settles in for a quick nap, hip-shod, head drooping.

Esther dismounts and a hand comes through some white brush and grabs Esther's shoulder. She screeches until the hand covers her mouth. Mr. Parrot has come up behind her.

The animals don't appear to have heard Parrot's approach, and she certainly didn't. She twists around at the same time in panic. Parrot steps next to her.

"You set my heart pounding, Mr. Parrot."

"We'd best git, girly."

"I didn't hear you come up," Esther exclaims, still clutching the base of her throat.

"Didn't mean for you to hear me," Parrot says. "Indian walkin' makes me a good spy. I don't even thank about doing it anymore. It's who I is."

"Is Mr. Wallace . . . "

"I was jest cookin' him some canned peaches right under them cottonwood trees when you come. But he's got a mighty poor appetite for such dee-licious eatin's."

Esther approaches me as I sit limply against the wall of the bluff.

The open, half-eaten tin of peaches nestles in between the roots of a giant cottonwood. Her stomach growls loud enough that Parrot chuckles. "I don't reckon you'd mind eatin' the rest of them."

But first Esther kneels next to me. I sit with my eyes closed, as still as death because it hurts to move. My bare feet are bruised and swollen. I couldn't wear boots now even if I had any.

Squatting in front of me, she can't stop the tears silently flowing down her cheeks. "Your features are so swollen and distorted I wouldn't have recognized you."

I wipe at the blood that drips from the open wound near the corner of my tender left eye. I can hear my own breathing, ragged and shallow. She touches my prickly cheek and says, "You're gonna be all right now."

It is true. My situation has greatly improved from morning to afternoon. I try to move, but it causes me to suddenly gasp, and my right eye springs open with the pain. There'll be no opening my left eye for a couple of days, I reckon.

I attempt a smile, but it ends in a groan. After I recover control, I growl, "Hello, Esther. Ya done real good."

"Ssh!" she hushes me. "Rest."

Parrot tilts his hat back on his head, revealing his broad white forehead. "Cain't rest much. We're not out of trouble, yet. We gotta get you to the widder's place by nightfall. Down those peaches, Missy. They'll give you strength to finish this up. Now that Preacher's outta commission, I gotta find you help and fast. We still don't know when they're gonna strike back at ya, but they will. At least we know who them *hombres* is, and they think Preacher's a goner."

"Not for long," I croak. "When they don't find my belt buckle and skull, I reckon they'll come a-lookin'.

"Then we can't go home," Esther says.

"You gotta go there, Miss Esther," Parrot insists. "He cain't move far, and 'sides, I'll bring help 'fore the sun rises twiced. I'll leave ya well armed."

"Help me on my horse." I struggled to move. "We might as well git this over with. It ain't gonna hurt any less an hour from now."

With Parrot on one side and Esther on the other, they half drag and half carry me to Chief's side. Thank goodness the horse knows how to stand still.

"Tie my legs to the stirrups and my hands to the horn."

"No!" Esther objects.

"Yes," I insist. "I can't stay on long by myself, and we need to make time."

"He's right," Parrot says, ending the argument.

"At least wrap my petticoat around his wrists to cushion the ropes," Esther urges. "If you don't, he may never regain use of that left hand. He's already so cut-up, it'll be months before he's healed."

In spite of the binding petticoat, I cry out when Parrot tightens the ropes. Esther turns away, saying, "I wish I could bear some of the pain, but this time I can't."

After we commenced, Parrot, leading his extra horse, keeps glancing back over our shoulders, and once he disappears for about twenty minutes. When he catches up, his lathered horses snort and puff, tack squeaking under the strain of the rough country.

"No sign of folks follerin' us. I snuffed out our trail, best I could, but they'll figure out he didn't burn and they'll come a-lookin'. Can ya find yer way back home from here, Miz Stokes?"

She nods.

"If ya can git him off the horse by yerself, I'll head on out toward Ranger camp in Frio City and try to bring help."

"God be with you, Mr. Parrot."

"God be with us all, Miz. Stokes."

Then, mercifully, I lose consciousness.

CHAPTER
THIRTY-EIGHT

The barking of the collie brings me to alert. Unshed tears fill Esther's eyes. "We're home."

The dog meets us at the edge of the garden.

"Quiet, Worthless, quiet!" When the dog realizes who his visitors are, he scampers beside us, trying to jump up on the horses. With her usual efficiency, Esther calms the dog and begins planning the tasks she needs to accomplish.

"You're to go right to bed."

Reining the mare in front of the house, she slips out of the saddle and reaches for me, but I stop her by croaking, "Barn, not the house."

"You're going into my bed," Esther protests. A flush creeps up her neck when she realized the implications of what she said. She obviously hopes I didn't notice, but I know she suspects the grimace on my face is a grin.

"That's what Albert'll figger."

"Oh." She now realizes if trouble comes, they wouldn't expect me to be in the barn. "Can I build a fire in the stove?" she asks.

I responded with a positive nod. Entering the house, she rolls the mattress off the bed as best she can, then carries the bulky bundle to Trail, who accepts the load without complaint. Then she leads Chief and me into the barn. Trail follows. If I hadn't been slumped over the gelding's neck, I wouldn't have fit through the barn door. It is not a big space, perhaps twelve by fourteen. After kicking the hay into somewhat of a level plane, she carries over the mattress and drops it.

"It will have to do."

She maneuvers Chief as close to the bedding as she can before she begins to work on the knots holding me in place, but the knots are too tight. The onyx knife in her pocket holds the solution to my quick release. She grunts as she struggles to slit the bonds off my feet and then my hands, and I tumble onto the mattress with a holler. My ribs did not like that action.

She backs Chief into the other stall next to where I lay. The horse seems to know I am injured, because he waits patiently as she removes his heavy tack.

Then she is bending over me bathing my brow with a cool cloth.

"I wish we had some laudanum."

If I ingest the herbs from my war bag, I will be of no use to her. But what use am I without them? Either way, I realize I cannot protect her. It is all up to God.

"In my war bag, in my medicine pouch. A drug that'll kill pain, but I'll be no good to you if trouble comes."

Esther begins digging around in my saddlebags.

The beaded pouch is old, the leather soft and pliable. She loosens the drawstring and dumps the contents into her skirt. She picks up the plug of tobacco, "Good for wasp and scorpion stings, but the other objects are a mystery to me."

"Red string."

Sorting through the tiny bundles of herbs, she discovers each is tied with a different colored embroidery thread.

"The red bundle! Let's see if I can remember what you did when Billy broke his arm. You spit in your hand and made a ball. How much?"

CHAPTER THIRTY-EIGHT

"'Bout half."

She spits into her hand. As she rolls the herbs into a ball, it becomes gooey. "I don't know the magic song," she says, unable to stop the tender smile that touches her lips.

"You know it, Esther, you sing it ever' day in ever' thang you do."

"Ssh!" she gently places her finger on my split lip. "Save your flowery speech 'til you get well." As her finger rests on my lip, she suddenly eases my jaw open and shoves the pill down my throat with her forefinger, as she had seen me do to Billy. "I've heard it's powerful' bitter."

I gag, then swallow. She quickly moves to the top of the stall rail where she'd thrown my tack and removes the canteen off the saddle's horn. She holds my head as I sip the water. It dribbles past my split lip and across my swollen cheek onto her skirt. When I finish drinking, I began to feel the effect immediately. Peace rolls over me as my limbs numb. I sigh and drop back onto the mattress.

"Bring me the shotgun," I whisper before the darkness engulfs me.

Almost immediately I'm breathing heavily.

"You'll never be able to use it," she mutters.

My eye flies open, startling her. "Do it," I insist. "Bring me the gun, then do your chores, then . . . " I fell asleep before I finished the sentence.

When I wake up, Worthless lays next to me whining and nuzzling me. Esther comes in and shoos the dog outside. The shotgun is next to me. I wonder if she'd checked the weapon's load.

Then the fever starts. The quaking rattles my teeth. Esther comes back carrying several colorful quilts.

"Does the fever mean internal injuries?" she asks.

I don't know. But it isn't good.

As she tucks the hand-stitched blankets under my bruised and battered feet, my teeth continue to knock together. It's August in Texas and I'm freezing. I think I whisper, "I love you, Esther Stokes," but it could have just been whimpering and groaning.

If she hears it, she doesn't respond. And I think I fall asleep.

My stomach growling wakes me up. She uses a soft cloth soaked in warm water to bathe my face before she spoons a soft scrambled egg into my mouth. I doubt I can stomach it. The pain washes over me in waves.

"Small bites," she encourages. "Try to keep it down, your body will heal faster if it has nourishment."

But after two bites I am done.

Later, I dream I can hear her singing softly. I imagine Parrot is on his way back with help at his side riding on the clouds, but I have no concept of time. Have I been here hours or a month?

I mutter, "If this depredation isn't stopped, it won't be because you didn't try, Esther."

She pats my good hand to comfort me.

As she bathes my tortured feet and pulls out the cactus spines, she talks. "I made chicken soup. It always helps a body get well." Then she mutters quietly to herself, "They must have dragged you behind the horse, the tops of your feet are scraped raw."

I stir restlessly because there is something I need to tell her . . . but I can't remember what it is.

"Tomorrow," she continues, "I'll bake biscuits and we'll have vegetables from my neglected garden. Maybe tomorrow we'll get you into a bath. I'm gonna bathe in a bit and I don't need you worrying after me. You need to sleep. Healing comes in sleep."

Then Worthless begins to bark a danger bark. Fast and High.

"What a fool I was to let down my guard!" She jumps from the pallet and heads to the barn door. "I thought we'd have more time before they discovered us!"

I struggle to sit up. But it is useless—I have no strength. The drugs run through and whirl around my body, wrapping me in a tight cocoon.

She hurries to the barn door. The sun's last glow permeates the sky. Thank goodness the wind usually dies down with the sunset. This has been the longest day of my life. I see her squinting. Her weak eyes directed toward the collie. Now the dog's outcry isn't an alarm, it is a threat—growls punctuated by vicious snaps.

"He's at the chicken coop." She stands riveted to the spot. "Two weeks ago, I would have marched straight to the coop with no fear, now terror freezes me at the door."

I can hear the hens squawking and screeching. Something—man or beast, is in the hen house.

I whisper, "If it's a coyote, your delay could be costing you hens."

"If it's a man," she whispers back, "it could cost me my life."

"You cain't let fear rule yer life, Esther."

"I know I'm acting silly. But I don't think I can shoot someone even if they threaten my life."

"When you see the threat, you'll do what you need to do. Ever' thang else is just supposin'."

She pulls the dirty wet boots onto her feet and runs to the coop. I hear the dog, snapping and barking.

I hear her hollering, "Come, Worthless, sit! For once, do what I say." I try to rise up on my elbow, but it feels as if an invisible hand holds me down.

Within a few minutes, Esther comes back into the barn wrestling the dog between her legs and holding a handful of its neck fur. It whines and yelps as if she is hurting it, but Worthless only wants back outside.

"Rattlesnake after my chicks," she says breathlessly.

After they settled down in the hay, I croaked, "What did you do?"

She said, "I took the hoe and killed it. If I hadn't, it would have come back and eaten chicks all summer."

"That's what evil is like," I try to clear my raspy throat to no avail. "It never has enough. If good folks don't stand in its way, it takes over, and they'll be no more good folks. Remember that."

"But good people often pay for standing up against evil with their lives."

I shut my eyes. "That's what it costs."

"I need to let that snake be a lesson and not let down my guard again."

I don't know if she's talking to me or herself, but the blackness swirls over me again. But I need to help her . . . to tell her . . . "set traps . . ."

I wonder if I said that out loud before my mind floats away like a butterfly.

CHAPTER
THIRTY-NINE

I wake with a start. Esther's head rests on my shoulder; my right arm wraps around her. Her breathing even, measured, and her warmth soaks into me. I'm glad she is sleeping. It had been a rough week. How she had gotten in my arms? I don't know, and instinctively I know she wouldn't be pleased to wake in my embrace, so I set out to extricate myself. The pain shoots through me, threatening to send the oblivion swirling around me again.

I exhale slow shallow breaths, trying to dismiss the pain.

The barn, still pitch black and hot, even in the pre-dawn hours, seems peaceful. I remain still and listen, but everything seems quiet. Esther stirs, rolls over, continues sleeping. I can't see her face, but I hear her quiet breaths.

I wonder what this day will bring. Will we both still be alive tomorrow at this time? Would the company of Rangers show up today? If they don't, will I be able to help her if trouble does come?

I have been in dangerous situations like this often in my life, but I've never been beaten this badly. Never been this helpless. How can I take the pain without blacking out? Can I take the pressure without breaking? It is dreadful to have no strength. It is a terrible thing to stand in the gap between civilized people and wolves. I ask God to have mercy on us both.

The almost full moon is setting. It still casts a bright light, allowing contrasting moon shadows to play across the ground. A rooster crows. But no faint gray-pink glow has yet begun to light the horizon. In several hours the sun will be up, and another hot summer day will begin.

Suddenly I think I hear something. Maybe rats in the grain. With hay quietly rustling, I struggle to sit up, but once again that giant, unseen hand presses me back into the hay.

I try to classify the noise . . . a coyote yip? But Worthless would never allow a coyote in the yard.

Then it happens. A cacophony of noise erupts. Clattering and banging, stomping and cursing—then two gunshots ring out.

Esther springs up and pulls the shotgun out of the hay. She steps toward the barn door closest to the house that she closed before she settled down to sleep. Peeking between the weathered boards of the door out into the early morning darkness, she whispers, "I can see inside the house. Someone lit a lamp. The door is open. I can see the silhouette, but I can't tell who it is. Maybe it's Parrot."

I wanted to tell her to be patient and wait, but my words come out as a groan.

She continues whispering, "Surely, if it's Parrot, he'll call out." She clutches her hand to her throat as if to still her wildly beating heart. She adds with resignation, "So it must be Albert. Once he realizes we're not in the house, his next stop will certainly be the barn."

She rushes back to my side and pulls the quilt over my head. "Remain still. You'll be no help to me and you'll get in my way. If they think you've gone with Parrot . . . they'll leave me alone. They don't know I was in Mexico with you."

I grab her arm. I want to say, hide with me, but my mouth won't work. I knew they would never leave us alone. I feel her covering the quilt on top of me with hay. I have never felt more helpless in my life.

"I've set booby-traps to buy us time."

Then I hear a man scream profanities. Another man laughs.

"Danged woman left her rake face up in the yard. I stepped on it and durned if it didn't make a goose egg on my forehead."

It is Albert all right.

"There is no one in the house, *señor*."

Albert calls loudly, "We know you're here, Esther."

Esther wisely keeps her mouth shut. Then I hear her move out of the stall where I lay. She takes the shotgun.

"Come out the front of the barn and we won't hurt you."

I hear movement, soft, like a little mouse. I doubt it could be heard outside.

"We'll burn you out if we have to."

With a loud squeak the barn's back door opens. The back door to the north. Not the front door that faces south and the house. I hear her pivot, knocking the scattergun against a support post.

Just as suddenly the front barn door flies open. I hear her spin back toward it. I hear an "uumph" and I realize someone has fallen. A pistol discharges, and curses fly from Albert's lips.

Tomás then says, "*Señora, hay un arma en su cabeza.* Drop it. Step toward the portal."

I am pretty certain *cabeza* means head. I feel her set the shotgun down on my feet as she follows Tomás's instructions.

Then, flesh contacts flesh as someone hits her. She whimpers and I feel strength surge through me. It takes all my self-control to stay still. In my weakened state, I need to reserve my strength. Surprise will be my greatest asset. I have to do this right, or both of us will be dead.

"You have caused many problems with *El Rey* and *El General*."

Relief washes over me when Albert intervenes, "That's not the way to handle a woman."

"Stop it, Albert," she demands, her voice higher than normal.

"Where's C. W.?"

"I have searched, señor; he is not here."

Esther interjects, "He rode for help."

"That's a lie," Albert protests. "He was in no shape to ride."

"Then how did he get here?" she challenges his logic. Being

smarter than Albert does not sit well with him.

"Too bad he left you here alone. Too bad for you, and too bad for him, since we'll have to hunt him down. But not to worry, Tomás's good at ambushes with a knife."

I suddenly know Albert refers to the death of her husband, Jobe Stokes. I'm not certain Esther will realize what he is saying.

"Your name's known by the Rangers," she threatens them. "It's in that book he carries."

"Are you sure? You haven't had time to go anywhere, and C. W. probably isn't up to riding fast. We'll catch him before he talks."

I hear the desperation in her voice. "He rode with another Ranger."

"What's one more? We'll kill him too."

"Kill her and be done with it," Tomás urges. "Let's get back across the river before we have a whole company of *rinches* on us."

"Go burn the house. I'm gonna have me a lady. It's been a long time since I've had a lady."

"You had a señorita last night."

"I said a lady, not a whore. Go do what I said."

As Tomás moves to leave the barn, I hear panic in Esther's voice. She asks something in Spanish, then adds in English. "I thought *El Rey* was to give you this farm."

Tomás stops, "*¿Que?*"

"I was at the Cantina la Paloma. I overheard you and the Castilian. Are you going to burn down your own house?"

The malice in Tomás's voice surprises me. "You have spoiled everything. I can never live on this side of the river now."

"I'm sorry," Esther says, "I wish none of this had happened. But you hurt those who were kind to you. You killed Jobe, didn't you? He treated you fairly—paid you more than fair wage. He dealt with you honorably. And so did I! Assuring you ate and got paid when I went without."

She is keeping them talking—smart!

"Tomás," she calls, "I know even as he died, Jobe told you that God loves you and he loved you."

"He crawled on his belly, whimpering."

"Because he wanted you to know he forgave you."

"*Violación!* Rape her," Tomás says, the viciousness plain in his voice. "Kill her, then slit her throat and shut her up."

I can hear someone moving closer to the stall where I am. It is Tomás. I can hear him screaming insanely in English and Spanish now. "I'll slit your throat first, and then your God can save you." Tomás seems to lunge somewhere, roaring in rage. Albert grunts. A scuffle follows.

Where is Esther? Are they fighting each other? *Good,* I think. *Let 'em kill each other.* I just hope Esther is out of the way.

Then someone slams against the wall and stumbles out of the barn. Albert laughs.

"I've always wanted you, Esther."

"I know," she says quietly, "but lust and murder are not the same sin. Your . . . "

"Shut up!" He screams. "What makes you think they'll find out? After you and those two Rangers are gone, there'll be no one to carry the tale."

"I forgive you," Esther responds. I hear her scrape along the wall away from Albert, toward me. She continues to speak. "You'll know, Albert. And you'll have to live with yourself. With the type of company you're keeping, you aren't likely to live with the burden too long."

The smell of smoke wafts through the air. I wonder why the dog isn't barking. Then, I hear another familiar sound—Tomás is killing her chickens. She is being robbed and murdered. She must have realized it, too, because her voice took on a supernaturally calm sound.

"There will be a no-good end for you, Albert. Change now. Repent. Walk away."

"Come with me, Esther. We can live like kings in Mexico."

"What about your children?"

"Ma will see to their raising."

"It'll be a terrible burden for Inez, raising all those children without a man."

"I never wanted those brats anyway. The oldest ain't even mine. He's C. W.'s, and because of that, I've punished that boy ever' day of his life. And the day I kill C. W. Wallace, I'll tell him how I tortured his brat. Then I'll kill that boy just like I killed Matilda."

"Albert!"

"I was doin' it to her as I slit her throat—and maybe that's how I'll do you now."

Esther scolds, "Matilda died of a fever. I helped nurse her. I was there when she died."

"That's not how I remember it . . . but you may be right. I killed her so many times in my head."

"C. W. told me Jesse stopped him from seeing Matilda. That's why he killed Jesse."

"So, the brat's Jesse's."

"I think that boy is yours, Albert. The shape of his lips and brow matches yours exactly. It's like you're looking in the mirror."

I hear a slap and know Albert has struck her. The blow must have ricocheted through her body, leaving her paralyzed with pain, because no sound follows the strike. I wonder if he has knocked her out.

Albert rants and raves, "That boy is not my seed!" His voice rises to a high-pitched scream. "He's not my seed!"

Then I realize Albert is not rational. He's a crazed animal. I wonder if Esther knows.

Esther squeaks, "You're hurting my throat, Albert, stop squeezing it."

"Come back," he demands.

Good! She's obviously pulled away from him. I feel her footsteps on the quilt next to me. She has come into the stall where I am.

"Whores," Albert screams. "Whores! The lot of you. Casting your eyes to and fro . . . " Albert ends growling like a dog.

She gasps and gurgles. I realize she can't breathe. In my mind, she is drowning in the Rio Grande once again . . . with ears ringing and stars dancing before her eyes. But it's me that cannot move. My mind is swirling in the current again, reaching without grasping, kicking without breath. The pain I feel is a log in the river. I push back the quilt and claw through the hay as I slowly start to stand.

I have to act before Albert knows what's happening. *If I don't act now, she'll be dead soon.* An unearthly groan springs from my chest as I stand. Albert is backed into the stall within my arm's length. I spin him around and throw a right punch into his middle. He doubles over and drops the knife from his hand.

Esther gasps for breath. As oxygen reaches her brain again, she has sense enough to kick the steel blade into the hay.

Maniacally, Albert tears into me with a combination of left, right, left blows to my already beaten head. At least it isn't on my broken ribs. The dull sound of flesh meeting flesh penetrates my brain, but because of the drugs, it takes a moment for the pain to hit me. But when it does the shocks almost cause me to black out. Frantically, Esther advances and pummels Albert's back. With a roar like a bear, Albert reaches back, grabbing her hair and waist and throwing her into a heap in the center of the barn.

But this break gives me enough time to wrap my elbow around Albert's throat. I squeeze with all my might. His knees buckle.

Esther screams. Albert has clutched his six-gun and pointed it directly at her.

"Let me go," he croaks, "or I'll kill her."

With a surge of energy Albert twists out of my grip. He stabs the pistol to touch Esther's heart. With a click, he cocks the trigger and snarls at me. "So, you're not dead after all. How many times I gotta kill you before you quit comin' after my ladies?"

"She's not your lady."

"Then she's nothing to me. I'll have her or I'll be done with her, but you won't get her."

"Leave the lady out of this. This is about the law, not her. Your lawbreaking ends now. It's between you and me. It's always been be-tween you and me."

"You think you're better than me, C. W.—but you're not."

I grab at Albert, but my left hand is useless. He spins around, pointing the pistol at me, "You got no guts. You never had. Without your hit-and-run Injun tactics, you're no good."

CHAPTER THIRTY-NINE

I raise both hands in a gesture of surrender.

Esther inches along the floor to where the shotgun is.

"You stole everything from me," Albert hisses.

"I stole nothin' from you, Albert."

Esther's gaze contacts mine as her fingers touch the steel of the barrel where it is half buried in the hay.

"Everything—Esther, Matilda, even the affections of my own Ma and Pa."

From her sitting position, Esther quickly lifts the heavy shotgun to her shoulder. "Drop the pistol, Albert." She speaks so forcefully I can hardly believe the resolve in her voice. Her tone is firm and steady "Please, put it down, Albert. This is over."

Albert freezes and slowly shifts his eyes toward her. A strange leer smears his countenance. He laughs. "You can't kill me, Esther. You're a Christian and Christians can't kill."

I grab for the pistol in Albert's hand and we begin to struggle again, a strange dance, chest to chest.

Unexpectedly, a shot rings out, shattering the night.

It startles us both as we struggle arm to arm, causing us to pause and look around.

More shots ring out as Tomás steps into the barn blindly firing both revolvers, spraying gunfire into the dark corners around us. Reacting, almost without thinking, Esther levels the heavy firearm at her hired man.

"*¡Alto! Señor,*" she screams.

I take advantage of Albert's distraction and smash my foot into his knee and shove him back with all my might. He lands hard on his backside. Tomás's bullets fly wildly around us. I jump on Albert and try to pin his arms down. Stars sparkle behind my eyes. I struggle to remain conscious. He reaches up and grabs my ear, pulling my head down. Pain shoots through my neck and back. I groan with pain and the effort as I twist out of his grip and retreat, rolling back a couple of feet.

Tomás turns toward the sound of Esther's voice and fires. The bullet whizzes past her head, splintering shards of barn wood as the slug impacts near her ear. We hear the click of the pistol's cylinder turning, and I see the barrel of Tomás's six-shooter aimed at her heart.

Then she squeezes the shotgun's trigger.

The gun kicks her flat into the hay. She loads another shell into the chamber before she looks up. Tomás leans against the threshold of the door, dots of red spreading onto his white flour-sack clothes.

"You have shot me, Señora." A sense of surprise rings in his voice.

Distress washes over her face.

"I am dead," he says.

She struggles to free herself from the tangle of her skirts so she can go to him.

"Oh, God, help him," she prays.

Tomás slides to his knees, his back to the door.

"Forgive me, Tomás."

Fear lights his pasty white face.

"Oh, Tomás," she cries out, "tell God you're sorry for the things you've done wrong."

"Burn in hell, Señora."

CHAPTER
FORTY

A bruptly, the life disappears from Tomás's eyes. He slumps into the dirt, his open eyes looking into space, a snarling grimace frozen on his lips forever. In horror, Esther stares at his body.

In the chaos, I am able to drop my full weight onto Albert and grab him as he lies on the ground. We are gut to gut. I put my injured left arm across his neck. His Colt pokes into my belly. With my right hand, I grab the weapon's barrel and twist it back toward him, best I can.

Two rapid reports of the six-gun cause Esther to whirl toward us. In the dim shadows, Albert and I are face-to-face in a bear-hug. Fire explodes through my hand and shock washes over me as if blood is draining out of my body.

In tandem, we struggle to rise as Esther rushes to us.

"Git me somethin' to stop the bleedin', Esther."

It is obvious she is uncertain who has been shot.

Then the pistol thuds on the barn floor as I move slightly, and she can see my right hand pressed against Albert's abdomen. Blood spurts between my fingers. She gathers her skirt and jams it against my hand. I slide my hand out from under the wadded material and place it on top of hers. Pain wracks me in waves, but I know I'm not in danger of dying. Albert is.

"I meant that bullet for you, Wallace. I don't know how that gun got turned around."

"Sssh! Sssh," Esther touches his lips with her forefinger.

"We should have burnt this damned barn down," he whines, "but you escaped through fire once, I was thinking you might do it again."

"Sssh! Sssh! Albert, don't talk," she urges.

"I'm done fer. . . gut shot."

"We'll get the bleeding stopped," Esther said, "then I'll sew you up." She looks desperately at me for confirmation of her words, but I shake my head no. I can tell by the way the blood's spurting and his terrible groaning that he's done for.

Only then do I notice that I'm gut shot, too. Only grazed across my belly like a barb wire tear.

"You got time, Albert," I say, "but only some. With the way that blood's gushin', the bullet hit somethin' crucial. You better make peace with your Maker now."

"He never did nothin' for me. I'm not about to grovel up to him here at the end."

"He gave you a fine family, a strong body, a good ranch," Esther challenges him. "You've been blessed, but you don't see it. All you have to do is change your mind to save your soul."

"We don't have time for a long theological discussion," I warn. "Albert, you've heard the Gospel. You know the right thing to do. Repent the choices that led you here. You see they were wrong choices. Can you say you're sorry?"

"God's got a love for you that you can't imagine," Esther whispers. "He made you, Albert. He knows how to love you the way you need to be loved. His grace is amazing. His mercy is never-ending. He'll forgive ever' wrong thing you ever did. You just ask him. Then he'll take you into eternal fellowship with him to a place where there's no more tears or suffering, no shame, failure, or sorrow."

Esther drops her gaze and begins to pray quietly. Her skirt is soaked with blood. She raises her head and meets my eyes.

"Albert, don't spend the rest of eternity living with one more wrong decision," she pleads. "Let us tell your mother . . . "

Albert writhes in agony, spitting out in anger, "I know I'll have no power or prestige in heaven. I'll see what it gets me in hell!"

Albert shudders in fury, and just when he seems ready to sit up, he exhales. His eyes stare blankly at the rafters. His jaw gapes open, his thick lips go slack.

Slowly and deliberately, I wipe my bloody hand into the straw, then reach over and close Albert's eyes and mouth.

I draw back to stand up. But my legs won't move.

Tears streak down Esther's cheeks. I touch her elbow with my good hand. It humbles me to ask, but I have to. "Esther, can you help me up?"

Her attention shifts to me. The cooling bloody wad of her skirt lifts from Albert's wound and falls heavily around my arm as she stands and assists me back to the pallet on the hay.

"Are you shot too?"

I shake my head no. *Why tell her now?* Haltingly, she moves to the barn door, grabs the rough jamb, and holds on. It reminds me of when I first saw her cling to the porch post.

I feel detached and numbed. With the immediate danger gone, the energy drains out of me. I rub my face like a weak puppy, smearing dirt and sweat across my brow. And blood.

Through the barn door I can see the edge of the milk-white moon setting behind the old mesquite tree, and in the east, streaks of dawn glow. Then I realize it isn't really dawn. Her house is afire. She walks out to the yard and I want to follow her, but I don't have the strength. Unnatural heat radiates from the inferno that engulfs her home, and I hope it won't jump to the barn, because I can't take being burned alive again.

She stands watching—obviously too tired to cry or scream, too sore to grab a bucket and try to douse the flames, and too sad to mourn the loss of a house when two lost souls lay on the dirt inside her barn.

She walks over and looks down at me with a sad smile. "I now know what's really important in life. To love and be loved is a great gift. One I'll never take for granted again. Everything else is just an earthly possession destined to burn at the end of the world."

I struggle to sit up, grabbing at her legs to steady myself. She kneels, then sits next to me and wraps her arm around my shoulders. We sit there silently watching the house burn.

Finally, as true dawn breaks, I croak, "Go wash up, Esther. We'll load Albert's body onto his horse and take him home to his mama."

Turning to face me, she says, "We can't tell her . . . "

I touched her face with the back of my good hand. "She knows, Esther. Maybe not the details, but she knows his character. I don't think we'll have to say much. She's made of stern stuff, like you. She's a Texan. At least he won't end up posed in a coffin in front of the barbershop. He'll get buried next to Matilda."

Esther whispers, "You're . . . "

Uncharacteristically, I hear him before I see him. Parrot's coming hell-bent for leather.

As we continued to stare in the direction of the trail, Parrot finally comes into focus. He pulls his lathered and trembling horse to a stop and jumps from the saddle.

"Saw smoke. You hurt?" He studies the blood on Esther's skirt.

I point to the bodies on the barn floor. "We must look like war."

"This sure 'nough looks like a fight, but you're standin', sort of," he says, "and they're not, so I reckon you won."

"We could've used your help an hour ago, Mr. Parrot," Esther scolds.

"I reckon I been a day late and a dollar short all week. Eight days ago, before you saw King Fisher in Mexico, the cap'n arrested him without much of a fight and put him in jail in Eagle Pass. But he was released 'cause his name wasn't in the Book and he had no record in court. Now, with your corroboration, we should be able to lock him up for keeps."

I shake my head with regret, "We cain't corroborate nothin'. Sure 'nough he was sittin' at a table with Albert and Tomás, but we didn't see, or hear, him commit a crime. He was just sittin' with some fellers who did."

"Dadburnit! Pardon me, ma'am," he nods in Esther's direction. "I got one other piece of bad news, Preacher. Cap'n turned command of the Rangers over to Lieutenant Robinson and sent 'im to Oakville, but the cap'n went to San Tone'ya. His health's so bad, I don't know if he'll be back. He asked for you to come to him as soon as you can."

I nod grimly. "We'd best be going. If you can help me."

Esther opens her mouth to protest, but Parrot continues, "Doctors don't give him long."

I counter, "Those doctors say that ever' time, and he manages to rally."

Parrot looks somber. "But this time, I reckon they may be right."

CHAPTER
FORTY-ONE

gnoring the prone bodies of Albert and Tomás, Esther walks out of the barn toward her burning house. A growing roar, whoosh, and crackle accompany the disintegrating building. Flames formed eerie new walls, blending odd orange-colored lights and shadows with the brightening dawn.

I struggle to limp up behind her, but the action costs me. I don't think I can go any farther, and she comes back to me. I wrap my arm over her shoulder to steady myself. She doesn't reject my action. Parrot comes and stands next to us.

The porch collapses with a bang.

Parrot claps his hands. "I got work to do."

Esther says to me, "You should lie back down."

"Cain't, gotta go to the cap'n."

Turning to face me, she gently puts her hand on my torn and battered arm and deliberately uses the name my mother calls me. "You're hurt, Nels, he'll understand that you can't come."

The firelight casts an odd pallor over her bruised face. But it isn't the bruises that tear at my heart; it's the thought of leaving her behind. I feel like a child ready to cry.

CHAPTER FORTY-ONE

"Go with me."

"Inez will need me."

How can I leave her here? And how can I not go to the cap'n?

"He's dying, Esther. If I don't see him now, I won't see him 'til heaven. And he's like a brother to me."

I can't stand any longer, and I cave in cross-legged into the dirt. She squats down next to me and pets my cheek in a way that reminds me of my ma. "Behind the barn, I've got an old buckboard. If Chief will consent to the traces, at least you can lie down when you get too tired to sit. Then you won't have to be tied to the saddle."

Parrot hollers, "I'll take care of the hitchin'. What do you reckon we oughta do with Tomás's body?"

"I don't know how to contact his family," Esther confesses.

Parrot disappears into the barn. In a few minutes he emerges with the old split-handled shovel. He walks up the hill to where Jobe is buried and begins to dig.

"Esther," I inquire, "Do you want that scoundrel up there next to Jobe?"

Esther runs her fingers through her tangled hair and smiles sadly. "It will be a symbol of God's forgiveness. I know Jobe wouldn't mind, even though, after the hateful way Tomás spoke, I'm not sure Tomás would want to be next to Jobe."

"I reckon his soul is in a place where he'll never be happy with anything."

Parrot helps me move to where I can sit back against the barn while he and Esther work. I watch as Esther slowly walks up the hill. Parrot carries Tomás's quilt-wrapped body over his shoulder. The body is wrapped in the double wedding ring quilt Esther had brought from the house to the barn for me to lie on. I see her bite her lip as she recognizes what Parrot has done. Instinctively I understand—that the quilt is a symbol of her marriage to Jobe. Now, like the rest of her old life, it is being buried. She is burying a dream.

I hear her say, "The Methodist Church provided the nice marble marker for Jobe's grave. The grave is covered with wildflowers. Every year there are Mexican hats, Indian Blankets, Prairie Primrose,

Paintbrush, Blue Bonnets, Texas Stars, Winecups, and Horse Mint. Each blooming in its season, if it's watered."

After an hour of hard labor, Parrot rolls Tomás's body into the hole. But instead of covering the body with dirt, Parrot comes down the hill for a drink.

From the top of the hill, Esther calls, "Worthless, here, boy." She whistles and whistles. But no dangling tongue and wiggling tailless behind answers her call. Perhaps the dog has been injured in the fight. I note Esther's growing sense of despair as she frantically searches for the animal. Finally, under the farthest peach tree, she finds the lump of black fur. The dog isn't moving. And then I know she won't find him alive.

She kneels down next to the bob-tailed collie for a long time with her hand on his fur. Her faithful companion and friend is dead.

The dog had probably approached Tomás in a trusting manner, and the man he thought of as a master had slit his throat.

I hear her faint sobs and know she is crying for the trials of the last eighteen days and her burned possessions as well as her beloved pet who has been her daily friend and comfort. I feel like crying too, but I have no tears.

The yelp of the dying dog probably initially alerted me to trouble. So the dog hadn't died in vain.

Esther gathers the beloved collie in her arms and carries her slain protector up the hill. Parrot and I watch her in silence.

The dawn has fully burst over the hills, filling the land with light and heat. She places her dog in the open grave on top of the man who killed him. By the time she comes back down, the warm summer wind has dried her tears, but their trails remain cut into the dirt on her cheeks.

Esther declares loudly, "I will not cry over this anymore. God is sovereign and all is right with the world in the eternal scheme of things."

Parrot climbs back up the hill and starts shoveling dirt into the grave.

Esther walks slowly back to the barn, gathers one of the quilts tossed on the barn floor, comes outside, and puts it next to where I sit.

"You'd best lie down, Nels. Mr. Parrot and I are going to set that hand before you leave here."

"I don't relish the sound of that."

I lie on my back, and before my one good eye drifts shut, I notice high, puffy cumulous clouds lit with gold. In the light breeze, smoke from the smoldering house curls upwards and slowly drifts toward Mexico.

Trial by fire, I think, as Esther kicks some of the coals of her former home into a mound and brings the coffee pot that she left in the barn to set on them.

After a while, she wakes me, helps me sit up. She tries to hand me two cups—one with coffee, the other with a soup of vegetables and boiled chicken. I hold out my right hand and she sees blisters have risen from where I held Albert's pistol by the muzzle.

"I grabbed the muzzle and turned it around and it went off," I say lamely, as a way of explanation.

She sits down next to me and feeds me, although I can see the exhaustion engulfing her.

"Come with us, Esther."

She shakes her head. "You know I can't. I'd only slow you down, and after I clean up here, I've got to go to Inez. She's been a good neighbor to me. She'll need me to help with those young'uns."

I nod. I knew that would be her reaction. "I reckon our course a' actions must be played out 'til they're finished. I don't know when I can . . ."

She stills my words by gently laying her fingers on my split lips.

"If God wills, I'll see you again."

But I protested, "I hate to go without makin' you some promises, but if I made 'em and couldn't keep 'em, I'd bust."

An uneasy laugh escapes her lips. "Our lives are in flux, Nels. They have been for thirty days. We both must do what we must."

I kiss her softly and to my surprise she kisses me back—gently, for which I am grateful. My split lip hurts something powerful.

She breaks the kiss. "I love you, Nels Wallace. Have I told you that?"

The kiss and her declaration give me hope we can find a future together one day.

"No, ma'am, you hadn't, but I'm real glad you did." I try to smile but my torn face aches too much.

"Hurts to smile, does it?"

"It does. I reckon I look a sight."

She laughs gaily and the sound rings strangely among the ashes of her life.

"It will heal."

"Yes, ma'am, it might take a spell, but with God's grace, it'll heal."

I see her touch her lips. I hope she'll remember what my kiss feels like when I am gone.

"We're wasting daylight," Parrot pronounces as he comes carrying two sticks and six inches of flat barnwood, much like I'd done for Billy. Esther holds my shoulders as Parrot pulls and sets the hand. I yelp, stifling my scream with a groan as I harkened back to the days when I was a boy among the Apache. Scream and they beat you until you could scream no more. Then Parrot binds my arm and hand with the two sticks and barnwood. It feels better with the support.

As Esther sits with my blistered right hand cradled tenderly in hers, Parrot loads Albert's body into the back of the rickety vehicle that will carry him home and me to Uvalde.

She asks, "You think that old wagon'll make it as far as San Antonio?"

I hate to cast aspersions on her gift, but I doubt it will make it to Uvalde. She squeezes my shoulders and then gets up to complete the chores necessary to get us on our way. She loads several plucked chickens, fresh vegetables, and water under the seat as Parrot helps me stand and hobble to the buckboard.

"We'll eat and drink like kings," Parrot comments.

With a groan, I try to hoist myself onto the seat, but that won't work, so Parrot helps me lie down in the short bed next to the body of my old enemy. My feet dangle over the edge. Although Parrot has greased the axles, the little wagon creaks and groans as if it is dying. Chief and Parrot's horse stand side by side under the traces, although their swishing tails and stomping feet indicate that this isn't their favorite arrangement.

With a tip of his hat, Parrot says, "Take care, Miss Esther." She grimly nods as he flicks the lines and starts the rattling buckboard down the overgrown path.

"What should I do with Trail?" she calls.

"Keep her 'til you hear from me."

We watch each other until we are out of sight. I can't stop looking at her, even though I know she probably can't see me clearly because she has no glasses. I feel myself praying for God's mercy and grace to be extended to her. Her hens are dead, her life in a shamble. She has nothing but my love. And a lot of good that can do her.

FORTY-TWO

The days after the cap'n's funeral pass quickly. I wished I could have said goodbye, wished I been there for the funeral. I barely remember that Parrot brought me home in his picture-taking wagon so Ma could nurse me back to health. The first month is the worst. I am so debilitated I can't get out to the outhouse. I feel like a baby. I wonder if I will ever be able to easily move about again. Ma's left to do everything for me and even has to spoon-feed me. But eventually the ribs and blisters healed and the wounds and cactus pricks grow less infected.

At first, I consider writing to Esther to tell her I am mending, but I don't have the strength. And who would carry the letter to her? Later, it had not seemed appropriate.

My left hand remains a problem. I have no strength in it and it aches unmercifully when it rains. I cannot make a fist, and I'll never hold a pistol with any accuracy in that hand again.

My body is broken, but when I'm not sleeping, I can't keep my mind from working. And my mind works on one thing—Esther. I wonder if the nightmares visit her like they do me. Although I know

Albert's body is rotting in the ground by now, but you wouldn't know it by his frequent appearances in my dreams.

God is taking care of Esther, but I worry about how she is eating. She had so little to begin with. I know she stored her empty jars in the barn, so I wonder if she's been able to salvage some of her summer garden and the dead chickens. I hate the thought of her living in the barn, especially during winter, so I determine, regardless of my health, before winter, I am going to get her. Her confession of love towards me is a promise that she returns my affections.

By the Fourth of October, I pull on my boots for the first time without grimacing in pain. Two weeks later, thanks to the hired men helping me, I mount Chief for the first time, but after a turn around the yard, exhaustion overtakes me and I know I cannot make that ride into the Strip.

Frequently, with nothing but time on my hands, I contemplate the brave people, like my ma and pa, or Inez and Moses Hindes, who risked everything to make a life of freedom, and to create civilization out of rocks and thorns, drought and flood, sulfur-tasting water, and loneliness. I remember all those Rangers who died trying to stand in the gap between lawlessness and civil behavior, Rangers like the cap'n. Sometimes I wonder if Texas is worth all the pain and trouble that comes with trying to live an honest life. But I seen the life evil men live, how they whine what they've lost, curse their bad luck, and ignore the human suffering they scatter along their trail. And since misery comes to the evil and the good, I'm resolved it's better I suffer now for doing right than suffer forever for doing wrong.

CHAPTER
FORTY-THREE

NOVEMBER 1, 1877

Kinney County, Texas

◐ *Waning Crescent Moon*

A nip in the air whispers of the change in seasons. The world is gray with a heavy fog. Visibility is about twenty feet down the old Indian trail, ten feet into the brush. Good deer hunting weather. The world is quiet in the heavy air. Moisture drips off the many brown and gold leaves that remain dangling from the limbs. In the distance, I can barely hear the creek. I sit and think as the sun begins to rise and the pea soup starts to dissipate.

I think about Esther, imagining her at her ranch, but I hope she's still with Inez. I figure I can build up my strength to be ready to ride the hundred miles into the Strip to see her if I ride Chief two hours in the morning and two hours in the evening every day for two weeks. If she's still there. She may have decided to go to Uvalde or Austin. I just don't know.

Way down the shrouded path, a mockingbird begins to fuss. Perhaps I imagine it, but then I hear a whistle split the air. Three notes.

CHAPTER FORTY-THREE

It's the family signal that all is well. The signal pierces the lingering fog. I answer the whistles with one long note.

A horse nickers and I can hear its footsteps shuffling through the fallen leaves, but I can't see it.

"Hello, the house," she calls.

I instantly recognize Esther's voice. I've heard people say their heart leaped, but I'd never known it to happen to me. But then I think, maybe I'm imagining her.

When the horse emerges through the fog, it is the little black mare I left with her. Glory be! Esther is here. I stand up and cling to the porch post as she comes nearer, and I remember how she was clinging to a post when I first saw her.

"Esther, you're home."

AUTHOR'S
NOTE

The Nueces Strip is a real place south of the Nueces River and north of the Rio Grande. In 1876, Governor Richard Coke determined to clean up the Strip with the help of the Texas Rangers. Leander H. McNelly was a real Texas Ranger captain who formed the Special Force Texas Rangers and led them into the Nueces Strip. He wouldn't allow swearing or gambling or drinking in Ranger camp. He encouraged the Rangers to preach the Gospel to criminals before they were executed. He employed civilian spies (including women and people of Spanish descent), and he worked with a Ranger named Parrot who often posed as a photographer. McNelly died from tuberculosis at age thirty-three.

If you get the opportunity to visit the town of Uvalde, please note the opera house with the dragon weathervane on the town square. Take the opportunity to visit the First State Bank to look at the outstanding art collection, and ask to see the McNelly Room.

King Fisher was a real person who became a flamboyant sheriff of Uvalde County. His reputation is still debated and talked about in the town of Uvalde. He often "stole" cattle in Mexico and drove them back north of the river, returning many to their rightful owners who were his friends. Some people loved him, many feared him. He was known to wear tiger-skinned chaps. Although arrested by Rangers several times, Fisher was never convicted of a crime.

In South Texas, Dick Heye saddles, covered in silver conchos, were stolen and some were recovered by the Rangers. I've used the saying "one riot, one Ranger" much ahead of the time period in which it was coined, but it is a motto associated with the Texas Rangers. One Ranger often did do the work of a whole posse. "Bigfoot" Wallace was a colorful early Texas Ranger who lived in Frio County.

Esther and Nels are figments of my imagination, drawn from the stories of courageous Texans I heard in my childhood. Lastly, I must give thanks to George Durham and Clyde Wantland for their book *Taming the Nueces Strip: The Story of McNelly's Rangers*, to Clinton L. Smith for his book *The Boy Captives*, and to O. C. Fisher with J. C. Dykes for their book *King Fisher: His Life and Times.* And to Elmer Kelton and Louis L'Amour for walking before me. I want to thank Lee Barton Works, Diana Layne, Anna Carmichael, Wayne Carmichael, Lois Buchter, Cathy and Frank Wolter, Jeannette Scruggs, and Glen Doans for their early read-throughs. We want to thank the great staff of TCU Press: Dan Williams, Molly Spain, Kathy Walton (for new eyes to see the manuscript), Wafa Shaikh, and our anonymous reviewers for their prescient objective input. Lastly, I want to thank Noah for not pestering me, and Jerry for paying the bills, giving me his two cents' worth, and doing the marketing while I write.

MZ

ABOUT THE
AUTHOR

MCKINLEY ZUMWALT is a writing team borne of a love for adventure and authenticity in storytelling. Theresa, a fifth-generation Texan, grew up herding goats and reading novels on the back of her horse in South Texas. Raised an Air Force kid, Jerry lived and performed stories around the world as an actor, teacher, and broadcaster. Follow us at mckinleyzumwalt.com.

Photo by Noah S. Zumwalt

CPSIA information can be obtained
at www.ICGtesting.com
Printed in the USA
LVHW040055160922
728310LV00004B/9